The Mom Group

Jennifer A. Jones

Ryaly Books

For Lenny, Alyssa, and Ryan.

And for all moms, including those who have been like a
mom to other people's children.

Prologue

My name is Erika Thompson, and I have hurt people. Seriously hurt people. Wait, that sounds ridiculously ominous. I have not physically hurt anyone, of course. I'm not a psychopath. But I undeniably crossed a few lines. Have I caused some mental and emotional anguish? Definitely. Could I have destroyed families? Maybe so. Essentially, I used my own suffering as an excuse to create the same outward chaos that I felt internally.

Happily married. I don't think that's what I am. I could blame my husband, as he isn't the partner I imagined he'd be when I said "I do" more than twenty years ago. Or maybe I'm not the right wife. In any event, I should accept it for what it is and just be happy. After all, the very comfortable home we share in Fort Worth, Texas is so much more than what I had growing up. More than I ever could have hoped for back when I was still living with my sorry excuse for a mother.

Overall, my life should be ordinarily fantastic. But I am not where I want to be, nor am I who I want to be. My children think I'm a wonderful mother and virtuous human being, and I am thankful for that. But not everyone thinks the way they do. My kids would be ashamed if they knew how much heartache and turmoil people have experienced because of me.

My sister is another story, having had our ups and downs over the years. We spend some time together and try to do sisterly things, but there is always this barrier. I wish we were closer. It seems as though we should be best friends, as she and I have shared too much of the same heartache to have such an arduous relationship. We think we know our family. We love them because we are supposed to, and yet, with mine, there is something missing. I can't quite put my finger on it, and I don't know how to fix it.

Strained relationships, inappropriate behavior. How do we begin to forgive ourselves for all the things we did not become?

Chapter 1

I'm sitting at home, waiting. I do a lot of waiting these days. My husband, Levi, spends nearly all of his time at work as vice president of software development something or other at a major technology firm. He spends more time away from home than here with me, and so I wait. I really shouldn't complain. Levi's work has allowed us to build this grand home, complete with a pool and outdoor kitchen, which is supposed to be perfect for parties and whatnot. The only problem is that, with Levi's work schedule, there is no time for entertaining.

Truthfully, I don't even have much in the way of friends to invite over. Well, not true friends. True friends are the ones you meet for happy hour so you can spend hours drinking wine and mapping out plans for vacations you will probably never take. The ones who are there to offer advice about what to get your mother-in-law for her birthday. They honestly, but kindly, talk you out of chopping off all of your hair. And they recommend a great book that you know you'll love because they loved it too. I don't have that. Not anymore.

I had a best friend once. Amy and I were inseparable until she moved away after high school. Sure, we have kept in touch throughout the years, but it isn't the same. In college, I had some friends out of convenience, but nothing solid. The idea of friendship fell to the wayside after my kids came along, so I never really tried. Now I am left with a part-time husband whom I rarely see, children I see even less, and a dog.

Realistically, I understand why my children don't want to live at home and commute to college. I didn't want to when I was their age. Although, my home life growing up was much less stable than what Cora and Henry experienced. Still, young people want to be independent, and I get that even if it does sting a little. I left my hometown in West Texas to attend a women's college in North Texas, not knowing where it would ultimately lead me. After taking a course called Social Issues, I decided to major in sociology and work in some sort of social work setting. Young, motivated me was ready to change the world.

I was barely in my twenties when I sat across the desk from Ms. Layla, the no-nonsense manager of the domestic violence center where I was applying for a job as an intake coordinator.

"What do you foresee as the biggest challenge of this job?" she asked.

"Well, the overall situation surrounding domestic violence is challenging. But I think the job at the center itself shouldn't be as long as I follow the procedures that were put into place to ensure the safety of the clients and staff. Basically, if I follow the rules, everything will be fine." I got the job, but I was wrong.

After my shift one Friday night, that familiar uneasiness washed over me while walking through the dark parking lot. I brushed it off, focusing on the lake picnic

Levi and I had planned for the following day. As I neared my car, a man came up from behind me and grabbed my arm. I screamed and unsuccessfully tried to pull away from him. He tugged me closer, snaked his arm around my waist, and began to whisper in my ear. The stench of sweat and liquor filled my nostrils.

"Hi there, sweetheart. You're very pretty. Listen up, I believe that my wife, Theresa Moore, is in your building there. You can either tell me, or I can get it out of you. Your choice."

I was shaking, crying, resisting. He only gripped me tighter, hand on my ribs just under my breast, nuzzling my neck in some sick attempt to frighten me. It worked. I nodded a confirmation that she was in there. He then shoved me to the ground and made his way towards the locked front door. I quickly got up, and with trembling hands, tried several times to get my key into the car door. I sped away towards home as fast as possible. Levi called the police once I told him what had happened. Physically, I had bruises on my arm and a swollen knee from hitting the concrete. Emotionally, I struggled, teetering between the guilt of disclosing that woman's whereabouts and the thought of what could have happened to me if I hadn't. Levi was fuming, but also worried. He didn't want me to go back to that job. Honestly, I wasn't sure if I wanted to go back either. I called in sick every day until I eventually quit. I had only been there for about four months.

I wrestled with the guilt of failing. I hadn't changed the world, and it was likely I wasn't going to. Safety was a requirement for my next venture, so when a local bookstore offered up a position, it felt perfect. It was only part-time, but Levi's career was taking off. Once my son was born, I left the bookstore and became a full-time mom to him and also to my daughter who arrived two years later. Throughout the years, I kept busy with their school and activities, helping teachers cut out construction paper for crafts, setting up winter parties, taxiing Henry to swimming and Cora to soccer. Before I knew it, they were growing up and needed me less and less. Henry left for college a couple of years ago, and Cora left this past August. With more time on my hands, I have toyed with the idea of finding a part-time job again or a fun hobby. I did sign up for an eight-week-long creative writing class at the community college in hopes of trying something new and making a friend or two. Unfortunately, after the second week, the instructor became ill, and the class was canceled.

The microwave beeps signaling that my vegetable lasagna dinner is finished. It's my third ready meal this week, and I am getting quite tired of them. It's nearly eight at night and Levi is still at work, but my mixed breed lab-mutt, Ozzy, is keeping me company, per usual. His full name is Ozzy Pawsborne, Prince of Barkness, a tribute to my obsession with 80s rock music, but we call him Ozzy for short. My sweet boy is always by my side when I'm bored. Or lonely. Or eating. Ozzy is the one I can always count on.

"Come on, Ozzy, let's go outside."

I open the door and feel a gust of air grab hold of it. This spring wind is no joke. I head back into the kitchen to top off my depressing dinner with a bowl of coconut milk mint chip ice cream. This carton is just for me as Levi refers to it as frozen toothpaste in a bowl. Our disagreement over ice cream flavors is just one star in an entire solar system of differences.

After starting my music playlist, Cinderella's "No-body's Fool" fills the room. I'm no Tom Keifer, but since there is no audience, I belt out the lyrics with nearly as much feeling. This type of music is my happy place, my sanctuary. Of course, Levi hates it, so I play it when he isn't here, meaning I play it all the time. Plopping on the couch, I pick up my phone to check Holler-Hub, the only social media platform on which I actually have an account. Sharing isn't my preference, as nobody wants to see a photo of me painting my nails or cares that I bathed Ozzy. Looking through the posts, I see that Amanda from high school is baking cookies for a school fundraiser. My former neighbor, Naomi, took her granddaughter to the park today. Fanny from the library ate spaghetti for dinner. Blah. Blah. Blah. Apparently, nobody else has anything newsworthy either. My half-hearted scrolling is interrupted when my sister's face appears on my phone.

"Hey, Olivia," I say. I always get an odd pang of anxiety when she calls. I never know what to expect on the other end of the phone.

Olivia is three years older than I am but easily looks ten years younger, which is fairly annoying. She owns a boutique called Ever After in a cute, upscale shopping area of University Park near Dallas. My sister could undoubtedly be a model for the fashionable clothes she sells. She tries to encourage me to branch out of my usual leggings and t-shirt, nagging that I need to put in the effort. No matter how much effort I put in, I will never look like Olivia. With thick copper hair that she dyes to match her stunning copper eyes, she is truly beautiful on the outside. The inside could use a little work.

"Erika, what are you doing tomorrow night?"

"Not much. I thought I might try a new vegan queso recipe," I say. I don't know that I actually will, though. I've found that I'm more a collector of recipes than a cooker of food.

"Ew. Gross. Why?"

"Um, because dairy causes digestion problems," I tell her for the millionth time.

"You really need a job or at least a hobby. With 'Jeans' constantly at work, you have too much time on your hands." My sister likes to refer to my husband, Levi, as some sort of denim moniker. "Anyway," she exhales, "can you watch Minnie tomorrow? I'm supposed to babysit for Cass, but I have a date."

This is not surprising. Olivia dates fairly regularly, although lately, she seems to have slowed down some. She kiddingly says she is giving other women an opportunity. She has recently been focused on spending time at the gym, getting her eyebrows threaded, or applying face serums. I think she keeps her aesthetician on speed dial. With age creeping up on her, she is putting up a fight. When Olivia is determined, not even Mother Nature stands much of a chance.

Cassidy is Olivia's daughter, making her my niece. Minnie, as in Mouse, is Cassidy's three-year-old. Cass is obsessed with Disney. Thankfully, she chose Minnie over Rapunzel or Maleficent, although those were seriously being considered.

"Sure, I can watch her," I say.

"Great. I'll drop her by tomorrow on my way out."

"Hey Olivia, are you—" I start to ask her if she is free this weekend, hoping we can grab lunch, but Olivia already ended the call. "Um, you're welcome," I mutter to myself.

With Ozzy back in the house, I head upstairs to run a bath. People always say that taking a bath is supposed to be relaxing. I keep trying it, but I don't get the fascination and usually just end up wrinkled and cold. I gather up my shoulder-length, wavy light brown hair into a ponytail holder. Now that I am forty-four, the gray hairs have been making an appearance more than usual, reminding me to schedule a salon appointment. Before getting into the tub, I decide to apply a little eye cream to the crow's feet that have also recently appeared. God, is that a white eyebrow hair? I turn away from the mirror.

After the bath, I put on sweet pumpkin-scented lotion and my favorite pajamas. They are peach-colored and covered in tiny ducks and donkeys wearing flowered leis. They are adorable, and one of the few items I have purchased from Ever After.

Once under the covers, I text Levi, "Will you be really late again tonight?"

As I wait for his reply, I go back to HollerHub and browse through the Recommendations section where, I assume, HollerHub has conducted some scientific analysis and pretends to understand me well enough to recommend items of interest. The first is a page for people who like to hike. They missed the mark with that one. There is a group about loving the 80s. Okay, I relinquish, they are getting warmer. One of the recommendations does pique my curiosity – Mom Group. I click on the link and am taken to a page that advertises itself as: "A place for local moms to get together for support, friendships, play dates, Moms Nights Out, and recommendations. We are a fun bunch of gals and accept moms of all aged children, working or stay-at-home. No men allowed."

A group just for moms. Huh. I don't need much parenting advice at this stage in my life, but it would be wonderful to meet some other local women so I can get out of the house, maybe meet up for coffee or a drink. I have had some mom acquaintances throughout the years, parents of the kids' classmates, and such. But nothing like my friendship with Amy.

I click the "Join Now" button in the Mom Group and am taken to a set of questions that I must answer before I am let into the group.

1. What city do you live in? Answer: Fort Worth
2. Age of your child(ren)? Answer: 19 & 21
3. Do you agree to follow all of the group rules, which include: not advertising your business, being kind, no drama, and keeping information shared within the group confidential? Answer: Yes

I hit submit and am in. The wide variety of topics are interesting. Some moms are looking for therapist or dentist recommendations and others are complaining about jobs or husbands. Some are just posts of funny pictures.

"I am looking for swimming lessons for my 8-month-old. Any recommendations?"

"The mosquitoes are eating my little Sammy alive. What all-natural products have you used that worked to keep the bugs away?"

"My husband is such an ass. He won't help me with any housework. I take care of kids all day and am tired too. He is so inconsiderate and doesn't understand where I'm coming from. But I don't care. I need help! Do y'all have a good housekeeper you use?"

I stop at this entry to read some comments, pleased to find that many of the other women commiserate with the original poster. They also have husbands that don't offer much help or support. I feel a twinge of anger in my chest thinking of the countless times Levi left all the housework to me when I was home with the kids. He believes in housekeepers the same way atheists believe in God.

I take a quick peek at my text messages and am peeved to see that Levi has not yet replied. Back in the Mom Group, there is a lady who is working from home and needs "the best office chair ever." This I can help with, as I recently redesigned my home library with an amazing steel and wood writing desk and paired it with exactly the best office chair ever. I offer up my own advice.

"I recently purchased an X-Chair. It's leather and has cooling, heat, and massage. You can choose your color and even add a headrest like I did. You won't be disappointed. It's very high quality."

I add the link so she can easily find my recommendation and am pleased to have officially added my first comment as a part of the group. Admittedly, satisfaction washes over me as I think about the possibility of friendship and belonging. I'd love to find my own close-knit group. I have never had a group of fun and supportive friends who shop together, travel together, laugh and cry together. I need that.

I try calling Levi and am sent straight to voice mail. It is already close to ten. I'd like to be able to say this is particularly unusual for him, but it isn't. He works hard for our family, and I should be thankful, as it is truly a blessing. Isn't that what everyone says? Your children are a blessing. Your husband working long hours so you can live a comfortable lifestyle is a blessing. So, I continue to whisper that to myself as I spend day after day and most evenings alone. Still, in a dark place deep in my heart, resentment is undeniably there. This wasn't the plan for my life. If I'm being honest, I don't know if I'm irritated because I miss Levi and want him at home with me more often, or if it's because Levi is the man that I chose to be my husband all those years ago.

I met Levi during our senior year of college, although we weren't at the same school. I was living in an apartment near my campus with two roommates that I wasn't particularly close to but who were nice enough. One afternoon, I accompanied one of them, Hailey, to what was known as the oldest restaurant in Dallas. Hailey wanted to go for the history aspect of the place. I wanted to go for the food.

"Did you know El Fenix opened in 1918?" Hailey nearly shouted, partially due to the noise around us and partially from excitement. "There are now several in the metroplex, but this was the original location. Although," she animatedly explained, "the actual original building was across the street. It closed down and this one opened. Check out the beautiful archways!"

I was more interested in looking at the beautiful enchiladas on the menu, which I ordered. After the waitress left, I made my way toward the bathroom. On my walk back to the table, I locked eyes with a guy whose crooked smile made me take in a tiny gasp. I hoped he hadn't noticed, but his smile grew wider, so I wasn't too confident that my face was as indifferent as I tried to make it appear. His chair nearly toppled as he leaped into my path.

"Hi. I'm Levi," he said, extending his hand. He was wearing shorts even though it was forty-degree weather, and his hoodie bore a logo that I wasn't familiar with. His dark brown hair was perfectly disheveled, and then there was the crooked smile.

I shyly took his hand and said, "Erika." It was a struggle to not smile so eagerly.

"Erika," he repeated in a deeper, softer tone, "would it be too forward of me to ask for your number?"

My face grew hot, and I knew my cheeks were turning ruddy as they often do when I'm nervous or self-conscious. I gave Levi my telephone number. He squeezed my hand, gave me a wink, and promised to call. Butterflies danced in my stomach, but I tried to keep my expectations in check.

"Did you know 'El Fenix' means 'the phoenix' in Spanish?" Hailey was still reading historical tidbits from the back of the menu. "And it used to be open twenty-four hours a day, seven days a week. During World War II, there was a city-wide curfew in Dallas, so all restaurants had to close from midnight until six in the morning. Only on that first night, none of the restaurant employees could find a key to lock the door. Isn't that crazy? They had to call a locksmith to have the lock changed."

I smiled, trying to match Hailey's enthusiasm. "This place is super cool," I managed to utter. And it was. But my thoughts were otherwise consumed. When my meal arrived, I felt too nervous to eat much. My encounter with a cute boy was unexpected and slightly unsettling. Encounters like this often happened for people like Olivia, but they were not commonplace for me.

Later that evening my apartment phone rang. My heart skipped a beat when I answered it and heard Levi's voice. We made plans to meet up for dinner the following Saturday. He offered to pick me up, but I am slightly paranoid by nature. I didn't know this guy and certainly wasn't going to get in the car alone with him. I'd read enough horror stories about women going missing, so I told him I would meet him at the restaurant.

On our first date, my paranoia quickly turned to infatuation, as Levi asked me about my interests, my family, my dreams. He was sweet and attentive, holding my hand across the table. On our fifth date, Levi asked me to marry him. The floor swayed under my feet as I asked him to repeat the question.

"I said, will you marry me? I know it seems fast, Erika, but when you know, you know. And I know."

But I didn't know. Not really. I had no experience in this area, and it all seemed really fast and slightly crazy. "Can I think about it?" I asked nervously. I didn't want to be rude, but this was a decision bigger than any I'd made before.

"Sure," he said, smiling, "but don't take too long. There is no doubt in my mind that you're the one for me."

A few weeks later we were laying on the floor of Levi's apartment, our fingers entwined, staring up at the ceiling. "Have you thought any more about my question?" he asked.

"I've been thinking about it."

"Listen," he began, rolling over onto his stomach to lock eyes with me, "I love you. I know it seems reckless and may be too soon, but it's how I feel. I love you."

"I love you too, but why marriage? We can just date for a while longer. See how things go, can't we?"

"I don't want you to be my girlfriend. I want you to be my wife. We are both about to graduate, and life is going to start moving along. I want you by my side as a permanent fixture."

"I'm not a fixture, Levi," I teased.

"That's not what I meant, and you know it," he assured, playfully tapping my arm. "But I do love you. I love you so much, and I just can't imagine my life without you. I want you. I choose you."

And there it was. Until I heard Levi say those words to me, giving me that tiny crumb, I hadn't realized how hungry I was to hear them. Nobody had ever really wanted just me. I couldn't remember the last time someone said "I love you" directly to me, just to me, and truly meant it.

Six months later, right after graduation, we tied the knot. It was a small ceremony that included my mom, Olivia, and Amy, all of whom had spent the prior six months trying to talk me out of it. Only Levi's brother, James, attended from his family. Levi's parents lived out of state and were largely estranged. We pressed our bodies together during our first dance as Skid Row's "I Remember You" played. Levi didn't mind my music back then. He thought it was endearing. We were so happy.

During that first year, I became pregnant with our son. Levi was invested in his career, which was on a fast track with promotions happening regularly. He was a small fish in a large corporation, swimming like hell every day. Once my precious Henry arrived, I quit my job at the bookstore, loving my new full-time role.

I click off the lamp on the nightstand but want to check my HollerHub notifications once more before trying to go to sleep. I see that several people have responded to my chair recommendation. Eager to continue my group participation, I click back on the post.

"Um, that chair is over $1,000. We are not all bougie."

"Ha! And maybe I can buy a solid gold desk to go with it."

"I'm not sure if this is a joke. If it is – good one! Like most of us can afford to drop 1K on a chair. If it's not a joke, ouch! Way to let us know you are loaded LOL."

My skin instantly turns warm and my stomach drops. I was trying to be helpful, and these women are just judging me. I'm not sure if they are being rude or if I'm being overly sensitive. I don't know what I did wrong. In any event, it is apparent that my comment is not helpful, so I hastily delete it. Maybe I'll just be a Mom Group voyeur for a while until I get the hang of it.

I must have fallen asleep because I suddenly wake up in a room that is completely dark apart from the sliver of light shining from under the bathroom door. Levi is in the shower, and it is just past midnight. When he climbs into bed, I pretend to be asleep. Not that it would matter if I were awake. Our level of interaction would be the same.

The next evening isn't much different. Olivia picks up a sleeping Minnie just after midnight. "Where is 'Denim'?" she probes.

"At work, as usual."

"This late? Erika, doesn't it seem odd to you that he stays at the office deep into the night, over and over again?"

"Well, I don't like it, but I don't know what I can do about it. He works hard for our family so he can take care of us all. He makes sure we don't want for anything."

"Do you feel taken care of?" Olivia knowingly whispers. "Do you not want for anything?"

I become agitated as I take in her words. "Again, what am I supposed to do about it? Of course, I wish I had a husband here at home with me, to share meals and cuddle together on the couch, laughing at stupid movies. We are finally empty nesters. I wish we could start planning vacations for just the two of us and take a cooking class or a salsa dancing lesson or something else that couples without young kids do. But he has a job that takes all of his time. There is no time left for me. That's just the way it is."

Olivia gives her head a little shake but says no more. With a sleeping Minnie cuddled in her arms, she turns as she steps onto the porch. "Salsa lessons? You know that doesn't involve tortillas chips, right?"

I give her a look and say, "I'll see you later." Closing the door, I make my way to Ozzy. He gives the best cuddles, anyway.

Maybe Olivia is right. Nothing can be done about Levi's work schedule, but maybe I need to do something more to take care of myself. Being a stay-at-home mom was never my original plan, as I always intended to be fully engaged in the workforce, doing something I loved. Once the kids came, I embraced the opportunity to be home with them, but it came with its own set of challenges. We have never been filthy rich, but Levi makes a very comfortable living. Still, I have felt guilty about not contributing financially to our household. I also experienced a significant loss of adult interaction, and when I did find myself around other women, it felt as though I had to justify what I did all day. This is almost laughable because there is not a free minute for moms who stay home. There is always homework to oversee, meals to make, field trips to attend. There is never a day off, no calling in sick. It is a full-time job in every sense of the term. There was always that balance of desperately needing a break and never wanting to miss a single moment. Now several months into being an empty nester, I realize how much I miss both my children and my husband.

Chapter 2

O n Sunday, I am up early, getting ready for brunch. There was an event scheduled in the Mom Group, and I was brave or stupid enough to sign up. It's at a local restaurant called Mash'd known for its delicious Avocado Toast Pizza. I'm an avocado addict, and this is the perfect comfort food. I have a feeling I'm going to need it.

My stomach turns at the thought of walking into a restaurant and sitting at a table with a bunch of women I don't know. What makes it worse is the thought that they are already friends, making me the solo outcast. Okay, I decide, I'm not going. I don't know what I was thinking when I said I would go, but I'm definitely not going. I open HollerHub and go to the event page to change my RSVP to "Will Not Attend." I see a note pinned to the top of the page: "No last-minute cancellations, please. We have a reservation and it looks bad on our Mom Group if people don't show up." Dammit.

Clothes are strewn all over the bed before I finally choose jeans and a gray blouse with small white dots. I apply a little mascara, tinted moisturizer, and lip stain. My hair is its own disastrous project, so I run some leave-in conditioner through it to tame the flyaway frizz.

It doesn't really work, but it's getting late, so I abandon my hair. I grab the car keys, kiss Ozzy goodbye, and head out the door.

In the restaurant parking lot, I sit in my car for a minute working up the courage to go in. I give myself the kind of pep talk I would give Cora, and now understand why she rolls her eyes at me. I'm not buying it either. Finally inside, I tell the host I'm part of the Mom Group party and am shown to a table. All the seats are already taken. I wipe my clammy hands on my jeans and peek at my phone, noting it's only ten minutes past the start time. The host adds a chair, forcing everyone to scoot down to accommodate me.

As I introduce myself to everyone at the table, some women smile at me, some nod, and some don't look up from their menus. The woman to my left is wearing a cute red dress, a gold star stud in her nose, and has gold stars painted on her fingernails. She says to me, "I'm Ashley. I have three kids all under the age of six."

"Wow, that must keep you busy."

"They do, but they are so great, you know. Like, so self-sufficient already."

"Your kids are already self-sufficient?" I repeat.

"Totally. Like yesterday, Ziggy made dinner for us all. I mean, it was peanut butter on toast and grapes, but still, he's like only four. And that is like super helpful because I run a business out of my home."

"That's impressive. What's your business?"

Her voice softens as she says, "I help couples, you know, in the bedroom. How old are your kids?"

I am not exactly sure what she means by helping couples in the bedroom, but I don't ask. "My kids are older. In college."

"Oh, so you must have like tons of time. What do you do?"

The dreaded question. Should I be honest and say that I spend my days reading, cleaning, and hanging out with my dog? That I sometimes cry because I'm lonely? Since my kids moved out, I have completely lost my sense of purpose and don't know what I should do? I don't know who I am anymore or maybe I never did? "I'm a stay-at-home mom. Well, I was. Now I guess I'm a homemaker."

"I don't know what that means," Ashley purrs.

Thankfully the waiter comes by and takes our order, cutting the conversation short. I spend the next thirty or so minutes listening to the other women share stories, laugh, give advice. I try to play along, chuckling at appropriate times. But honestly, this lunch just feels exhausting and weird, and I'm ready to leave.

Instead, I muster up the courage to turn to the woman on the other side of me. She appears to be a little younger than I am, but definitely in her mid to late thirties. That is close enough to my age to have some things in common.

"I'm Erika. I have two kids in college. What's your name?"

"Sheila," she says with a smile that doesn't quite reach her eyes. "I just have one, and she is in her terrible twelves." She laughs at her own joke.

"I remember that age. It can be rough, for sure," I fib, as that was not my experience at all. Henry and Cora were what I would call "rule followers" and pretty easygoing.

We make more small talk about our husbands and our hobbies. She loves that I love vintage music, which is how she describes it. Sheila seems nice, and I decide I would like to explore a friendship with her. I work up the nerve to say, "Would you like to grab coffee sometime?"

"Sure, sounds good. Hand me your phone, and I'll enter my number."

Sheila joins a different conversation, but I've accomplished what I came to do. I met a new friend. I hear a ding and a few women pick up their phones to check for an incoming message, including me. "It's mine," I say, as I see a text from Levi.

"Have to fly to DC for a meeting. Leaving late tonight. Will probably be gone all week." That familiar pit forms in my stomach.

I use this text as an excuse to make my escape. "It was nice meeting you all, but I need to run," I say, holding my phone in the air as evidence of something important calling me away.

"Bye, nice meeting you," a few women mutter.

"Bye, Jessica," another calls out to me.

I don't bother correcting her because I'm past the point of caring much about this lunch or the women who didn't talk to me. I met Sheila, and that is good enough for today.

Later that evening, I go into the bedroom to find that Levi has moved my clothes from the bed to the floor, so he can use the bed to pack. "Jesus, Erika, did you empty out your closet? What were you doing?"

"Just looking for something to wear," I snap back. Then, a bit calmer, I tell Levi about the mom lunch.

"That's great. I'm glad you finally got out of the house. But it would've been nice if you'd cleaned this up. I was also hoping to come home to some sort of dinner. I know you don't cook much, but I thought maybe you'd have something here to eat. That isn't too much to ask considering I had to work on a Sunday, don't you think?"

I don't bother responding to his question. It wouldn't make a difference.

Then I do say, "Why do you have to go out of town so suddenly? Usually, your out-of-town trips are scheduled weeks in advance."

I don't know if he is stressed about work or nervous about this trip, but I can feel the exasperation dripping off of him. "Sometimes these things are out of my control. I don't schedule all the meetings. When my boss tells me to go, I go."

"I know. It's just—it seems like you are gone more and more these days. Always working late and on weekends. And now you have more trips. I don't like being by myself all the time."

His voice softens as he says, "I know it's difficult for you, but I'm doing this for us and for the kids. This is the career I've always dreamed of. Have you thought about going back to work in the field you had always dreamed of? I'm sure there are plenty of non-profits that have job or volunteer opportunities. Or why don't you find a hobby so you can make some friends of your own?"

Levi might have a point, but I respond by stepping over my clothes and out the bedroom door. I go downstairs, hold up Ozzy's leash, and ask him if he wants to go for a walk. He happily runs to the front door. Safety is never a concern in our neighborhood, even for a woman walking a dog alone at night. As I bend down to put on his leash, I put my hands on both sides of his face, scratching behind his ears. "I love you so much, Oz," I whisper. He licks my face and dances around, anxious to go.

I admire the beautiful landscape in front of my neighbors' homes, all visible with strategically placed accent lighting. With the early warming of spring, flowers and trees are blooming. I decide I will go to the garden center tomorrow and buy new flowers for the planters out front. Turning winter's brown, dried-up flower bed into an array of happy colors is cathartic. Levi prefers a uniform color scheme, but I love a variety of flower types and colors. The yellows and reds mixed with pinks and purples are so cheerful.

The following day, I unload my nursery purchases onto the front porch, including yellow lantana, purple pansies, white alyssum, and a pink hydrangea bush. I also picked up the cutest garden gnome. He just looked like he belonged in front of the house. Ozzy barely lifts his head when I go inside and grab a glass of sweet tea from the kitchen. Back on the porch, I sink into the cushioned rocker to mentally map out my planting. Water beads down the glass when I take a sip. As I try to enjoy the sunny afternoon, my mind keeps wandering to other bothersome areas of my life, like my marriage for one. And something else nags at me too. Unhappiness? Maybe boredom? I call my daughter.

Cora is nineteen, with thick, curly hair, dark like her father's. She often wears a smile that lights up the room. Cora the Explorer, as I lovingly call her, decided to attend college in Colorado, which caused a slight wound in my heart. I held on to hope that she would want to stay close to home. It's hardly surprising, though. She is a free spirit, and I always knew that as soon as she graduated from high school, she would want to branch out on her own. With the cooler weather, mountains, and outdoor lifestyle, Colorado is definitely tailored to her. Cora must have also gotten her outdoorsy gene from Levi, as I'd prefer to be curled up on the couch with a great cup of coffee and an even better book any day of the week.

"Hey, Mom," she answers on the third ring in her normal chirpy voice. "What's up?"

"I'm just calling to see how my fabulous daughter is doing. I miss you."

"I'm doing just fine and miss you too. I joined a club on campus called the Colorado Mountaineers. We go on scheduled hikes and camp outs. It's pretty fun. You'd hate it."

"You know me well," I chuckle. "I'm glad you're having fun. How are your classes going?"

"They're fine. I'll be so glad for summer. Statistics class is kicking my butt. I'm taking a class called Women in History, though, and it's super interesting. The other day, my professor, Linda, talked about Yvonne Brill who was the first female rocket scientist back in the 1940s. She invented a propulsion system that keeps satellites from slipping out of their orbits. It's still in use today. And," Cora huffs, "can you believe that when she died, a newspaper printed an obituary about her that started out talking about how she made awesome beef stroganoff? Like seriously? She is a female rocket scientist in the 1940s, and that's what was first highlighted. Of course, they reprinted it and took that out, but still. Anyway, it's amazing to learn about all the women who have made such a huge impact throughout history."

"You call your professor Linda?" I ask.

"Yes, Mom, because that was the point of my story." Cora sighs with exaggerated annoyance.

"Oh," I exclaim, changing the subject. "I have a new friend. Her name is Sheila, and we met at a mom's lunch. We're going to meet up soon. She gave me her number, but I don't want to appear too anxious. God, it's like I'm dating again."

"That sounds nice. You should text her, Mom."

"Is that better than calling? I was thinking of calling her later today."

"Text her for sure. People aren't too big on phone calls these days. Okay, I need to run. I'm meeting a few friends at the student center and still need to stop for some coffee. Love you," Cora sputters in the way she does when she is ready to go.

"Bye, Cora. I love you and can't wait to see you." I glance down at my phone, and see she is already gone.

I send a text, "Hi Sheila. This is Erika. We met at the Mom Group lunch. Would you like to meet up for coffee later this week?"

As I wait for a reply, I sit back and stare out at the two Crepe Myrtles beginning to bloom, one white and one red. Levi planted them for each of the kids when they were five and seven years old. Cora was so ready to help that she came out of the house wearing rain boots, which she proudly proclaimed were her gardening shoes, and one of my floppy hats that fell so low on her head she nearly tripped as she skipped to where her daddy was digging. Henry, on the other hand, couldn't care less. I chuckle to myself remembering how he dramatically whined as if we'd asked him to help dig a hole for a new swimming pool. A few days before the tree planting day, he had received a new video game, and it took everything to tear him away from the living room.

My phone dings and Sheila's message comes through, "Let me check my schedule and get back to you."

"Great! Can't wait!" I immediately reply.

The flowers are patiently waiting to be planted as I click over to the Mom Group to see what's been posted recently. A new event has been created – Mom's Night Out at a local winery that I definitely plan on missing. I think I'll just work on my friendship with Sheila for the time being. I read through some recent posts.

"In search of a good tattoo artist who isn't booked for the next two months. Every local place I call isn't taking walk-ins. My dog passed away, and I want to get her paw print on my leg but looking to get it done this weekend."

"My son has these wart-like growths on his hands. Does anyone know what they are? Pictures in the comments. Bonus points for home remedies."

"Have any of you ladies had weight loss shots? If so, which doctor did you use, and did it work? My doctor won't give them to me as she thinks they aren't safe, so I need to find a new doctor. I've been gaining weight since having my kids and I'm ready for a change. Thanks, friends!"

I stop at this post and read some of the comments. The ladies are encouraging, but none have said they actually received weight loss shots. I feel a little concerned for her, as she said her doctor is refusing to provide them. I add a comment, "I have not received weight loss shots. However, I would not recommend them. It's apparent that your doctor is apprehensive so you may want to take her advice. You should just eat a well-balanced diet and exercise three times per week. Shots and other quick weight loss plans are gimmicks and a waste of money. If they worked, everyone would be skinny. Be patient and put in the work and you will see results. Weight loss can take a lot of time, especially as we get older."

Before I close out of the Mom Group, I'm excited to see notifications that there are immediate replies to my comment. Wow, that was fast.

The first reply reads, "Not helpful. She didn't ask you for advice on ways to lose weight. She asked if you have had the shots. If you haven't, move on."

My excitement is replaced by knots forming in my stomach as I read the next response. "Erika, you are so rude. This lady is trying to do something to be healthier and more confident and you are just shitting all over it. Of course, we all know about diet and exercise. Obviously, that isn't working for her. And she isn't old like you seem to be from all the wise advice you have shared. If you can't be nice, fuck off."

"Oh my God," I say aloud. The phone begins to shake in my hand as I delete my comment, but not before noting who wrote that last response – Nicole Hastings. I click on her picture to go to her profile. I want to see this person who feels the need to be so cruel. How can she take a few sentences of what was supposed to be helpful information, and make me out to be a monster of a person?

Nicole's profile photo shows her laughing as her husband lifts her off the ground. They are at some sort of park with a backdrop of gorgeous mountains. She is wearing a white cropped top, showing off her flat stomach and shimmery black leggings. Elation radiates from this picture at the same level that apathy radiates from my profile picture. The camera lens sees into the soul, capturing both true joy and true sorrow.

I've been sitting under the cover of the vast front porch, but my face burns as though I've been staring into the sun. Why don't I do or say the right things? I don't understand why these women don't like me. I'm a nice person and try to be a good citizen. I hold the door open for people and return my shopping cart at the grocery store. I sometimes pay for the coffee order belonging to the car behind me at Starbucks. I buy Girl Scout cookies from the neighbor's kids. This bothers me, and I feel almost heartbroken that these women wouldn't care if I fell off the face of the earth. I would not be missed in the Mom Group, that's for sure.

I send another text to Sheila, "Hey, how is your schedule looking for this week? Did you get a chance to check?" I stare at my phone for a full thirty minutes, waiting for a reply.

Finally, Sheila responds, "This week isn't good. I'm pretty busy most of the time with my daughter and her activities. You know how it is. I don't think getting together is going to work out anytime soon."

Suddenly no longer in the mood to work on the flower beds, I leave everything on the porch and head back into the house. I get in the shower, tears mixing with the warm water running over my head. The failed Mom Group interactions replay in my mind, as I try to determine what I should have said or how I should have responded so these women would want to be my friend. It's like high school all over again, the popular kids against the outcasts. I then sink into the king-size bed, sharing it only with Ozzy this week. "Why don't they like me, Oz?" I whisper, as he softly grunts in his sleep. "I feel so hurt."

Chapter 3

I do not feel hurt. When I wake up, it's still dark out. The time on the alarm clock shows 3:13 in the morning, but I am no longer tired nor am I sad. The hurt has been unmistakably replaced, and the fire coursing through my veins stems from fury. I am pissed off. Who the hell do these women think they are to treat me this way? That Ashley and the other women who all but snubbed me at the Mom Group lunch. The women who called me names when I tried to be supportive and helpful. Sheila ghosted me. And Nicole. That witch doesn't know me, but she's about to. I've allowed the people in my life to walk over me too many times and for too long.

I go downstairs and pour myself a glass of wine. Anger is an excellent motivator, but a little liquid courage never hurts. With the push of a button, my laptop comes to life. I create an alternate email address, which I then use to open a new HollerHub account. I need to think of a fake name I can use to set it up. I choose Candace Tanner because Cora loved the TV series "Full House" when she was little, and Candace is the actress who played her favorite character, DJ Tanner. I search the internet for a photo of what could reasonably be a twenty-something mom and upload that as my profile picture. I don't feel good about stealing another person's photo, but I'm sure people do it all the time. It is the internet, after all. In the "About Me" section I write, "I am a mom of two, who loves her husband bunches! I like wine, dancing, and hanging out with my girlfriends."

Candace is everything I'm not – happy, bubbly, social. She makes me want to hurl, but she will fit right in with the Mom Group. I ensure the settings are private so that nobody will be able to tell that Candace has no friends and is, therefore, not a real profile. It is time to click the Join Now button, answering the questions as Candace:

1. What city do you live in? Answer: Fort Worth
2. Age of your child(ren)? Answer: 3 & 6
3. Do you agree to follow all of the group rules, which includes: not advertising your business, being kind, no drama, and keeping information shared within the group confidential? Answer: yes, of course!

Candace is in.

I search through the Mom Group posts, looking for something I can comment on to integrate Candace as a member of this community. I want these women to like Candace. To trust her. She needs to become one of them, even if only behind a screen.

"Looking for summer camp ideas for ages seven and ten. My kids want to go places and do things, but my momma heart wants them to stay home with me. Anything that's only a half-day, maybe?"

"I need a photographer for family pictures. It will be for my husband and me, our five kids, and my parents. Any recommendations? Also, trying to find coordinating outfits. Where should I shop for that?"

"I have to brag on Simply Nails. My nail tech, Kim, is amazing. She did these for me and I love them!!! It took her forever to add the tiny crystals, but so worth it!"

I take a closer look at the picture. God, those are awful. How does she wipe her butt with those nails? They are nearly three inches long. And with all of those glittery things on them, she would probably blind herself if they ever reflected the sun. I start to giggle thinking that she is probably so thin because she can't open any packages of food or hold a fork. But Candace thinks they are amazing because she is one of the girls, and so amid my excessive eye rolling, I reply, "Oh my gosh I love them! They are so you! Beautiful!"

I get immediately likes on Candace's comment and the original poster replies, "Thanks so much, Girl! You are too sweet!"

I feel a jolt of pleasure at the positive responses I receive from these women, then quickly remember that it isn't me they are responding to. It is Candace, and she is nothing like me. I keep scrolling through posts about diaper rashes, jogging strollers, and gluten-free cookies, but suddenly stop at a picture of a very attractive shirtless man with a post that reads: "This is my boss. We had a company lake party last summer, and I snuck this picture. I'd never pursue this because he's my boss (and because I'm married LOL), but I wanted to share this beautiful creature with you all. Do any of you have secret real-life hot guy crushes?"

There are eighty-six total comments and replies. Wow. I scroll past picture after picture of primarily attractive men with captions such as, "my cute neighbor" or "my hot stepbrother." Wait, a woman has a crush on her own stepbrother? They aren't technically blood related, but that is pretty revolting.

Amongst the masses of photos, there is one by none other than Nicole, the person who was extremely rude to me. A handsome man with dark hair and sea blue eyes stares dreamily into the camera with a post that reads: "This is my husband's best friend. I'm secretly in love with him – just kidding, kind of! But is he not the hottest guy ever? His body is just as perfect as his face. He is always at my house hanging out with my husband, and I'm definitely not upset about it LOL. I could stare at him all day long." I screenshot Nicole's comment for safe keeping.

On Friday, I tidy up the house in anticipation of Levi's return. We barely communicated all week, sending only a few texts about the landscaping company, scheduling a dentist appointment, and other mundane matters. Memories flood back to a time when Levi went out of town, and we would talk on the phone for hours, deep into the night. Even the most typical daily activities were shared and appreciated. While he was in meetings, he would send me "I love you" texts and share cute photos or videos that he thought I would enjoy. I would tell him about Cora's and Henry's adventures at school or tease him with the promise of alone time to make up for our stint apart. Our bond was special. We shared actual joy. I can't pinpoint the exact time our relationship went from mind-blowing to mind-boggling. How strange it is that strangers become partners and lovers, and then strangers once again.

Levi arrives home well after midnight. I step into my slippers and walk downstairs and into the kitchen where he is rummaging around. "Can I make you something?" I ask.

"Jesus, Erika. You scared the hell out of me. What are you doing up?" He comes over and gives me a brief hug.

"I heard you come in and wanted to say hi. How was the conference?"

"Like every other conference, partly stimulating, mostly boring. What have you been doing all week?"

"Not much of anything. Talked to the kids. Listened to music and read a lot."

"You're right, that isn't much of anything. Isn't there some hobby that interests you, or maybe you can find some friends?"

"Yeah, I tried that. It didn't work out."

"Erika," Levi says, sighing, "you always focus on the negative. When you focus on negative things, you are setting yourself up for a lifetime of unhappiness. You can choose to be miserable or choose to be strong. Make the better choice."

"Was that inspirational quote printed on the conference swag they gave you?" I ask, not bothering to hide my eye roll.

"I'm trying to help, but clearly I can't talk to you," Levi snaps, as he abandons the food and walks out of the kitchen.

"You never actually try talking to me anymore," I mutter to myself. I had short-lived optimism for a happy reunion, hoping Levi would see me and be overcome with the need to hold me and tell me how I'd been missed. It was an unrealistic fantasy, as likely as a cold day in July, so I'm not sure why I still had that glimpse of faith. I wanted to tell him I missed him, but I knew that wouldn't change anything, so I kept pretending I didn't.

No longer tired, I go into the living room and sink into the slate gray couch, positioning the fluffy pillows around me to get comfortable. I open HollerHub with the intention of checking out Nicole's profile and scrolling through more of her photos. One is of her in a restaurant with her husband, tagged in the picture as Chris Hastings, along with the man she has a crush on, AJ Johnson. Both of the men's profiles state that they work for the same company, Master Metals & Materials. A quick search on the company's website tells me that it is a steel manufacturing company located here in Fort Worth. On the "About Us" page are several photos, including one of Chris with "Owner" under his picture and one of AJ with "Account Manager" under his.

Chris is also a very attractive man. How tawdry of Nicole to have a thing for AJ. Is her husband not enough for her, or is her lack of respect just that blatant? There is a message in the way she treats him, and he needs to know.

In addition to names and photos, individual email addresses are listed. This is perfect, as I'd prefer to not send this type of message directly through HollerHub. Once that happens, Candace will be banned from the Mom Group for sure. I open up the Candace email account and begin a new message to Chris and AJ:

"You don't know me, but I thought you should be aware that Nicole is very open about her attraction to AJ. This was posted in a group of nearly a thousand women in the area. I'm sure many of them or their husbands know you or are familiar with your business. This is highly inappropriate."

I upload the screenshot with the photo of AJ and Nicole's comment, but pause before hitting send. I believe in karma and a world where actions have consequences. The most fundamental example of karma is that when a bird is alive, it will eat ants. When the bird dies, the ants will eat the bird. The question is, do my actions constitute karma where Nicole is concerned, or is it up to the universe to determine her fate?

I reason that karma is too busy to pay attention to the inner workings of a mom group. Nicole created the drama with me, so I will create the karma for her. This isn't revenge so much as returning the favor. Plus, this needs to be nipped in the bud before Nicole has an affair. She may not realize it now, but in the long run, this message will help more than harm. The email is sent with the swoosh of something that can't be undone. I feel a smidgen of guilt, knowing the disruption this will cause. That guilt is quickly replaced by a touch of satisfaction. I am tired of being stepped on. I will easily match people's respect, but I have finally reached the point where I will also match their disrespect. And Nicole definitely disrespected me.

Chapter 4

Apparently, Chris read the email because it is "Moms Gone Wild" in the Mom Group. Nicole did not hesitate to post about the unfortunate email her husband received.

"Someone sent an email to my husband telling him that I am in love with his best friend. First of all, I am not in love with his best friend. Second, it was a stupid post that was just supposed to be a fun game. I was KIDDING. It was a JOKE. Of course, I'm not secretly in love with his best friend. Third, which one of you bitches took that screenshot and sent it to him? I swear to God if I find out, you will be sorry! I can't believe I trusted all of you and someone would do this to me. My husband is so pissed at me. I have been crying all night and trying to explain to him that it was a joke. This is so messed up. You suck!"

There are copious amounts of comments under Nicole's post, all reiterating her sentiments. Some of the women are now fearful of posting in the group, others claim to be sad or disappointed that a woman would do this to another woman. Funny, I don't remember anyone being sad about Nicole's offensive comment to me. Still, there has been a lot of feather-ruffling and one thing is for certain, these ladies are enraged.

A decision is made to make a clear, succinct post about the rules, stating that anyone caught taking a screenshot of a post in the Mom Group will immediately be banned. That almost seems more like a gift than a punishment, but what do I know. They also plan to have an in-person meet-up to discuss this infraction. All active members are welcome. I certainly can't attend as Candace but would love to go as myself. I am not a particularly active member of the group, but previous efforts were made. I sign up for the event, which is taking place the following week, and I'm actually looking forward to it.

With Levi back home from his latest travel venture and still working long hours, I decide to treat myself to a make-over. I'm not typically audacious, but I am tired of the same old Erika staring back at me every time I pass a mirror. Feeling exceptionally spirited, I begin calling local salons to see if there is any availability.

Finally, I find one. "We can get you in with Shandra at two o'clock, will that work?"

"Yes, I'll take it."

To fill time before then, I drive to Monkey and Dog Books, a place that I love. It is the cutest indie book-shop that maintains the charm that is often lacking in larger chain stores. They also have author events, which are exceptional because they are always so intimate. I breathe out a sigh of contentment when I walk through the door. I make my way to a table set up at the front and begin thumbing through the books on display. Levi is not much of a reader, but I passed on my love of reading to both Henry and Cora. We are three bibliophiles at heart. Reading always gives me someplace to go when I feel stuck where I am.

My phone starts playing Poison's "Nothin' but a Good Time," and the only other customer in the shop gives me a side-eye as I dig in my purse. It's my sister, and I consider sending her to voice mail, but ultimately step outside. "Hey, Olivia."

"Have you talked to Mom?"

"Not in a while, why?"

"She's coming out to visit."

"Oh, God," I cry louder than I mean to. "When?"

"Sometime in the next week or two. She'll only be out for a week and asked if she could stay with me. But," Olivia draws out, "it's just that with the store and Cass and Minnie and my dates. It's so crowded at my place."

"No, no way. I don't want her to stay with me. Can't we put her in a hotel?"

"Erika, she is our mother. That would hurt her feelings. And you have plenty of room. She could practically have her own wing."

"I didn't know she was capable of having feelings," I shoot back. Olivia waits me out with silence. "Fine. She can stay with me, but you are taking her out and spending time with her while she's here. I'm not going to have her nagging me all week."

"Deal. Thanks. Hey, I have to run. Talk to you soon," says Olivia and hangs up. And within that minute-long phone call, my mood turned sour.

Instead of going back into the bookshop, I get in the car and drive to the salon. I'm early for my appointment, so the girl behind the counter entices me with the promise of a full face of beauty. Apparently, the make-up artist is available to give a free demo using some new cosmetics they are sampling. I wonder if I should be concerned that nobody at this salon is booked. But I agree and go to Sharla's station.

"Are you and Shandra related?" I ask.

She eyes me strangely before saying, "Nope."

"Oh, okay. It's just because your names are similar. I thought maybe you were sisters."

"Nope, not sisters. Can you close your eyes, please?"

I quickly comply as Sharla begins brushing my lids. "Not too heavy. I don't usually wear a lot of make-up."

"You should. Wear some at least, I mean. The right amount of color and a good liner will really open your eyes. I can recommend some products for you."

Thirty minutes later, Sharla holds the mirror in front of my face, and I see a brighter version of myself. "Wow," I nearly shriek, "I look pretty good."

I buy one of everything Sharla used, tip her for the service, then make my way to the hair stylist's chair. "Just a trim, please, and maybe a few highlights to cover the gray," I say to Shandra.

"You know," she says, "you'd look fantastic with a deep, almost black shade. It would cover your grays and match your eyes."

My hesitation is not hard to miss, so Shandra adds, "I know it sounds drastic, but you'll love it. I promise. It will be perfect for you." Her facial expression convinces me nearly as much as her words do, so I agree to the change.

I try to relax and enjoy the pampering. When Shandra finally spins me around to the mirror, I'm shocked. The results are pleasantly astonishing. It's a much more polished version of me. "Add red lipstick," Shandra teases, "and the men won't be able to stay away."

Levi comes home earlier than usual that night. There is no dinner ready, as I have stopped expecting him to be home by dinnertime. He does a double-take on his way up the stairs. "You look great. I like your hair. Do you want to go out for a bite to eat? Italian maybe?"

"Sure, sounds good," I say, somewhat surprised. "I'll just grab my purse."

The restaurant is simple yet charming, as is the menu. After we order, there is an uncomfortable silence between us. We used to be able to sit in silence for hours, but now it feels strained.

"You really do look very nice," Levi says. "I like your hair that color. Why the change?"

"I just thought I could use some sprucing up. There's nothing like fixing the outside to make the inside feel good." My slight chuckle acts as a weak attempt at humor.

"I'm sorry I have to work all the time. There just isn't anything I can do about it. I think it would be so beneficial for you to find something to do," he says kindly.

"I did join a mom group on HollerHub. That has been—" I pause to search for the right word, "entertaining."

"That's good. So, what does the group do?" Levi asks, taking a bite of bread.

"Well, it's basically just a bunch of local moms who give each other parenting advice and meet up for lunch or drinks, stuff like that. I'm watching more than participating, but I did go to a lunch once. It didn't go too well."

"That's not good. Do you think maybe you didn't put yourself out there enough? You can be so introverted and quiet that it's off-putting." So much for being kind.

"Heaven forbid I be off-putting," I say, rapidly blinking to prevent the drops that have instantly formed in my eyes from spilling over. "I know I'm not charming and well-spoken like you. Good-time Levi. Everyone's best friend. Well, everyone except me. You have your entire life to be a jerk. Why not take today off?" The words are out before I even know what I'm saying.

"Why would I want to hang around you if this is how you're going to act? I compliment you and take you out to a nice dinner. I'm trying to help you find friends or a hobby or something, and all you do is spit in my face. I'm trying here, Erika."

"I don't need your help to find a hobby. I need my husband. I need you. Sitting home by myself all the time gets so lonely."

"I don't know what to tell you," Levi admonishes. "I have a busy career. It takes up my time. I can't sit at home and babysit you. I have to work."

Angers swells quicker than I can control it. I snap back at him, "So work then. I'm not looking for a babysitter. I just want my husband back."

"Your husband," Levi says almost mockingly, "is making a good living to buy you all the nice things you like to have and ensure our future is secure. Isn't that what you want?"

"I'd give back all the material things if it made a difference," I whisper, defeated.

I spend the night tossing and turning while Levi lightly snores beside me. I try to think back to when things changed. When Levi became more distant. It was around the time he received his last promotion four or five years ago. The vice president title came with countless additional responsibilities, resulting in more time away from home. It has always bothered me on some level, but it wasn't so glaringly noticeable when my children still lived at home. They filled the silence with their comings and goings, friends, and activities. Since they've been gone, the house is so undeniably empty.

Chapter 5

I scroll through the Mom Group before heading out to the lunch event which was set up to discuss the screenshot incident and the general group rules. There are still some lingering posts about the Nicole debacle, but they have mainly died down. Thirty-two women have confirmed their attendance at today's lunch. This is a popular event, and I'm hopeful to perhaps blend into the background. I don't spend nearly as much time perfecting my outfit as I did for the last event I attended. I'm not here to socialize and make friends, but to listen and perhaps gloat, internally, of course.

An entire back room is cordoned off to seat all of us. The lady who created the Mom Group, Allison, makes an announcement.

"Thank you all for coming. Since there are so many of us, to keep things simple, I hope it is okay that we pre-ordered several appetizer plates for all to share. Everyone can have one alcoholic drink and then soda after that. The bill will be split evenly amongst us all. If you would like additional alcohol, please open a separate tab for yourself. Thanks so much for understanding." She gives a half-smile and continues. "As you know, someone in our Mom Group family has taken a screenshot of a member's post and sent it to this member's husband. This is not only unacceptable, but it is rude and frankly, lacks class." Allison places her hand over her heart and tries to emit sympathy. "It's been devastating for this fellow mom and caused a serious problem within her marriage. We are a group of ladies who should be lifting each other up, not tearing each other down. The fact that someone is so untrustworthy just breaks my heart. I want you all to know that I'll be extra vigilant in watching what happens in our Mom Group. This behavior is not to be tolerated. Now, I'll open it up for comments or questions." Allison sits back down, and the comments start flying:

"This person is a monster. Why would someone be so mean?"

"How could a mother do something like this?"

"I say we make everyone sign a Mom Group oath if they want to stay in the group."

"I don't think that is legal. Is that legal? I'm not signing anything."

"Maybe we can weed out those who won't sign it. They must be the culprits."

"Can someone pass the fried cheese?"

I stay quiet, taking it all in. These women are acting pissed off, but honestly, they seem to be enjoying the additional drama this has caused. Anything to have something to talk about, as long as they are not at the center of it. I would bet money that many of the women here create their own storms and then complain when it rains.

"Excuse me," I say, and a few heads turn towards me. But just a few, as most of them are focused on bruschetta and garlic bites. "There is no way to tell who the person is who did this, right? So, I don't understand how making people sign oaths or threatening them with expulsion is actually going to help. I mean, people can sign whatever and still take screenshots."

Allison looks as annoyed as she sounds when she says, "Yes, I know we can't wave a magic wand and people will automatically follow the rules. However, if people feel like they're being held accountable, then they'll act accordingly. We need them to know that doing the right thing is expected."

"Okay," I continue, treading lightly, "but I still don't understand how this is going to work. Don't they already know the rules? We had to accept the rules before we joined the group." My initial plan to hide in the background has clearly failed. I can't help myself.

"I'm sorry, what is your name?"

"Erika Thompson."

"And how long have you been a part of the Mom Group?"

"Oh, I don't know. A month maybe."

"Right," Allison says through a tight-lipped smile. "So, you really don't have much experience in our group. We are really happy to have you here at our events. Truly. But perhaps it would be best if the decisions about the group are left to those of us who have been here for years. Since the beginning for some."

There are a few murmured agreements and a giggle or two, so I bite my tongue and decide not to engage any further. I realize how tightly my jaw is clenched when I have to forcibly relax it to take a sip of wine. I'm slowly learning that I shouldn't waste my words on people like Allison who deserve my silence.

"I only have one more thing to say before we go back to enjoying our lunch," Allison resumes, unfolding a lavender-colored piece of paper. "It's a quote by the famous and well-respected Marilyn Monroe, and it goes, 'This life is what you make it. No matter what, you're going to mess up sometimes, it's a universal truth. But the good part is you get to decide how you're going to mess it up and how you will make it better.' Isn't that just so inspirational?" She once again places her hand over her heart for emphasis.

I want to stick my finger down my throat in response. Is she serious? I look around the room to see if others share my bewilderment but see heads nodding in what appears to be sincerity. It's time to pick my chin up off the floor and focus on my untouched plate of food. I don't know what to make of this lunch and feel like I'm in some alternate universe. I'm aware that I'm not for everyone. Hell, I'm barely for me. But honestly, if I were to become actual friends with the women at this lunch, I better run out and buy a lottery ticket because the impossible is happening. Do these people genuinely like Allison or do they want to befriend her because she created the Mom Group? Like it gives them some special VIP access. There appears to be a lot of Allison ass-kissing going on.

"Moms," Allison says in a loudly exaggerated drawl. Goodness, here she goes again. The room hushes instantly as she continues. "As you can see by all the laughter and conversations going on around you, we are still just the most amazing group." She lifts her glass in the air. "Cheers to you, Moms. You are brave. You are strong. You are valued."

Everyone is quick to raise their glasses in response, murmuring words of affirmation back to our host. Allison is eating it up, as she obviously has an exaggerated sense of self-importance. She expects to be recognized as superior to the rest of the moms in the group, but I won't feed her ego.

I extend the one-drink cap from lunch and pour myself a large glass of wine as soon as I get home. "Oz, want to play outside?" There is no response. I try again, louder. "Ozzy?"

He bounces down the stairs, grabs his favorite stuffed toy raccoon, and accompanies me out the back door. There is a slight cooling breeze, confirming how much I love spending time in our backyard, especially before the Texas heat forces me indoors. The patio furniture is cushioned in brightly colored yellow and white bold stripes and the huge Talavera pots show off various plants and blooming flowers. Ozzy begins his game of dropping the raccoon at my feet, so we can play fetch. He doesn't tire easily for an old boy.

Back on HollerHub, regular activity has resumed in the Mom Group.

"This is a little embarrassing, but I have recently developed back acne. It's so bad, I don't want to take my shirt off in front of my husband. Does anyone else struggle with this? How have you treated it?"

"I'm looking for a lactation consultant. Preferably one that will come to my home. Does anyone have any recommendations?"

"Please spam me with all of your party recommendations. I'm talking balloons, cookies, cakes, decorations, venues, and more. It's for my daughter's thirteen birthday. Thanks!"

I scroll past several posts, none of which I bother commenting on. I stop when I see a post made by Allison right after the Mom Group lunch. "Just wanted to give a shout out to my lovely admin team who help run this group. There is a lot that goes on behind the scenes, and with recent events, even more work has been put into the group. You ladies rock!" I roll my eyes so far back I practically see my own brain losing cells.

Allison. Condescending, righteous Allison. Let's see what all she has posted in the Mom Group. A search of her name reveals a very long list of posts by the infamous group leader.

"Y'all, I have to brag on my little peanut! She started walking at seven months old! I kid you not! I'm not surprised considering she clearly said 'mom' at only three months. Should I start saving for Harvard? LOL!" Well, this is certainly boastful and potentially hurtful to other moms whose children may not be composing their first symphony by age two.

"Check out my toes, ladies! My nail gal painted the cutest little ladybugs on my big toes! I'm ready for sandals!" I make a face. Toes kind of weird me out. They are just these gross, collectors of sock lint. Levi used to make a game of touching me with his bare toes, bending and making them crack and pop. I'd move away from him, shrieking for him to stop. Once the kids were old enough to know what was happening, they joined in on the fun. Well, fun for them, pretty repulsive for me.

I step over a now sleeping Ozzy to refill my glass, bringing the bottle back out with me. The Bordeaux is smooth and earthy as it slides down my throat. I top off my glass and go back to perusing Allison's posts. Am I being stalkerish, I wonder? My third glass of wine convinces me that I'm being curious, but not crossing any lines. After combing through dozens of unexciting posts, one in particular gives me pause.

"Y'all, I hate my job. My boss is a total you know what. He comes to work every day stinking like a skunk that's been smoking cigarettes. What's worse, he acts as though he knows more than all of us when he is totally clueless about our work. Like, he is pretty much an idiot. I used to enjoy going to work, but since he joined the company, it's been awful. It's so hard for me to leave my position because I make so much money and have lots of vacation time. But really, y'all, what do you think?"

What I think is that I've hit the Mom Group jackpot.

I take a screenshot of Allison's disgruntled employee post. Now to do a little digging which, of course, is going to require another glass of wine. I empty the rest of the bottle into my glass and sit back, ready to investigate. Her personal HollerHub profile doesn't list her place of employment so I continue to search through Allison's entire page. There are lots of pictures of her kids and an equal number of selfies. Loads of selfies. Allison in her car. Allison leaning on a gigantic tree at a park. Allison posing with a margarita raised to her lips at an event. In the background of the event photo is a sign with a blue circle and a large M in the middle. A quick Google search is all it takes to find it. Manning Tax and Accounting Services. I go to their website, and after a few clicks around, Allison's face is staring back at me. Underneath her headshot is the caption: Senior Administrative Assistant to the Vice President of Business Accounts.

I can't believe how easy this is. Or maybe how lucky I am. The internet undoubtedly has eliminated all forms of privacy. If people want to find out something about you, they will. My search is interrupted when the back door slams and Levi appears and says, "I've been looking for you. I need to go to Atlanta for a few days. I'm leaving on Friday."

"Why do you need to go over the weekend again?"

"There's a team dinner Friday night and golf on Saturday. I should be back the following Wednesday."

"Don't forget my mother is coming this weekend, so she'll be here when you get home."

"In that case, I'll be staying all week," he says only half-jokingly.

"Honestly," I say, sighing, "I don't blame you. I don't want to be here either. I can't believe I let Olivia con me into letting my mom stay here. I know Olivia has the store, but she pays people to work there. Why can't they cover for her? She should be able to take a few days off. And Cassidy can certainly care for her own daughter for a few days without Olivia's help." Olivia is busy, and I'm not as sympathetic as I should be, but when it comes to my mother, it's all I can do to keep from feeling irritable.

"Well, I can't blame Olivia. And it's not like you have much of anything else going on."

"Yes," I say, suddenly fuming, "I'm well aware that while Olivia has an eventful, fulfilled life, I'm over here with nothing. Zip. Nada. My life consists of feeding and walking Ozzy, and literally nothing else. It's fine. I'll take my mother out shopping. We'll go out to lunch a few times. Hopefully, the week will fly by."

I glance at Levi who is still standing over me. "Something else?" I ask.

"I'm worried about you. Do you day-drink alone often?" He says this in a way that mimics sincerity, but in actuality, he knows he's just being a jerk.

"I shouldn't even dignify that with an answer. But no, I do not regularly day-drink by myself. But if I want a glass of wine, who else am I going to drink it with? You're never here."

"Here we go again with that. When are you going to get over it? We've been round and round this same conversation for what feels like years. I have to travel for my job." He over-enunciates each word of that last sentence. "And," he calls out while going back into the house, "I doubt that was just one glass of wine."

The wine glass shatters as it hits the back door.

Chapter 6

I open my eyes with a startle. The clock shows that it's past ten o'clock. It can't be this late. Oh, my God. How did I sleep past my alarm? My mother's plane landed this morning at a quarter before nine. I grab my phone and see several missed calls from both Olivia and my mom. I call my mom back first.

"Where were you?" she says with an expected amount of irritability.

"I'm not sure what happened to my alarm, but I'm on my way," I say breathlessly, as I rush around getting dressed.

"Don't bother. I took a taxi, and I'm almost at your house. You can pay for the cab when I get there."

"Yeah, sure no problem." I sit back on the bed and catch my breath. I send a quick text to Olivia to let her know Mom's pick-up mishap has been resolved. This is a visit that I have been dreading ever since Olivia called me with the news of my mom's visit.

Neither Olivia nor I were close to our mother. Or rather, she was not close to us. We both tried throughout our young lives to win our mom's love and attention. But Marlene Marie Gatlin was much too busy for any nonsense involving her kids. She worked full-time as a bartender in a hole-in-the-wall sports bar, raising us as a single parent in a small town in West Texas. Our father attempted to have a relationship with Olivia and me when they first split. I was only around four years old at the time but was aware of the constant berating my mother dished out to my dad every time he came around to see us. She used us as a weapon, threatening to withhold visitation and communication unless he met her demands, which usually involved giving her money above and beyond court-ordered child support. Eventually, he stopped showing up. I harbored some resentment towards him for his abandonment, but on some level, I understood it. He had a sudden cardiac arrest and passed away when Olivia and I were teenagers, so the opportunity to restore our relationship was forever lost. My mom has always been toxic, and it's hard to blame anyone who chooses not to be around her. It's a choice I have made time and time again, but somehow she is still in my life.

Olivia and I practically raised ourselves, as our mother was usually off with this man or that one, sometimes bringing them into our home. We would wake up to find Marlene's conquests eating our cereal or sitting on our couch when we came down for breakfast before school. In an overly chipper voice, Mom would say things like, "Say hello to so-and-so," but I typically gave them a dirty look and hurried out to the bus stop. One morning, Mom grabbed my arm and said, "You will not spoil this for me. I have a good thing going. You brats have messed up my life for the last time. You and your sister are ruining any chance I have at happiness." It took years before I realized that any responsibility for my mother's happiness did not belong to us girls.

As an adult, I distanced myself from my mother. Her moving to Phoenix nearly ten years ago made that even easier to do. Olivia is closer to her, regularly keeping in touch, but I no longer have much interest. My relationship with her is just civil. I finally realized that I couldn't change someone who didn't see an issue with her actions, so I stopped trying to please her. Marlene is a narcissist and always will be, so all the previous effort I put into the relationship was a complete waste of time.

A car door slams, and I hurry down to open the heavy mahogany door. Ozzy gets up to greet my mom but lays back down when he doesn't get so much as a pat on the head as she brushes past. "It would've been nice to know you weren't going to bother to show up. I could've called your sister."

"Hi, Mom," I call after her as she heads straight to the kitchen. I run out to the waiting taxi driver, press some bills into his hand, then hurry back inside to find my mom rummaging around in the refrigerator. "Like I said, I really am sorry. I did set my alarm, but I must have been exhausted and slept through it. I'm glad you made it here okay."

"What are you exhausted from? Living in your fancy house?" she scoffs, looking around for emphasis. "Anyway, yes, I'm here now. Hello, Erika." She hugs me and then turns back to the fridge. "I'm starving. All they gave us on the plane were some pretzels and a soda. Didn't even have peanuts. I asked, but because some people are allergic, they stopped with the peanuts. Isn't that the dumbest thing you've ever heard? What if I was allergic to gluten and couldn't eat the pretzels? I guess they didn't think of that. So do you have anything for lunch, or should we go out?"

"Um—" I start to disagree with her peanut and pretzel analogy but decide against it. "I have fixings to make sandwiches, or we could go out."

"I just have to pee, and we can go." This is going to be a long week.

After we order, my mother sits back and brushes her brightly dyed red hair out of her eyes. She lowers her voice and solemnly says, "Erika, I have cancer."

"What?" I nearly choke on my lemonade, my chest tightening. "What kind of cancer? When did you find out?"

"Well, I haven't technically found out. Not officially anyway. But I've been having these awful headaches, and so I just know that must be it. Haven't made it to the doctor yet with the high deductible and all. Perhaps you can help with that, so I can begin treatment."

I am completely exasperated, and we've only been served our drinks. "Oh, my God. You do not have cancer. You probably need new glasses or something."

"Well, I can't afford that neither."

"I can take you to the eye doctor while you're here, Mom. I'll call them tomorrow. You can't go around telling people you have cancer. It's inappropriate."

"I'm not telling people. I'm telling you. And you don't know that I don't."

"You don't know that you do," I say crossing my arms. "And until you have an official diagnosis from a doctor, stop saying that."

"Look at you miss bossy pants. All grown up and now you have an attitude. Money must do that to a person. How is that handsome, hardworking husband of yours? He didn't even come out to say hello."

"Levi is fine, and he isn't home. He's at a work conference until later this week."

"A work conference over a weekend?" She raises one eyebrow and grins.

"Yes, a work conference over the weekend. His company has business associates, and they play golf and have dinners on Saturday and Sunday and work during the week. It's very common," I justify, annoyed with myself for feeling like I need to provide her an explanation.

"If you say so," my mother trails off as a plate of food is set before her.

Back at home, my mom is napping, and I am enjoying the quiet with only Ozzy's occasional sleepy sighs to fill the silence. You don't realize how much you value peace until that peace is disrupted. I fish out my phone to check my email, delete a dozen junk messages, then open HollerHub. I haven't checked in on the Mom Group lately, and there is still some unfinished Allison business. Two new events have been added – a playdate for moms with young kids, so not applicable to me, and a Mom's Night Out meet-up in Sundance Square: "Kick up your heels and join your fellow moms for a night of bar hopping and dancing. We will start the night at the Red Goose Saloon. Where we end up will be anyone's guess." I'll pass on this one too. Allison and her friends are challenging enough when they're sober. They can't possibly be any better drunk.

It's time to close out of there and return to the Manning Tax and Accounting Services website, where I locate Allison's photo once again and take note of her title, Senior Administrative Assistant to the Vice President of Business Accounts. Now to find the Vice President of Business Accounts, who is apparently a smelly idiot. I don't see anyone with this exact title, then notice there is a separate tab for Executives. A click on that presents a handful of men dressed in suits. They are all wearing black suit jackets with white shirts, but each has a different colored tie. It's almost like looking at an Andy Warhol painting. Turquoise tie guy and brown tie guy both have Vice President of Business Accounts titles. Better to be safe than sorry. I copy both of their email addresses into a new message which will be sent from the Candace email account:

"Good afternoon, Gentlemen,

Your company seems to be very distinguished, and I am sure you have several important client accounts. Therefore, it would be remiss of me to not share an embarrassing situation involving one of your employees. I won't go into too many details, as a picture says a thousand words. Please see my picture below. I am sorry to deliver this disheartening news."

I am not one teensy bit sorry. The screenshot of Allison's derogatory post is added, and I immediately hit send. This time I don't feel the need to pause and consider the consequences of my actions. Sure, one might say that I shouldn't be taking screenshots of other people's posts. And to that, I would reply that people shouldn't post things they wouldn't want everyone else to see. Allison was unkind to me. She was certainly being unkind to her boss by blasting him like she did. And to me, kindness is everything.

Chapter 7

It's Tuesday morning, and I've hardly heard from Levi since he's been gone. Yesterday, I reached out to Olivia to remind her that she promised to not abandon me with our mother all week. She was also out of town but is due back today. This was news to me, as I thought our mother couldn't stay with her because she was busy with the boutique and Minnie. I send her a text asking what time she is coming back, and if she can meet up for a late lunch with mom and me. She responds that she can, and we make plans for this afternoon.

I walk past the guest room on my way downstairs to fix breakfast and see that my mom is not in her room. A quick peek into the guest bathroom tells me she is not there either.

"Mom," I call out, heading downstairs. "Where are you?"

I go past the empty living room and check in the kitchen, but it's quiet. I walk all around the house calling out, but get no reply. I stick my head out the back door and yell for her, but again, no response. I open the door leading to the garage and see that it is dark. I'm beginning to get concerned, but am not aware of my mother having any sort of tendency to wander off. After dialing my mom's phone number, it begins to ring. I follow the sound back to the living room and find the phone sitting alone on the couch.

Now on the front porch, I'm nearly screaming, "Mom. Mom! Where are you?" I try again and again before heading across the lawn to look down the sidewalk in case she went for a walk. As soon as I step onto the grass, a cold, wet sensation seeps through my socks. The sprinklers must have gone off earlier in the morning. Groaning, I go towards the driveway to peel the socks off my feet. I place my hand on the hood of the car for balance, and when I do, I find my mother sitting in the passenger seat. She is dressed, has on a full face of make-up, and is clutching her purse in her lap. Apparently, the only thing she is missing is her phone.

"Mom?" I say, a little worried. "What are you doing in the car?"

"You said you were going to take me to the eye doctor to see about my headaches. I've been here for three days, and we haven't gone yet. I figured the only way I could get you to take me was to wait in the car."

My concern quickly morphs into aggravation. "I forgot to call. Let's go in the house and get some breakfast, and I'll call for an appointment."

"You probably can't get me an appointment at this point. I'm only staying a few more days. Let's just drive up there and check in."

"That's not how it works. We need to make an appointment."

"Look, I told you I needed to go. It's not my fault you forgot. Now let's go." Her tone scolds in a way that almost makes me feel like a teenager again.

And just like a teenager, I give in. "Fine. Give me a few minutes to get ready."

She glances at me before saying, "I think you need more than a few minutes."

My mother has always had a way of making my blood boil, but I run inside and quickly get changed. Then I call the optometrist's office anyway and ask if they can squeeze us in, explaining that my mom is suffering from severe headaches. "She's only here until tomorrow," I lie. Thankfully, they are gracious enough to work us into the schedule.

After the doctor completes her exam and writes a new prescription for glasses, my mom says, "How do you know it isn't cancer?"

"I'm going to go up front to pay and arrange to have your new glasses shipped to your home," I say, not wanting to subject myself to this conversation.

As soon as we get home, I pull into the driveway, click the garage door open, and turn to my mother in the passenger seat. "Go ahead inside. I'll be back in a bit."

"Where ya going?"

"I just have a few errands to run. No need for you to come along. I'll be back soon."

"Pick me up something other than wine while you're out. I'm tired of drinking that crap. Maybe some brandy and not the cheap stuff either," she says while exiting the car.

I nod and speed away as quickly as possible without causing alarm to the neighbors. My mind is swirling with anger and anxiety. I drive with no direction, past the places I regularly see in my city. The huge Baptist church with the gigantic steeple where there is an exceptionally large number of cars in the parking lot considering it isn't Sunday. The bustling shopping center with nearly a hundred stores and restaurants, filled with moms and kids, husbands and wives. Happy people doing happy things.

I turn off into the local cemetery, driving down several of the windy rows, past wilted flowers and weathered stuffed animals. This isn't the first time I've been here. I park at the curb and begin to walk between the plots, reading names and dates as I pass. I remember reading somewhere that fifty years after burial, all the body's tissues are liquefied. After eighty years, the bones begin to crack and soften. A century in and even the bones have largely turned to dust. The teeth will still be there, though. I shudder to think that eventually we are reduced to dust and teeth. I am not sure which is stranger, life or death.

I don't know anyone lying underneath the grave markers and headstones, but I want to be here just the same. It has been a while since I've visited. It's calming to realize that there are hundreds of individuals here, each one a person with a life and a story, all different. Everyone rushes around in their daily lives, trying to achieve something greater in life. Greater than themselves even. This cemetery reminds me that many of the things that bother us in our daily lives don't really matter in the end. We all end up here. How can that time between birth and death be filled with so many ups and downs? It's exhilarating, stressful, joyous, and excruciating all at the same time. I would actually welcome some of those ups and downs. Well, the ups anyway. Lately, my life has been stuck in an endless loop of mediocrity with some stress and sorrow thrown in for good measure.

I am sitting on a cement bench, listening to the birds sing and to the cars creating a low rumble off in the distance. I soon become lost in thought about Levi, my mom, the ladies in the Mom Group. My mind only pulls itself back to the present when I hear several car engines grow closer. A funeral procession has entered the cemetery gates. I make my way back to my car to leave but am not ready to go back home. Back to my mother. I end up at the Fort Worth Water Gardens, which truly is a beautiful architectural phenomenon. To describe this as merely a fountain does not do it justice. I pick a shady spot away from the handful of people scattered about. It's a weekday so it isn't crowded, leaving this outdoor oasis mainly quiet except for the soothing gush of running water. It makes me think of my honeymoon where Levi and I spent three blissful days at Niagara Falls.

We were poor kids just out of college and thought it would be a smart idea to drive to the Falls for a few days. We were too thrifty to pay for airline tickets, so driving twenty hours each way made perfect sense. I laugh at the memory, feeling the same flicker of the warmth I felt then. It became a whole trip, stopping to tour Graceland in Memphis and buying matching keychains that read "Taking Care of Business." Seeking out the small hole-in-the-wall restaurant that Levi's colleagues said we had to try. I can't recall the name of it, but we drove around for an hour trying to find it, deciding that it was definitely worth it once we finally sat down to eat. I don't know if the food was that good or if we were just starving by that point.

When passing through Cleveland, we drove by the actual house from the movie "A Christmas Story." It's open to the public now but wasn't at the time. I've always wanted to revisit the house and walk through the inside but never made it back to Ohio. But the time we spent inside the Rock and Roll Hall of Fame was magical. I remember walking up to the glass pyramid, which, at the time, had only been open for around five years. Hours were spent looking at memorabilia, photographs, and instruments from some of the most famous rock musicians in history.

During that last stretch of our drive to New York, Levi and I made up what we thought would be the ideal album. My selections included bands like Ratt and Mötley Crüe. Levi's adds were more along the lines of Oasis and R.E.M. In the end, we had a complete album of twenty songs that we both agreed would be perfect road trip material. Digital music was just emerging, and Levi promised to figure out how to create a mix CD for our next trip. I don't think he ever made that CD, but it was fun just the same.

Luckily, our hotel room overlooked part of the Falls because we didn't leave the room much. We did walk a bit onto the Rainbow Bridge but never crossed into Canada. The majority of our days and nights were spent lounging in bed or sitting on the small balcony, eating whatever food we picked up from places within walking distance to the hotel. I don't remember what we talked about during that time, but I do remember the way I felt. For the first time in my life, I felt safe. I finally knew what it meant to be important to another person. To be loved.

Back at home, I find my mother dozing on the couch. I tip-toe past her and into the kitchen to set down her brandy and the wine I bought to replace what she drank.

"Where've ya been? It's been hours," she says behind me.

"Crap. You startled me. I had to run a few errands, picked up the brandy," I say, holding it up to her.

"Give 'er here." She holds out her hand. "And get me a glass too."

I comply and say, "We are leaving in about thirty minutes to meet Olivia at the restaurant."

"Good. It'll be good to talk to someone else for a change. I need new conversation." She throws back the rest of her drink as I walk out of the kitchen.

At dinner, after the waiter takes our order, I turn to Olivia, "What did you go out of town for?"

"I had a meet-up with some new designers. It was like a mini-conference at the Four Seasons in downtown Austin. The hotel was beautiful. Five stars all the way."

"Wow, that sounds nice. Did you get any leads, or make purchases, or whatever it is that you were there to do?"

"I made some promising contacts," Olivia proudly shares. "And I think I may open a second location of Ever After."

"That's great, Olivia. Really. I'm happy your business is doing so well."

"Yes, well," she continues, "we will see. I'm a little short of capital, so I may need to take out a loan or explore a partnership. I'm not sure what I'm going to do just yet. But enough about me. How has your visit been?" She looks from mom to me.

"It's been fine," I say at the same time my mom says, "Kind of boring."

I stare at my mother who shrugs and says, "What? It has been boring. You have all this time and money and all we've been doing is going to eat or walking around the mall. I can do that in Phoenix."

"I'm sorry," I snap, "I thought maybe you were out here to spend time with me, not just use me for my money."

"Here we go," Olivia mutters.

"Oh, Erika," my mother retorts, "don't be so sensitive. I'm only saying that I thought you would have planned some nice things for us to do. Spa days, tours of the city, fancy dinners. Otherwise, what am I even doing here?"

I stare open-mouthed at her, unsure how to respond. Olivia jumps in. "She's kind of right, Erika. Why didn't you plan some special things to do?" Obviously, Olivia didn't know the proper way to respond either. Olivia is so strong but morphs into a little girl again around our mother.

"Are you both being serious right now?" I turn to my sister and say, "We didn't exactly grow up in a loving home with a present mother. Perhaps if I had a proper familial role model, I'd know how to treat family better."

"Why are you speaking Spanish? And hey, I'm sitting right here," my mom says, picking at a roll.

"Yes, I remember," says Olivia to me, "but that's in the past. She is here now."

"That's what I said. I'm here now," my mom chimes in.

"Since you two are such peas in a pod, Mom can stay with you," I say to Olivia, as I push my chair back to leave. To my mother, I scowl and say, "Familial is not a Spanish word."

"Erika, don't be like that," Olivia argues.

"Oh, no. It's fine," I say, "you can have her. Feel free to stop by to pick up her things. I'll have her suitcase waiting on the front porch. Don't bother knocking."

"Don't forget to set out my brandy." I hear over my shoulder as I walk away from the table and out of the restaurant.

I don't realize how badly my hands are shaking until I grip the steering wheel. Tears sting my eyes, blurring my vision. I swipe my hand across my face to dry them, but it's no use. They are falling faster than I can wipe them away.

I burst through the front door and go straight to the guest room, throw all of my mother's things into her bag, and roll the luggage onto the porch. I consider not including the brandy out of spite but decide I don't want to risk her ringing the doorbell.

Next, I change out of my clothes and into pajamas. It's still early, but I'm not leaving the house again so might as well be comfortable. With a glass of wine in hand, I try to relax on the couch. Ozzy has been following me around the house and seems to be relieved when he can finally lay down near my feet. I open HollerHub and bypass the regular newsfeed, going straight to the Mom Group. I haven't checked it since sending that email to Allison's bosses.

That's weird. I can't find the group at all. I refresh the page and try again. Have I been kicked out? I don't know why I would have been. The searching and screenshots were all done while logged in as Candace, not that they would even be able to tell that. There is no reason I should have been removed from the group. I delete the HollerHub app and then download it again, thinking there may be some sort of glitch. I try to search for it. Again, no Mom Group.

I start to put my phone down when it pings. It's a text from Levi, "I'll be home tomorrow early evening. See you then. Your mom still there?"

"No, she's gone," I text back.

Chapter 8

I am outside pulling weeds. With summer approaching, the weeds will be a constant battle. They love the Texas heat. I, however, do not. Sweat is dripping down my forehead, mixing with the sunscreen I have diligently applied. I was in my forties before I even thought of a skin care routine, which is by no means fancy. It basically consists of sunscreen during the day and moisturizer at night, maybe some eye serum. I'm using a small spade to dig the weeds out at the roots, pulling at them with my gloved hand.

"Ouch. Dang it," I say out loud to myself and remove a glove to find a thorn has pierced my thumb. I pull it out, and a drop of blood trickles from the small wound.

In the bathroom, I open the cabinet underneath the sink and begin rummaging around for some alcohol and a piece of cotton. I apply the drenched cotton ball to my thumb, feeling the sting. I do this over and over until it doesn't sting anymore, then put on a bandage.

"What are you doing in there?" Levi groggily calls from the bed. He is using this Sunday morning to catch up on sleep.

"Just cleaning up a little. Sorry if I woke you."

"It's fine," he says, stretching in the same way Ozzy does upon waking. "I needed to get up anyway."

I sit on the edge of the bed, hold up my hand, and say, "Gardening catastrophe."

"Sounds dangerous," he says, taking my hand to inspect my thumb. I'm surprised when he continues to hold it. My hand knows this feeling. The warmth and texture of his soft hand, so familiar, yet foreign at the same time. We sit there in silence. I'm not sure what to say to this man with whom I have shared so much. All of my adult life has been a life with him. For our entire marriage, we have both been here in this house, in this bed. But I have not felt like I truly share a life with him in a long time. Silence can be empty, but this silence feels full of answers. I've been blaming my husband's work on the growing distance between us. But distance isn't what separates us, silence does.

I slowly pull my hand back and meet Levi's eyes. We linger for just a few seconds before I stand up and say, "I better finish up downstairs." I start to walk out of the room.

"Erika," Levi says.

I pause but don't turn around.

He continues, "I might run to the office this afternoon for a while."

I nod and walk out the door.

Back on the porch, I continue my war with the weeds, not exactly sure who is winning. My phone dings, and I use that as an excuse to take a small break. It's a text from Olivia, "Have a sec to talk?" I give her a call.

"Hey," she says answering immediately, "what're you doing?"

"Just working in the flower bed. What's going on?"

"I just wanted to let you know that Mom left. Well, she actually left a couple of days ago, but I thought you should know."

"Okay. Duly noted."

"You really should cut her some slack," Olivia says. "She did the best she could."

"Actually, no she didn't," I reply. "I just don't have the energy for her anymore."

There is a long pause before Olivia says, "Hey do you remember when we used to play 'Who's That Guy'?"

I half-smile and half-wince at the memory. When Olivia and I were around nine and twelve years old, we would hide in the hallway and peek out at whatever guy our mom happened to have in our home. We would take turns making up stories about him to completely define who he was, including his name, age, occupation, weird habits, criminal history, secret flaws, or whatever else we could imagine.

"Yes," I respond, grinning, "that is Peter Pumpernickel."

"He is one hundred and twenty years old and works as a dog food taster, choosing only the best kibble," Olivia adds.

"When he isn't eating canned Alpo," I carry on, "he likes to rearrange cereal boxes at the grocery store in an attempt to confuse fellow shoppers."

"Yes, and one time he was arrested for drive-by cereal swapping. He received a ten-year prison sentence and served his time in an animal shelter, where he had to taste dog food for free." Our stories are a little more creative now than when we were kids. We are both laughing by this point. It feels good to laugh.

That quickly dissipates when Olivia says, "But seriously, Mom needs us. You should try to talk to her more."

"The only thing Mom needs is money, alcohol, and someone to wait on her hand and foot. And that person won't be me. Hey, I need to run, Levi is calling for me," I fib.

"How is 'Jordache' doing?"

"He's fine. But he's leaving for the office in a bit, so I need to talk with him before he goes." I wince, wishing I could take back my words because I know what's coming next.

"On a Sunday?" She does nothing to hide her disapproval.

"Be there in a minute," I fake yell to a husband who isn't there. "I have to go. I'll talk to you soon," I say to my sister. Then I quickly end the call.

I sit back on the porch chair with mixed feelings. It was good to have that brief connection with Olivia, laughing over childhood memories, even if they were centered around some messed-up circumstances. However, just the mention of my mother did nothing to sustain that happy feeling. It's distressing because I know I need to let go, but there is some small piece of me that is still hanging on. Still waiting for the impossible to happen.

Back on HollerHub, I am surprised to see that the Mom Group has reappeared. There is a lengthy post from Allison pinned to the top so she can be sure everyone who goes onto the group's page sees it:

"Dear Moms, I am very sorry for any confusion you may have experienced with the recent disappearance of the Mom Group. I was forced to close the group for a brief period while I sorted out some very personal things that came about as a result of one of the group members. Before I go into the sordid details, I want to thank the lovely ladies who took the time to reach out to me directly. You showed that you truly care. The friendships I have made in this group are those that will last a lifetime. You are true momma warriors, and I'm so glad to be fighting on the same team.

"Now, for the ugly part. For the second time now, someone in this group has taken a screenshot of a post and used it for evil. It was seemingly worse this time, as the person who suffered was me. And I am still suffering from the consequences of your actions. You know who you are. Unfortunately, we don't know who you are, but we know what you are. You are a conniving, two-faced, backstabbing, pitiful, disgusting, repulsive, detestable, nasty person."

Wow, that was a lot of adjectives. I keep reading.

"You betrayed the trust that we moms have in this group. What's worse, you broke the rules. We should be able to discuss things freely without fear of judgment or repercussions. Without thinking that some idiot is going to screenshot our posts and send them to our bosses! Yes, that is what happened. I wrote a post about my boss. I was just letting off a little steam. It wasn't a serious post. I was just trying to add some humor to the group while slightly complaining about my current work situation. Now, unfortunately, it is my former work situation because your screenshot ended my career. Yes, ladies, I lost my lucrative job. Not only was I fired, but I was also mortified. My boss brought me into his office and reprimanded me like a child. He told me that I am an embarrassment to the company. Me! An embarrassment! I have only brought good things to that company, like my positive attitude, exceptional work ethic, and fashionably cute yet professional office suits. But he didn't even care. He said that he can't have someone working for a company who is so blatantly disrespectful. Fortunately, my husband, Jeff, has a good job, so we won't be poor or anything like that. He is being soooo super supportive and sweet to me. But that's not the point.

"I know this was a very long post, and if you've read all of this so far, thank you. I only have two more things to say: 1) Do not post anything private in the group. I know that is contradictory to the group itself as we are here to share, but someone amongst us cannot be trusted, and 2) I will find out who you are. I will, and I'm coming for you.

"Again, merci beaucoup, my friends XOXO!"

I read it all a second time and try to determine how I am feeling. Giddy. Energized. My skin tingles as satisfaction washes over me, awakening every square inch of my skin. I search for guilt, reaching into my core for anything that resembles remorse but come up empty. No guilty feelings here at all. "Miss High and Mighty" got exactly what she deserved. She was a horrible, vile, repugnant, wicked person to me at that lunch. I smile, noting that I'm also good at adjectives. Payback is gratifying. This may have even one-upped her and that's even better.

I read through the comments, and they are exactly what I would expect. They essentially imitate Allison's post, sharing the same sentiments. Everyone is being sickeningly sweet, bending over backward to write the best, most supportive responses to the Mom Group Queen. This whole episode with Allison and the other rude ladies lights a fire within my soul. A storm has been brewing inside me, deep and dark, waiting to be released. No longer will I be meek. I have found my voice, my strength. I've finally realized that there isn't one single person on this planet who is entitled to treat me poorly, especially not Allison. I pull a ponytail holder out of my back pocket and put my hair up, tucking the loose pieces behind my ears. "Bring it on," I whisper out loud, "I'm ready. Bring it on."

Back in the house, I run into Levi eating a bowl of cereal at the kitchen table and looking at his phone.

"Late breakfast?" I ask.

"Thought I better eat a little something. I'm not sure when I'll be able to get out of the office after I go in."

"You know," I say, still high off the confidence booster I just received, "I'm pretty sick of your job. In fact, I hate it. I hate your job. And I hate what it's done to us. It's your entire life, and I'm just over it."

Levi stares at me mid-bite, almond milk dripping off the side of his spoon. "Well, why don't you tell me how you really feel?" He resumes eating and looks back down at his phone.

I snatch the phone from his hand and set it a little too hard on the counter.

"Easy with that. What's wrong with you, Erika? Where is this coming from?"

"What's wrong with me is that my marriage is a complete joke. A joke." I'm nearly screeching by this point, but I don't care. "It's like I'm not even married. I might as well not be. You're only here to sleep, shower, and occasionally eat. I feel like I spend all of my time chasing something that should just be freely given to me."

"And what's that?"

"You," I scream. "It's you. I'm always wondering 'where's Levi, when's Levi coming home, I wonder if I'll see Levi today.' You used to choose me. Every day, you would choose me. Now I barely fit into your schedule. I'm a broken-down car that you walk past and never bother fixing. I'm a stamp that you've mailed and no longer has value. I'm the crumbs in the bottom of a bag of cereal." I hold up the box on the table. "I'm cereal dust."

Now I slump to the floor, sobbing. The confidence I felt only minutes ago, is quickly replaced with this incessant loneliness. I'm lonely in ways I wasn't even aware of. Ways I don't understand.

Levi comes over and crouches down next to me. "Get off the floor. It's going to be alright. It's my career, babe, I have to go when I'm needed."

"Ugh." I shrug his hand off of my shoulder. "Maybe you should stay here when you're needed."

He leaves the kitchen. Leaves me sitting on the floor. I'm not sure what happened or why I feel so emotional about this. In reality, I can understand that he has an important job. A demanding job. But in my heart, I don't care. I need a husband. The garage door closes, signaling that he is gone.

"Ozzy, come here, sweet boy." Oz continues to lay on the floor where he is, so I scoot closer to him. I pet his soft fur, and he lifts his head so I can give his neck a good scratch.

"Let's go outside," I say. The backyard is bright and sunny, but it feels like I'm standing under a rain cloud, waiting for a storm to hit.

I decide to text my son. Henry lives only about thirty miles away, but I talk to Cora in Colorado much more often. It must be a boy thing. "Hey, honey, how are you doing? Do you have time to talk?"

He replies right away, "I'm fine. In class. Talk later?"

"Sure. No problem. Call me later. I love you."

Henry has always been my calm, steady rock. He is very quiet, but not in a shy way. He likes to take his time assessing people and situations. It takes a while to earn his trust, but once you do, Henry is loyal for life. He is also very protective of his sister. Cora likes to throw around words like meddling or controlling, but Henry only has good intentions. And the kids do have a good connection even though their personalities are so different. It's an easy relationship that picks back up whenever they are together. I wish I had that with Olivia.

I text Amy next. I haven't heard from her in a while, but we were so close for so long that we always immediately fall back into a comfortable, easy friendship. "Amy! I miss you! How have you been? Are Jared and the kids doing good? Would love to catch up. Let me know when you have time for a chat."

Within five minutes of hitting send, my phone rings. Amy's cute face is on my screen. She has a slight gap in her front teeth that is actually quite charming and a light sprinkling of freckles across the bridge of her nose. Her hair is dirty blond, and she keeps it cut a couple of inches below her ears. It's an older picture, one where she is in her early thirties, but I love it just the same. It reminds me of who she was when we were younger, of who we were together.

"Amy!" I cry into the phone. "It's so good to hear from you. How are you?"

"Erika," she says with such warmth, "I've missed you so much. We are all doing well here. The girls are great. Sydney graduates this year, and Courtney is a junior in high school. I can't believe how fast time is flying. But I don't have to tell you that, with your kids already in college."

"And yours graduating, wow. I can't believe it. And how is Jared?"

"He is also great," Amy says. "We are in such a routine, but it's good, you know? Typically, we aren't all home at the same time for dinner with Jared and me working and the kids with their after-school activities, so we make a plan to eat breakfast together every morning. We don't all always make it, but we try. Even if we stand around for five minutes with a frozen waffle and a glass of juice. It keeps us connected when we are all just so busy."

"That sounds so nice," I say and mean it. "I'm happy that you're happy."

"And what about you? How's Levi? Ooh, how's the evil sister?" Amy laughs.

I laugh too. "Levi is fine. And Olivia is good. She stays busy with her store and her daughter. And her granddaughter. And the tons of men she juggles," I chuckle.

"Good, good," she giggles back. "Well, sorry to have to cut this short. I only had a few minutes, but when I saw your text, I thought I'd call for a quick hello. When we have more time, I do want to hear more about you, Levi, and the kids and the evil sister too, of course."

"Of course."

"Talk to you real soon, Erika."

"Okay. Talk to you later."

Olivia was the evil sister in Amy's eyes, and I understood why she felt that way. On the surface she really was. When Amy and I were freshmen, Olivia was a senior. I naively thought that starting high school would be easier having an older, popular sister already there. Of course, she would want to take us under her wing, introduce us to all of her friends, and pave the way for our own popularity, right? Wrong. Olivia wanted nothing to do with us, and she made that perfectly clear the night before the first day of that new school year. Amy was spending the night, and we were going to go to school together, hoping to hitch a ride with Olivia and her friends. Olivia cleared up any misunderstanding that evening when she advised us that under no circumstances were we to approach her, talk to her, or even look in her direction. "If you see me coming, move to the other side of the hall," she would say. She once tried to get me to use a different last name so that I couldn't be associated with her.

"How would that even work?" I had asked. "That makes no sense. The school records have my real name.

The teachers are going to call attendance." She agreed that wouldn't be possible, but the fact that she even mentioned it in the first place let me know how serious she was about nobody at school knowing we were related.

"We don't need her, anyway," I told Amy as we were laying down that night, too nervous to actually fall asleep. The start of a new school year always caused a pit in my stomach, but high school was a whole new ballgame. "We can take the bus to school."

"Aw, man," Amy said, "not the bus. We're in high school."

"Well, I don't know what else we can do."

"We can walk," Amy suggested.

"Amy, that's like four miles, and it's August."

"Yes, but it'll be early in the morning so it shouldn't be too hot," she said convincingly.

So, we walked to school that first morning. The clothes we carefully chose were splotched with sweat. The make-up we carefully applied was running down our cheeks. A car full of older kids drove by us and yelled something out the window, but we couldn't tell exactly what they said. Amy was disheartened, saying that we were the biggest losers. I nodded, but in my head, I disagreed. I had Amy, and that was enough. Even if I never made another friend in high school, I knew I'd never be alone.

Chapter 9

I decided to attend another Mom Group event. I don't know why I keep torturing myself. I am one hundred percent sure I will be completely miserable. It's a reconnaissance mission, I tell myself. I want to know what's going on in the group. Because I am nosey, yes, but also, I want to hear from Allison. I want to look into her eyes and see if that smug, patronizing face of hers is a little more humbled now that she knows she is just as vulnerable as the rest of us. Her perfect little world has been rocked, and I want to witness the fallout.

With summer in full force, I choose to wear a cute dress the color of sea glass and tan chunky sandals. I bought the dress from Ever After, and Olivia gave me the sandals from her own closet after deciding they would match perfectly. And they really do. I've gone back to get my hair colored, keeping it that same deep brown, almost black shade. I've lined my eyes, lengthened my lashes, and applied a light pink gloss. After one last look at myself in the full-length mirror, I am pleasantly surprised. I feel pretty darn good.

A Mötley Crüe album is blasting through the car speakers on the drive over to the restaurant. When my favorite song starts, I turn it up even louder and half sing, half scream. At a red light, an older couple is staring at me from the next car over. They turn their heads away when I begin singing right at them. They must think I'm insane, but I don't care. Today is a take no prisoners kind of day.

My attitude changes slightly when that familiar knot forms in my stomach the minute I pull into the parking lot. I attempt to convince myself to overcome this fear by saying, "You can do this, Erika. It'll be fine. These women mean nothing to you." I once heard that the words you speak to yourself can make an actual impact, especially if you change the emphasis of each word in a powerful sentence. I try it, saying aloud, "YOU are a bad ass. You ARE a bad ass. You are a BAD ass. You are a bad ASS." Okay, those last two sounded weird, but the point's been made. I don't know if I believe my own pep talk, but it's enough to get me out of the car and moving toward the restaurant. I have no friends in there so, at this point, there is nothing to lose.

There are many women here. I'm guessing at least fifty. We are all on a patio that is likely meant to hold only half that number. The wait staff weave in and out of us all, holding trays high above their heads, clearly looking irritated. Eyeing the room, I spot Allison animatedly talking to a growing group. She is standing tall, likely in designer heels, while the others are perched in chairs that have been dragged to form a semi-circle around her. It's like a shepherd and her flock. Wherever she leads them, they will go.

Again, due to the sheer number of people in attendance, food has been pre-ordered. I wonder how the restaurant is going to manage to split the bill between us all. They can't surely keep track of who paid and who hasn't. As if reading my mind, Allison makes an announcement, "Welcome lovely ladies. You'll notice you all signed in when you arrived. This is so we can keep track of the attendees. I am going to pay the bill upfront, and each of you will send me a portion of the bill once divided." My question has been answered, but I chastise myself for attending an event that will result in further interaction directly with Allison. "Now," she continues, "you are all aware of my situation and the pain it has caused me, Jeff, and my children, so I don't want to drag this out. Today is about fun and friendship. So have fun and make friends!"

I maneuver toward a table overflowing with hors d'oeuvres and add an avocado egg roll, a piece of garlic toast, and a club flatbread to my plate. I can feel perspiration forming under my dress and suddenly feel the need for some fresh air, away from this tightly-packed group. With my plate in hand, I again snake through the crowd and out the front door of the restaurant. To the right, a man is standing about ten feet away, smoking a cigarette, and speaking loudly into a phone. A large family is near him, engaged in conversation, kids running circles around their parents. I turn to the left and see a bench with a lone woman sitting on it. I head over and ask, "Do you mind if I sit here?"

"Not at all," she says, motioning to the other side of the bench.

She has thick, brown, perfectly straight hair that frames her pretty, narrow face. She is wearing satiny camo joggers that are cropped slightly below her shin, revealing a slender gold bracelet on her left ankle. The black t-shirt she is wearing is fitted and has a picture of an open book on it. Swirly stars are coming from the pages and underneath are the words "What are you reading today?"

"Troubles in Paradise," I say to the woman.

"Excuse me?"

"Your shirt. I'm reading 'Troubles in Paradise' by Elin Hilderbrand. It's the third book in a series. I love her books. I want to read her winter books, but I'm waiting to start them in December." I shove a bite of egg roll in my mouth to stop babbling.

"Oh, right. Yes, I've heard of those. Are you here for the Mom Group thing?"

"Yes," I exclaim. "But, honestly, I'm not sure if it's for me."

"No? Why not?"

"Well—" I pause wondering how much information to share. "I just don't feel like these are my people."

The woman laughs and says, "I get that. They aren't really my people either."

"Exactly." I relax into myself, thankful to have found an ally. "I mean, that Allison is kind of arrogant. Not to be mean or anything. I hardly know her. But she seems like—" I stop short again, trying to find the right adjective without sounding too harsh.

"A bitch?" the woman offers.

"Yes," I giggle. "That's the word. Well, as I said, I don't really know her. But I have been to a few of these events, and I see her posts in the group."

"Well, I do know her. She's my sister-in-law."

My eyes widen in surprise as my cheeks begin to burn. "Oh, I'm sorry. I didn't mean—"

She cuts me off. "Don't worry about it. I'm the one who said it. And she is a bitch." Her smile widens mischievously. She extends her hand. "I'm Elizabeth. But Liz is fine."

"Erika," I say, shaking her hand.

"I hate these events," she says. "And I wouldn't even be in the Mom Group if Allison weren't the one running it. She's my husband's sister. Alec, my husband, asked me to join the group when she first started it to be supportive, so I did. Then he asked me to come to these events to be supportive, so I do. Well, not all of them. But I try to make the ones I can. It's called keeping the family peace. Allison is, by no means, my favorite person, but it's fine. The Mom Group is okay too. It serves its purpose and can be helpful when looking for specific information so that part is good. Why did you join?"

"I'm not sure. It was a group recommended to me on HollerHub, so I thought I'd check it out. My kids are in college so a lot of it isn't really applicable to me. I guess I was hoping to make some friends, but that hasn't happened yet."

"Not true," Liz says with the first genuine smile I've seen today. "You met me."

A few weeks later, Liz is sitting with me on my back porch. I've assembled a bowl of strawberries, pineapple chunks, and grapes, cut up thick slices of watermelon, and made cucumber and tomato sandwiches. All perfectly light foods for this hot summer day. We are sharing lunch, wine, and gossip.

"Allison was a mess," Liz is revealing. "I'm sure there is more to the story than what she has shared with Alec or me, but we went to their house for dinner a few days after she lost her job. She said that she was in a room with several bosses from her company. They were all very upset with her, throwing accusations around, trying to find out if she has always been disloyal to their company. Apparently, Allison sat there crying as they berated her for being an embarrassment. It was pretty intense."

"Yikes. Sounds like it," I say, working to hold my face in a neutral state. In any other circumstance, I would feel horrible about someone losing a job, especially if I were the cause of it. This circumstance is a little different. Allison has a dark heart, and her altruistic appearance is artificial. She doesn't care about the women in her group. She only cares that she holds power over these women. They put her on a pedestal, and she not only likes it, she expects it.

"Honestly, I'm not super sad about it," Liz continues, apparently sharing my exact sentiments. "It knocked her down a few pegs, you know. She kind of needed that. She's a good mother, always doting on her kids. Her husband seems to worship her, so she must be an okay person. But there is something else. I don't know if he doesn't recognize it or if he chooses to not acknowledge it. Sometimes love knocks out the commonsense gene."

Glad I could be of service I think to myself. We spend the rest of the afternoon getting to know each other. Liz works part-time in the library at an elementary school. She fills her days reading with kids and organizing books. That sounds like a dream job to me. Maybe not the kid part, but the library part, for sure. She explains that they don't need the money. After all, Liz's husband, Alec, works as a physician's assistant in a gastroenterologist's office and makes a better-than-average living. She works there because she loves it. With her daughters both in high school, she found herself with too much free time.

"I was kind of going crazy," Liz confided. "The girls are never home, and Alec works ten to twelve hours a day. I just needed to find something to do. But I wanted it to be fun and rewarding."

"That's great that you love your job. And I know what you mean. Levi works at least that much and travels all the time. My kids are also busy away at school so it's just me. Well, and Ozzy." I reach over to touch him, and his tail gives a brief wag from his sprawled-out position on the outdoor rug.

"Maybe you should find a part-time job," Liz suggests.

"I don't know. I'm not sure what I'd even do. After I got married, before Henry was born, I worked part-time in a little local bookstore, and I loved it."

"Well, do that," she chimes.

I start to say that I will think about it when Levi walks out of the house holding a bottle of wine. He stops right in front of Liz's chair, holds up the bottle, and says, "I thought you two could use a refresher."

"I thought you were at work," I say. "Why are you home so early? What time is it?" I stare at him, confused by the sudden appearance.

"It's around four, and I'm home because my day is over." He looks at me, furrowing his brow, then turns to Liz. "I'm sorry we haven't had the chance to meet yet. I'm Levi." He extends his hand, but rather than take it, Liz abruptly stands up, putting just inches between them.

"Hi, Levi," she says, tipping her head to the side and displaying a dazzling smile. "It's nice to meet you. I'm Liz."

Levi immediately lowers his hand as there is no longer enough room between them to shake. They lock eyes for just a second or two, not long enough to make anyone uncomfortable, but long enough. Then, he quickly takes a small step back while matching her smile with his own famously crooked smile. A sharp pang hits me. It's a smile I haven't seen in a while.

Liz turns to me. "I didn't realize how late it was getting. I need to run so I can figure out what I'm making for dinner." She bends down to pick up her purse. I'm watching Levi watch Liz.

After we say our goodbyes, Levi takes a seat in the now vacant chair. "Want to share this bottle with me?" he asks.

Ordinarily, I would jump at the chance to drink wine with my husband on the back porch. In the past, a shared activity like this would have been spent talking, laughing, flirting. I can't remember the last time my husband and I flirted with each other. The feelings I should have had are clouded by Levi's reaction to Liz. It was so slight, and he could have just been acting polite, I reason. But I know my husband. I'm as familiar with his facial expressions and body language as I am with my own. He finds her attractive. And why wouldn't he? She is very pretty.

I tell myself that I'm acting ridiculous. Of course, my husband is going to find other women attractive. It would be absurd of me to think otherwise. It's common to think that someone other than your spouse is good-looking. It means nothing.

Still, I decide that sitting with Levi will likely not end well. Whether it's the wine I have already consumed or my growing irritation with him, I know myself well enough to know that sarcastic comments are coming, and we will end up in a full-blown fight.

I stand, pick up the bottle of wine from the side table, and head into the house saying, "Actually, since you're home, I should probably start dinner."

Later that week, Liz sends me a text early in the morning, "There is a new coffee shop that opened nearby. Want to grab a cup?" I am thrilled to hear from Liz again.

We make plans to meet in an hour. I jump in the shower, taking the time to shave my legs and condition my hair, both activities I often forgo. Liz is always effortlessly put together which has made me want to up my game. I put on some jean shorts and an olive-green shirt that ties over my right hip. I add a thin gold necklace with a tiny bee charm. It was a gift from Cora for Mother's Day several years ago. She said it was because I am always calling her and Henry "honey."

I start a map app on my phone and make my way to the coffee shop. My stomach is growling, so I'm hopeful they have muffins or pastries too. The coffee shop, called Sip and Spin, doubles as a mini music store. Liz is already at a table when I arrive, a steaming mug in front of her. She is wearing a one-piece black jumper and looks fantastic. Even though it's just coffee, I suddenly feel frumpy. I wave at her and make my way to the counter to order. There are shelves lined with older albums, memorabilia, and fun trinkets like keychains and bobbleheads. I spot one bobblehead of Alice Cooper and another that is supposed to be Gene Simmons.

"Can I help you?" an attractive thirty-something guy asks.

"I'll have a mocha latte, please. Hot."

"Thank you." He grins.

"Oh, no," I stammer, "I meant that I want a hot latte, not iced."

"I know," he says, smiling. "I'm just teasing you. I'll take it over to your table when it's ready."

I pay, thank him, and drop a few dollars in the tip jar. I sit across from Liz, realizing I forgot to order something to eat.

"Hey," she says, "isn't this place the greatest? I thought you'd like it, with your love of rock music and all."

"80s rock. I'm not into the current stuff. Some of it's too heavy for me with all of that screaming. But 80s rock is so nostalgic." I look around and spot a guitar on the wall signed by Darrell Abbott from Pantera. "That's really cool," I say, pointing it out. "He was from around here. Pantera was awesome."

Liz stares at me for a second and laughs. "You're full of surprises, Erika. I never would have pegged you as a Pantera fan."

The barista sets my steaming latte on the table. "Can I get either of you anything else?"

"No, we're good," Liz says not looking up.

"Thank you," I say smiling. He smiles back.

Chapter 10

Over the next several weeks, I visit Sip and Spin no less than a dozen times. Each time, Jimmy, the cute barista I met on my initial visit, is there.

"Hey, Erika. How're you doing today?"

It's silly, I know, but his smile always brightens my day. "Hi, Jimmy, I'll have my usual," I say, referring to a mocha latte.

"Actually," he says, with mischievous eyes, "I'm trying out a new drink. Would you like to be my guinea pig?"

"What is it?" I ask, unable to stop my own grin from spreading.

"It's a surprise, but I promise you'll love it. You aren't allergic to garlic, right?"

My eyes widen in horror, but before I can speak, Jimmy quickly says, "Kidding. I'm only kidding. Okay, go sit down, and I'll bring it out as soon as it's ready. It will be very, very hot." He winks at me in that way he often does when joking about our first encounter.

I sit at a corner table, the perfect place to people-watch both through the window to the street outside and in the shop itself. There are only a few people in here, which isn't surprising considering it's mid-morning on a Wednesday. I typically don't come in on the weekends – it's too crowded. A woman with a brightly colored pink shirt is typing feverishly on a laptop. Some teenaged girls, out of school for the summer, are sharing a table, each engrossed in a phone. A man a few tables to my left is reading a newspaper. It's been a while since I've seen someone reading a physical newspaper.

A steamy cup is placed before me. Jimmy meets my eyes and with a proud smile says, "It doesn't have an official name, but it's a vanilla bean latte with soy, two pumps of vanilla, three pumps of sweet cinnamon, a dash of nutmeg, and a shot of espresso."

I gently blow on the drink before taking a small sip. "Wow," I say, genuinely surprised. "This is good. I love my mocha lattes, but I'll definitely order this in the future."

He beams. "I know it's not super complicated or fancy, but our menu is pretty tame. I thought we needed to liven it up."

"It's really good." I take another sip. Jimmy is still standing there so I continue. "How long have you worked here?" We've only ever talked about coffee and pastries before, a little about music.

"Well," he says, sliding into the seat across from me, "we only recently opened, so since then."

"Oh, yes, of course. I should've known that," I say, shaking my head.

"I know it seems weird that a guy my age works full time in a coffee shop, but I really like it. My prior job in corporate America was stressful. I worked in finance and was breaking my back day in and day out. After about ten years, I decided that my mental health was more important, so when one of my buddies was opening up this place and needed someone to manage it, I jumped on the opportunity. I quit my old job, and here I am." He holds out his arms, gesturing.

"That's brave. Do you ever regret that decision?"

"To leave my old job? No way. When I go home, my time is mine. I'm not thinking about the presentation I have to give next week or the report due tomorrow. Sure, I can't go on lavish vacations or buy expensive cars, and I'm completely fine with that. The owner is a great guy, but he lives across the metroplex and has other businesses, so he doesn't come in very often. He pays me a pretty decent wage to keep this place up and running. Enough to live comfortably. It's just my dog and me in my apartment. It works."

"That sounds kind of perfect, actually. It's just my dog and me too, most of the time. My kids are in college and my husband works long hours and travels a lot. His name is Ozzy."

"Your husband's name is Ozzy?"

"No, sorry," I laugh. "My dog is Ozzy. He's older, almost ten, so not as rambunctious as he used to be. But he's outstanding company. I can tell him anything."

After a few more minutes of chatting, Jimmy excuses himself to return to the counter. I steal glances at him while he waits on customers and makes drinks. He is really nice.

On the way home, I find myself turning in the direction of the cemetery. I park in my usual spot and head over to the bench, where I sit in silence. The heat is in full force, but the huge oak tree nearby provides shade, casting an eerie set of shadows over the nearby gravestones. The slight breeze does nothing to help the temperature but makes the shadows dance ever so slightly as if there is more life than death surrounding me.

I pull out my phone and open the Notes app to make a checklist of the things I need to do. Call Cora to see when she is coming back home this summer and how long she is staying. Make an appointment for Ozzy for his annual check-up. See if Olivia wants to go out to lunch for my birthday in September. I know it's nearly two months away, but her schedule can get busy. Maybe Liz can come too. That would make it more fun. Text my mom to see if she ever received her glasses. No, scratch that. She would've called complaining if she didn't have them already. No need to open up that line of communication. Look for a part-time job. I add a question mark next to that last one.

I open HollerHub to see what is happening in the Mom Group. Activity has resumed back to its normal level so I scroll through to see if there is anything interesting.

"Help me settle a debate with my husband. Do you have a junk drawer? Maybe it's low-key trashy, but I need a place to put all the things that have no place to go. He thinks it's me being lazy and not organizing properly. What do y'all think?"

"Which zoo should I take my kids to, Dallas or Fort Worth? They are two and five, and it will be their first time."

"My eighteen-year-old daughter keeps sneaking out of the house. We are torn because, yes, she is eighteen and technically an adult. On the other hand, she lives in our house, pays no bills, and we feel she should follow our rules. Any ideas on how to handle this? Help!"

After reading that last one, I feel grateful that Cora and Henry are managing their own lives for the most part. And even when they lived with us, they didn't do anything like that. Not that I'm aware of anyway. At this point, if they did sneak out, I don't want to know. My scrolling is interrupted by a phone call from Levi.

"Are you in a cemetery?" he asks before I get the chance to say hello.

"Yes. How do you know that?"

"Your location service is turned on. What are you doing there?"

I could explain the real reason I'm here. That although I don't know the faces or stories of those that surround me, I know their names. I know when they were born and when they died. I know that they were beloved mothers and fathers, daughters and sons. I could tell Levi that I feel less lonely here, surrounded by these quiet, peaceful strangers in this quiet, peaceful place. I can contemplate, plan, decompress. But that's entirely too much to share, and he wouldn't understand. I offer the only plausible explanation. "Just sitting."

"But, why? That is weird," he accuses.

"Why is it weird? Because it isn't something you would do? Well, I'm not you. I like it here. It's serene and kind of beautiful. I feel like I can really think. Besides, the people here don't mind."

"What people?"

"The people buried here. They don't care if I want to sit here all afternoon."

"That is messed up, Erika. What's wrong with you?"

I sigh heavily, my frustration not contained. "What do you want, Levi? Did you call just to give me a hard time?"

"I called you because Henry is home. We were wondering where you are."

"Is everything okay?" An anxious tension wells up inside of me. Henry rarely just pops over.

"Henry is fine. He wants to talk to us about Cora."

"Is everything alright with Cora?"

Now Levi sighs. "Can you just come home?"

I throw my car into drive and hurry through the winding roads out onto the main street. My mind is racing with all the horrible things that could have happened. Was Cora in an accident? No, Levi would have sounded more panicked if she was in the hospital or something. Maybe she is sick. She went to the doctor and received some terrible test results. Some sort of disease like cancer. God, I sound like my mother.

The usual sights of the city are a blur, and muscle memory is managing my drive home. My mind is elsewhere. On Cora. I pull into the driveway. With purse in hand, I burst through the front door.

"Henry?" I call out. "Levi?"

I hear laughter coming from the kitchen and walk in to find them both there. Henry is drinking a Dr. Pepper. His dark brown hair hangs down over his ears as if offering proof that a busy college student can't be bothered with such things as a barbershop. He has my dark eyes and a watered-down version of Levi's crooked smile. He's a good-looking kid. Levi is standing across from Henry, drinking a beer. The label is half missing, and there are tiny scraps of paper littering a small section of the large granite island. Their lax behavior tells me that whatever is happening, it isn't exceedingly serious.

"Henry," I say, walking over to him. I give him a tight squeeze and then hold him back so I can look in his face. "What's going on? Are you doing alright? What's happening with Cora?" Questions are spewing out as if someone opened up a fire hydrant.

"Hi, Mom. I'm fine. Cora is fine. But have you talked to her lately?"

"We text fairly regularly. I think I talked to her last week sometime. Why?"

Nobody says anything. I look at Levi, who motions for me to sit down. I take a seat on the bar stool. The leather feels cool against the back of my sticky legs. I didn't realize how warm I am feeling. "Want something to drink?" Levi asks.

"No, I don't want anything to drink. Will somebody please tell me what's going on?"

"Cora has a boyfriend," Henry says.

"Okay, so? I mean, that's great, right?" I look at Levi, confused.

"He's forty-two," says Levi.

"What?" I practically yell. "Forty-two? Is she insane? She is only nineteen years old. That is not acceptable. Not one bit. How long has this been going on?"

"I think for a few months," Henry replies.

"A few months?" My voice is now several octaves higher than normal. "Why are you just telling us now?"

"Hey," says Henry, holding his hands up in surrender. "I haven't known for that long. That's just how long I think they've been dating. Besides, I wasn't sure if it was my place to tell you before now. It's just—"

"It's just what?" I scold impatiently.

"It's just that now I think it's getting kind of serious. And I thought you should know."

I turn to Levi. "And what do you have to say about this? Your daughter dating a man in his forties. That is our age, Levi. He is as old as we are. It's appalling."

"I agree," says Levi. His tone is much calmer than mine. "But what can we do about it? She's technically an adult." His response floors me.

"Are you out of your mind? You are her father. She is nineteen. She's no adult. Her brain isn't even fully developed yet. Which is obvious based on the types of decisions she is making." Anger is burning hot in my stomach. I try to relax my clenched jaw, forcing my shoulders to drop so I can speak again, calmer. "Cora is in no position to be dating a man that is nearly as old as we are. She is a young girl with her whole future ahead of her. We need to talk with her."

"I already tried," pipes in Henry. "It's not going to do any good. She thinks she's in love."

"Oh, God," I whisper, folding my arms on the island and laying my head down on them.

I wait a few hours to ensure I'm in a much better head-space. No good comes from a knee-jerk reaction. I want to talk to Cora rationally. If I approach her with too much emotion, she will respond in the same manner, and the whole conversation will be pointless. I've learned early on to never trust your tongue while your head is angry or your heart is broken.

After two rings, she answers. "Hey, Mom." Her voice sounds happy, normal.

"Hi, honey. How are you?"

"I'm doing good. How about you? How's dad?"

"We are fine here." I pause choosing my words carefully. "Listen, Cora, I'd like to see you this summer before school starts back up. It's already July, and time goes by so fast."

"I know. It's just that I have my friends here, and I'm really liking it, you know. There's so much to do in Colorado all summer long."

I take a chance at probing for a little information. "Could there be any other reason that you don't want to come home? Anything holding you back?"

There is a brief silence. "Have you been talking to Henry?" she asks. "Did he tell you about Brandon?"

"Brandon, is that his name? Your—" I cringe at the use of the word. "Boyfriend?"

"Mom, I can't believe my luck. He's just the most amazing man I've ever met," she gushes. "He is so intelligent and is always teaching me about the world and how things work. He shows me what it means to be treasured. Always taking me out for romantic dinners or evening hikes. He is just so special. My life has been so much better since we met."

I slump back in my seat. Cora's voice overflows with excitement, and the speech I had planned in my head is now useless. She is young and in love. I am not going to change her mind so I change my strategy. "Bring him with you," I say.

"To the house?"

"Why not? If he's as fantastic as you say he is, I'd like to meet him. I'm sure your dad would too. I'll make up the guest room for him. It'll be good."

"I don't know," she says, hesitantly. "But I'll talk it over with him and see what he says."

"Great," I say, as if something has been settled. I'm not sure what to do about this Brandon situation yet, but I have to do something. This relationship can't go on. My little girl deserves better.

Levi is back traveling, as usual. This time he is in Seattle for some sort of trade show. I would have loved to tag along. Even if Levi was busy all day, I could have kept myself entertained with all there is to see and do. I wouldn't consider myself a die-hard fan of grunge music, but some amazing bands emerged from the Seattle area. Touring around there would be fun. I have always wanted to visit the Central Saloon where bands like Nirvana, Alice in Chains, and Soundgarden played before making it big. I would stop to see the Jimi Hendrix statue and even his gravesite. And of course, the house where Kurt Cobain spent his final days would be on my must-see list.

But Levi insisted this trip wasn't for spouses. He would be busy all day and evening, and I likely would be bored by myself. He must think that being alone in Washington is different than being alone in Texas. Besides, he reasoned, we would have to board Ozzy and at his age, that wouldn't be too comfortable for him. That part was true, I conceded. So I'm here at home with Ozzy, and he is a happy boy for that.

Honestly, I don't know what Levi specifically does at his job all day. What I do know is that it is his passion. At one point I thought I was his passion. I'm not sure if I am angry, sad, jealous. Is it ridiculous to be jealous of a job? I used to be the kind of person who could be hurt or upset and push that negativity down. I could still look up at him and smile through it all. As the years have passed, my face no longer betrays my feelings. My mother didn't dole out wisdom very often, but I do remember her saying, "Pay attention to who's in your passenger seat. Some people will only ride with you as far as they can get on your tank of gas. After that, they will hitch a ride with someone else." Levi has been hitching a ride with his job for a long time.

I pour a glass of wine. It's a little early, not even nine in the morning, but I reason that mimosas are served with breakfast so there isn't much of a difference. Out back, I walk across the grass to a section of the yard filled with pea gravel, on which sit four Adirondack chairs. The old, splintered wood creaks slightly as I slip into the seat of one, indicative of several summers and winters gone by. In the center is a stone fire pit. Pieces of old logs covered in black soot and ash form a small pile, a reminder of summers long ago spent out here with the kids. I wipe away the beads of sweat already dripping down my glass, sunlight playing off the little designs etched into the side. The temperature is quickly rising.

Thoughts of Cora and her new boyfriend consume my mind. There is only one reason a successful, older man would want to date such a young woman who is still in college, who has yet to determine her direction in life. She is beautiful, but she is so much more. In addition to being a free spirit, Cora is the kindest person I know. The goodness in her heart is deeply planted. As a young girl, she once emptied both her piggy bank and her bookshelf to donate to her school's reading buddy program. When a blood drive was held for a neighbor down the street who was diagnosed with leukemia, she zealously cried because she was too young to donate her own blood. Cora once brought home a field mouse that she was convinced needed a home. While watching TV one evening, this mouse ran across the living room, causing me to shriek. Cora's little legs came running after it, as she was calling out, trying to coax the "little mousy" back to her room.

A piece of me does want to meet Brandon to see how he interacts with and treats Cora. Apparently, my curiosity and my common sense are not on the same page. I sigh, deeply inhaling the hot, humid air. I hope Brandon is just a phase. Cora has always danced to the beat of her own drum. It's one of the qualities I love most about her.

Someone is walking around from the front of the house across the grass. It's a woman, and she is heading right for me. I squint to try to put her into focus. I am nearsighted and have prescription glasses, but only wear them for driving or watching TV.

"Erika, let's go," she yells, still over fifty feet away. It's Liz.

"What are you doing here so early?" I yell back.

"I'm kidnapping you for the day. We're going out." She is closer now, her face coming into focus. "Get dressed."

I laugh. "Going out where? Want a glass of wine?" I haven't moved out of my seat.

"No, we can get wine later. Come on. We are having a ladies' day out." She spins in a circle, arms above her head and adds, "A full, carefree, and fun day. I have it all planned. I just need you to get dressed."

Now in front of me, she extends her hand, helping me up. These chairs were much more comfortable when I was younger. They need to be replaced with something not so close to the ground, something with cushions. "Where are we going?" I ask again. "What should I wear?"

Liz is wearing tan linen pants and a white gauzy blouse. Her pretty face is lightly made up with only hints of color on her lips and cheekbones. She looks at my current outfit, which consists of joggers and a Guns N' Roses t-shirt that I bought when I went to their concert in 2011. The shirt is faded and has several holes in it, but I can't bear to throw it away. Levi had given me tickets as a birthday present, and our seats were incredible. I've been out to watch some local live music over the years but haven't been to an actual concert since that one.

"Put on something nice, but comfortable. Nothing too fancy. But fancier than that," she says, her finger pointing up and down my body.

Inside, Liz sits on the couch, already engrossed in her phone, as I run upstairs. I walk into the closet looking at row after row of clothes, trying to make the right choice. I bypass the section of t-shirts that are screen-printed with bands, skulls, or funny sayings like, "Sorry I'm late, I didn't want to come" or "Hang on, let me overthink this." The next section houses my nicer cotton shirts and blouses. I thumb through them eventually removing a red blouse with tiny white hearts. I call it my Valentine's Day shirt, but I wear it year-round. Pants are definitely nicer than shorts, but it's so hot out, and I don't even know what we are doing yet. The thought of doing anything outside in pants, or worse yet, jeans, sounds unbearable. I compromise and wear a white skort. It's technically shorts but has a slightly dressier look of a skirt. Plus, the extra flaps in the front and back ensure that the white material isn't see-through. I top it off with my white chunky Dr. Marten sandals, which are decidedly cute and comfortable.

I brush my teeth again to remove any red wine stains, then hurry through a mini make-up routine, applying the basics. I pay careful attention to areas that need concealer and am generous underneath my eyes. I slather lotion on my legs and quickly slide the razor over them. I wasn't planning on going out today, so the stubble was definitely visible. Small gold hoops are looped through my ears before heading back downstairs. Liz looks up and smiles.

"Better?" I ask, arms outstretched, doing my own little twirl.

"Much. Okay, let's go."

I get in the front seat of Liz's car. It's the first time I've ridden in here, as we've previously only met up at places. She drives a medium-sized Acura SUV. I don't think I've ever been in an Acura, but I like it. It's very clean inside and smells like suntan lotion. Liz puts on oversized sunglasses, pops a piece of gum in her mouth, and starts the car. Low music from a local radio station begins playing. "Want some?" she asks, holding the pack out to me.

"No, thanks." Levi has pointed out on more than one occasion that I am a smacker when I chew gum. I've grown self-conscious about it and now only chew it when I'm alone.

"First stop," Liz declares, "breakfast. You haven't eaten yet, have you?"

"No, not yet. Breakfast sounds good. I'm starving."

"Good," she replies. "We are going to this fantastic breakfast spot in Dallas."

"Dallas?" I'm surprised. Dallas isn't terribly far, but with traffic, it will easily be an hour or more from Fort Worth.

"Yes," she says and smiles. "All of our activities for the day will be in Dallas. I thought we could use a change of scenery." She glances at me, gauging my response.

My smile feels genuine. "Dallas is great. And so is a change of scenery. Absolutely."

She nods her approval of my agreement, and I relax into the seat. "Can I put the back heat on?"

Liz laughs. "It's the middle of summer. Are you cold?"

"No, the air conditioning feels good. But the heat would help my back. It's a little sore from some gardening, I guess. Or just from being old."

"Ha." Liz reaches over and pushes the button, warmth instantly spreading across my lower back, relaxing my muscles.

As Liz drives, I notice her hands on the steering wheel. Small creases zigzag across the backs of them.

Tan sunspots are slightly visible. All telltale signs of a mature woman. They say that the hands are the first to age, even before the face and neck. I glance down at the wrinkles and spots on my own hands, noting that there seems to be more than I remember. Liz has nails that are too long to type comfortably, but not unusually so, each meticulously polished a deep shade of red. A gold watch is clasped to her left wrist. She wears a thin link chain on her right wrist, with two charms dangling from it. One is an open heart with tiny, scalloped edges. The other looks like the shape of a state that I can't make out from this angle.

"What is that charm?"

Liz glances at me then down at her wrist. "It's Arizona."

"My mother lives there. In Phoenix. She's been there for about ten years or so."

"What do you think of it?" Liz asks.

"I've never been."

Liz pulls her eyes away from the road for a longer look in my direction. "Your mom has lived in Phoenix for ten years, and you've never been?"

"We aren't exactly close. Are you from Arizona?"

"I am, yes. I was born in Mesa but grew up further south in the Tucson area."

"What brought you to Texas?" I ask. There are so many transplants into Texas. People move here due to jobs or the cost of living. Some because they love living in extreme heat for ten months wrapped in two months of cold with the constant threat of ice. I'm exaggerating a little, but not much.

"I'm not exactly close with my parents either. I grew up in a very strict household. This worked fine as a young kid, but when I started junior high, I pushed back, big time. My parents weren't having it, so they became even stricter. And I pushed even harder. Eventually, when I was seventeen, I split."

I can't tell from her expression if this subject is a sore spot, as Liz is maintaining a neutral face. I'm not sure if I should push the subject, but my curiosity is getting the better of me. "So, you just left at age seventeen? Wow, that is gutsy. Where in Texas did you go? How did you live?"

"My first stop was actually Oklahoma. I had a friend from high school that moved to Lawton, so I asked her if I could stay at her place until I figured things out. She lived in a two-bedroom apartment with three other girls. It was pretty crowded, and I slept on the couch. I got a job working at a convenience store for a few months so I could chip in for rent. I lived with her for a while until I met a guy in the Air Force who was stationed nearby in Altus. One night, we both ended up at the same party."

"Was that guy Alec?" I ask, wondering if she has been with her husband for about as long as I've been with Levi.

"God, no," she replies. "We dated for a few months and then moved in together. I was so ready to get out of that apartment. Anyway, he became very possessive. He didn't want me to go out, even if he was going to be out with me. He would say he didn't like his friends looking at me. But he went out all the time. Turns out he was screwing other girls left and right. He kept me at home, so I wouldn't know. One night while he was out with his friends, I took off in his car and headed for Texas."

"Holy crap, that's insane. Then what happened?"

"Then," Liz says, "I got arrested for motor vehicle theft."

"No way. You went to jail?"

"Nah, he got his car back and explained that it was a misunderstanding. They let me go the next day. But I was already in Dallas by that point. I worked small jobs here and there, bummed people's couches, and did what I needed to get by."

I'm surprised by Liz's story. She seems so pulled together and level-headed, nothing at all what I would imagine a runaway teen would become. "I never would have had the guts to leave like you did. Especially not at seventeen, out in the world alone."

"How did you get away from your mom?" she asks.

"I went to high school out in West Texas where I grew up but moved to the Dallas area for college."

"So, you ran away too. It just looks a little different from what I did."

We walk into the restaurant, past an indoor fountain topped with cement birds intentionally placed as though they are splashing about. The center of the ceiling is made up of glass prisms, sunlight playing off the water and illuminating the fountain and adjoining tables. The tables are dressed slightly differently, but all complementary, with linens in hues of cream and beige and golden flatware placed on white cloth napkins. The blush-colored candles sit atop golden holders of varying heights all intertwined with faux greenery and small white flowers. It's beautiful. I order an open-faced biscuit topped with a poached egg, creamy gravy, and finely diced onion. Liz orders a vegetable scramble and a cup of cubed melons. We both get an Americano.

"This is heavenly," I say, after swallowing my first bite. "I just don't eat out much anymore. I've almost forgotten what good food tastes like."

"I make my way to Dallas every few months, and I always stop here," Liz says, pleased that I'm pleased. "It's a must."

Our conversation is light but flowing. I like Liz. She is easy to talk to and fun to listen to. She tells me about her cat, Ginger, and I talk about Ozzy, even though she's seen him a handful of times already. I mention the books I'm reading, and Liz tells me about the latest art exhibit at the Kimbell Museum.

"What's next?" I ask. "Are you going to tell me, or is it a surprise?"

Liz laughs. "This is a fun day out, but not a super-secret spy adventure. We won't be doing anything today that you haven't done before. Hundreds of times before probably."

"I guess pole dancing is out." I smile.

"You haven't pole danced before?" Liz asks half-laughing, half-serious. "It's a tough workout. And great for the bedroom." Her smile slowly spreading wider.

"No, I'm too self-conscious. I could never pole dance in front of a bunch of ladies in a class. And I, for sure, couldn't do it in front of Levi without feeling like an idiot."

"You get used to it. It's a good confidence booster, and I'm sure Levi would love it. We'll plan that for next time." She winks and starts the car.

The next stop is a salon for pedicures. I'm suddenly self-conscious of my legs, certain that my quick shave missed some of its targets. I browse the wall of nail polish choices, looking for something bright to reflect my mood. I pick out a shimmery turquoise and sit back in the waiting area. Liz is there with a bottle the color of charcoal in her left hand. Her right hand is holding a glass. "Champagne?" she asks, motioning to the other glass on the marble side table.

"Yes, please." I take a small sip, the bubbles tickling my throat.

We are seated next to each other, feet in the hot, swirling water. I'm given a remote to control the massage features on my chair. We chat for a few minutes, then let the silence take over as we relax and enjoy the pampering.

Forty-five minutes and two glasses of champagne later, we are done. The pedicurist expertly slides my sandals back on my feet. We take our time walking back to the car, careful to avoid scraping our freshly painted toes. Liz turns to me and says, "How about a little boutique shopping? There are some cute shops in West Village."

"My sister owns a boutique in Highland Park," I say.

"Good idea. Let's go there."

Once we get to Highland Park, I guide Liz to the shop. "That's it," I say, pointing. "Ever After. Although, I didn't tell her I'd be coming by." I'm second-guessing my decision. "She might be busy."

"Nonsense." Liz tries to alleviate any tension she feels emanating from me. "It's your sister. Besides, we are customers. Nobody turns away customers."

I haven't been to Ever After in quite some time. A very long time, actually. The mannequins in the front window are skillfully styled in what I assume is the shop's summer line. We go in, and I immediately spot Olivia. She is fashionably outfitted in a pale pink dress with a thin matching patent leather belt. She hasn't noticed me yet, but another associate comes over to us. "Welcome to Ever After. Are you looking for something in particular that I can help you with today?"

"No, thanks," I say. "We're just looking."

"Whoa," says Liz, dragging her hand along each item as we pass. "There are some really cute clothes in here. This whole store is adorable. I love the ceiling."

I look up. I've always loved that ceiling too. It's covered in antique metal tiles, each one a different swirl of copper blended with patina. I once asked Levi what he thought about doing something like that in our den or study, but he wasn't on board.

Olivia catches my eye. "Erika," she says, hurrying over and enveloping me in a hug. "Welcome, welcome. What're you doing here? Looking for something to replace your leggings and t-shirts, I hope."

"Ha ha," I deadpan. "I'm just out spending the day with my friend, Liz." We both turn in her direction and see that she is holding a pale yellow lace-trimmed blouse up to herself in front of a large mosaic framed mirror.

Olivia walks over. "That would look fabulous on you." She extends her hand and says, "I'm Olivia."

"I'm Liz. It's nice to meet you."

The three of us are standing together now. "How did you two meet?" Liz asks.

"The Mom Group," Liz and I say in unison. This makes Olivia smirk.

"What is this Mom Group exactly? I've heard about it, but don't know much about it."

"It's just a place where a bunch of moms share parenting advice and meet up for lunches or drinks, things like that," I explain.

"Sounds riveting," Olivia scoffs.

"It's part helpful and part worthless," Liz offers.

"Part boring and part crazy," I chime in. We both laugh in agreement.

"Did you want to try that on?" Olivia asks, nodding towards the blouse in Liz's hand.

"No need," Liz replies, "I'll take it. And the gold and crystal earrings I saw on the front display table."

I also choose some new earrings and an oversized toiletry bag covered in skulls and hearts.

As the other associate rings us up, Olivia asks, "So, what are you doing in Dallas?"

"Girls' day," Liz says before I have the chance to respond. "We are spending the whole day treating ourselves."

"That sounds fun, actually," Olivia says. "Let me know next time you plan one. I'd love to tag along."

"We sure will," I say, hugging Olivia goodbye. "Say hi to Cassidy and Minnie for me."

Liz and I walk around the shopping area, wandering in and out of several more stores. A food truck is parked nearby, so we get two iced teas, then find a bench in the shade. We sit for a while, sipping our tea, watching the people go by.

"Your sister seems nice," Liz says.

"She is," I reply, tentatively. "But Olivia is a firecracker. She has a loud presence. Not in a bad way, but more like she owns whatever room she's in. She has a lot of opinions, and she isn't afraid to voice them."

Liz laughs. "That seems the exact opposite of you."

I think about this for a minute before responding. "I guess. I mean, I have a lot of opinions. I just think I go about expressing them differently than my sister. I'm definitely more reserved. Olivia is the fun sister."

"You're fun. We've been having lots of fun today. And we still have more to do," Liz says, and I appreciate her for that.

It is odd how two people can be born of the same parents, grow up in the same household, and share several of the same experiences, yet be so vastly different. I love Olivia. We have been through a lot together, and she is the only other person who really understands the childhood that I went through because she went through it too. We've become somewhat closer as adults, but as kids, we were vastly different. Age separated us, but that was just one factor. Olivia was born with self-confidence. She has always known who she is and what she wanted.

Once I started high school, I ran into Olivia regularly on campus, which she loathed. Not that we had much in the way of hallway conversations. But before that, when I was in junior high, I only saw her at home as we passed on the way to the bathroom or grabbing a snack from the kitchen. She was gone more than she was home, and I didn't blame her.

One day when Amy and I were in the eighth grade, we walked to a park a few blocks away. There was a baseball game going on, and with nothing better to do, we thought we would go check it out. We wanted to look extra nice in case we ran into any cute boys. I didn't own much make-up, but Olivia had tons. I'm not sure how she afforded it all. I always wondered if she stole it, but I never dared to ask her. I knew Olivia wasn't home, so Amy and I snuck into her room, using her eyeliner, mascara, and lipstick. We didn't have much practice, so the eyeliner looked like it was applied with shaky hands, and the mascara was clumpy, but we thought we looked fabulous. We were careful to put everything away exactly as we found it. Olivia would be furious if she knew we touched her things.

There were a lot of people at the park. Parents were watching their sons play baseball, high-schoolers were hanging out in clusters, socializing. Amy and I stood partially out of view, just under the bleachers. That's when I saw her. Sure, I lived with Olivia, so I saw her around our home, but not like this. She was in her element.

Olivia was wearing shorts that she cut so short from a pair of her jeans, the pocket linings hung lower than the bottom of the frayed hems. They were tight and hung low on her hips, revealing her belly button. The sun glistened off her smooth legs, the shimmery lotion she used catching the light. The top she wore was tight and cropped. But unlike the fitted shirt I was wearing, Olivia's was filled out on top, tapering down to her flat stomach. She was only sixteen, but in my eyes, she was so grown-up. So mature. I watched as she flipped her hair with one hand, playfully slapping a cute boy on the arm with the other. A different boy in the same group offered her a drink of something from a container he pulled out of his back pocket. Olivia drank it without hesitation. Near the baseball field at that park was the moment I realized how different I was from my sister. Many moments came later, but this was one of the first. People flocked to Olivia, even back then. She was a magnet, pulling them all in. They loved her, and she knew it.

The next stop Liz planned was a walk around the Dallas Farmers Market. It's been years since I've been here. This is no ordinary farmers market. It's made up of several buildings, each housing different vendors, shops, and restaurants. We begin in Harvest Lofts, wandering in and out of shops that offer authentic clothing and gifts from Mexico, handmade jewelry, and Texas souvenirs. I purchase a canvas handbag adorned with three tarot cards – the moon, the sun, and the lovers. It will be perfect for carrying my books to and from Sip and Spin.

"Interesting choice," Liz says, admiring it. "It's cute. I like it."

Liz and I each purchase a succulent in a brightly colored ceramic pot. We laugh when I show her a t-shirt picturing a row of succulents with "What the Fucculent?" written underneath. She matches my find with one of her own. It's a t-shirt of a cactus with the words "Don't be a Prick" written above it.

"Should we get them?" Liz asks, eyes beaming.

"Definitely," I say. "We can wear them to the next Mom Group lunch."

She squeals in response, her laughter igniting my own.

"Can you imagine what Allison will say?" In a high-pitched southern voice, Liz mimics her sister-in-law. "Now, lovely ladies, it has come to my attention that some of you are not behaving appropriately.

Showing up to a mom event in vulgar attire is unacceptable."

I continue with my own impression of Allison. "If you want to remain in my beloved Mom Group, you must act with the utmost honorable characteristics of a perfect mother. A good mother would never behave in such a crude manner."

Once our amusement dies down, we purchase our respective shirts, vowing to wear them to the next event no matter what.

On our way back to the car, we stop at a fruit stand and each purchase a large bag of oranges and another of grapefruit. As we sit in the car, ready to leave the farmers market, I turn to Liz. "Thank you so much for this day. It's been incredibly fun, and I didn't realize how much I needed it."

"The day isn't over yet," Liz replies. "We have one last stop."

We pull in front of the Statler Hotel and step out as Liz hands her keys to the valet.

"Why are we at a hotel?" I ask.

"You'll see." She smiles, confidently heading inside.

I follow her past the lobby and down a set of stairs. We end up in a small room with wood-paneled walls. The only items in here are a phone booth and a shoeshine station.

"I don't think my sandals need shining," I say. "And I have my own cell phone."

Liz makes a face and walks over to the phone booth, lifting the handle. She pushes some buttons, and something clicks. A hidden panel in the wall has opened, revealing a room behind.

"What is this place?" My eyes widen as she starts towards the door.

"Come on," Liz says, walking through. I skip to catch up.

"No way," I gush. "Is this a speakeasy?"

"It sure is."

My eyes try to adjust to the very low light. The place is small but exudes warmth. Brick and wood play off each other giving the place a slightly masculine feel. We take a seat at the bar, as a well-dressed bartender comes over.

Liz handles our order. "We will each have a Yuletide Mule and—" she pauses to study the short menu, "we will share the Artisan Cheese and Handcrafted Charcuterie."

"Oh," I jump in. "I try to avoid cheese."

"Okay then, how about—" she looks down again and says, "the B&B French Fries with Trio of Sauces?"

"Perfect." I nod in agreement.

"Why no cheese?"

"Dairy doesn't always agree with my stomach. I mean, I eat minimal amounts of dairy. I just try to avoid it when I can."

"I used to be vegan," Liz discloses.

"You did? Was it hard?"

"Not at all. I probably would still be, but Alec isn't so it's just easier that I'm not. But I make a lot of meatless meals for us and the kids. Meat doesn't need to be the focus of everything we put in our mouths."

We glance at each other for just a second before bursting into laughter. The bartender sets down our drinks, followed by the food a few minutes later. I know it's just fries, but they are truly amazing. Perfectly crispy on the outside, soft on the inside, and lightly dusted with salt. The dips just make them that much better. I take my time alternating between the spicy ketchup, truffle aioli, and guajillo, which is both fruity and smoky.

We get back to my house around seven that evening. It's not late, but I'm exhausted from the full day of adventures. Still, I feel the need to be polite. "Want to come in for a bit?"

"No, I need to get home," Liz says. "But I'll help you carry in your stuff."

We enter through the door laughing and talking. I'm surprised to hear Levi's voice. "Hello, girls. What have you two been up to today?"

"We had an amazing day," I say, setting my loot on the floor. "We went all over Dallas, eating, shopping, pampering." I hold up my foot so Levi can admire my toes.

"Very nice," he says. "Sounds like fun." He sounds different, playful almost. I am briefly reminded of the Levi of years before.

"Yes, it was, but Liz has to leave, and so our day has come to an end."

"Actually," Liz says, "I think I can stay for a little bit." She sits in the chair across from Levi, crossing her legs and making herself comfortable.

"Great," I stammer, but I'm so tired and was hoping to just shower and put on PJs. "I'm just going to put this stuff away." I carry the fruit into the kitchen, opening the bags and emptying the contents into two large bowls. I add a little water to the succulent pot and make room on the windowsill above the sink. Next, I take my new clothing and jewelry and walk through the living room, past Levi and Liz engaged in conversation, laughing. Liz is leaning in, telling a story, and Levi appears to be completely engrossed in whatever she is talking about.

"I'll be right back," I interrupt. "Just going to take these upstairs." Neither one of them looks in my direction. I'm glad Liz and Levi are getting along. But still, an uneasiness hits me on my way to the bedroom. I brush it away, chalking it up to fatigue.

Liz stays for at least two hours. The three of us sit in the living room the entire time. She does most of the talking, telling funny stories, quips about her job and her kids. Levi smiles at her, laughing at appropriate times. I try to smile and be engaged, but my smiles are often interrupted by my out-of-control yawns. Finally, Liz stands up and says she has to get home. I again tell her that today was really fun, and how much I appreciated my time with her. Levi gets up to walk her out. I walk upstairs to shower and go to bed.

Chapter 11

"I'll be home on Friday. Brandon is coming with me. We are only staying the weekend because Brandon has to be back at work Monday."

I stare at the text message on my phone, delighted that Cora is coming home. I sure have missed her. But I'm sad that she will only be here for the weekend. It's Wednesday so that gives me two days to clean the house, wash the guest sheets and towels, and shop for groceries.

I send her a text back, "I'm so happy to be able to see you. I wish you could stay longer, but I understand." I don't understand but continue typing. "What type of food does Brandon like or not like? I'm picking up groceries."

"He tends to eat organic, like me. But don't go to too much trouble. He wants to take you and Dad out for dinner."

That's a different spin. Usually, it's the parents taking out the daughter and her boyfriend. I guess when the boyfriend is the same age as the parents, all bets are off.

I text Henry, "Hi honey, Cora and her boyfriend Brandon will be by this weekend if you want to come over. What's his last name again?"

It takes nearly twenty minutes before he replies, "Brandon's last name? Pearson, I think. Not sure if I can this weekend, but I'll try to stop by."

I pull out my laptop and open a search engine to find Brandon Pearson. Lots of options appear. I try to narrow it down by adding his location – Colorado. The search gives fewer results but still isn't helpful. Without a photo of Brandon, I'm not exactly sure what to look for, just hoping something will be recognizable. I give up on my internet search and try to find him on HollerHub. This time, I'm presented with a neat list of profiles so I start clicking on each one. The first is of a guy pictured with his wife and kids. Hopefully that's not him. The second is one of a guy that looks to be in his seventies. Profile after profile I search, but nothing seems to fit. Finally, I click on one that shows we have a mutual friend – Cora Thompson. Bingo.

Brandon's profile is not private so I can see every-thing he has posted, albeit there is not much. He is a handsome guy who has dark hair, with slight wisps of gray at his temples, just barely visible in his photographs. His nose is a touch crooked, as though it's been broken before. Stubble appears to have been intentionally left on his face, covering his sharp jaw line. I can't blame Cora for being attracted to him.

Brandon's profile picture shows him seated at a table holding up a wine glass and looking directly at the cam-era as if saying cheers to the person taking the photo. Funny, since Cora isn't even old enough to legally drink. I keep scrolling and see that he made a fifty-dollar do-nation in support of a fundraiser for veterans. That was nice of him. There is a photo of him on a boat, a photo of him in a suit wearing black-framed glasses, and a photo of him with several other people on what looks to be a hike. But I'm not finding what I'd hoped to – evidence that he is a bad guy. He seems normal. Maybe likeable. I'm sure he would be if he weren't dating my daughter. I close my laptop.

That afternoon, I do my grocery shopping. I'm not sure what organic foods Brandon particularly likes, but I don't think I care. If he is polite, he will eat what I make and pretend to like it whether he does or not. I decide to buy ingredients to make black bean and potato enchiladas. My kids have always loved this meal. The enchilada sauce is homemade, and I drench each tortilla in it before adding the filling. It's good comfort food. I also grab an organic fruit tray, organic blue corn tortilla chips, and almond milk. I throw in a case of beer and a few bottles of wine for good measure.

As I'm loading the groceries into the back of my car, I look up just in time to see Levi driving past the parking lot. He is not heading in the direction of our house. That's odd, I think, looking at the time on my phone. It's only three o'clock. Levi's office is twenty miles away so there is no reason he would be back in this area. He's rarely home from work this early. After I start the car and turn on the air conditioning to hopefully spare the produce, I take out my phone once again to check Levi's location. His location service is turned off. Okay, now that is really strange. I have no idea what he's doing, but I need to find out.

"Will you be home for dinner?" I text him.

I sit in my car for a full fifteen minutes but get no response. On my drive home, my phone dings. I glance at it and see, "Not sure yet, but don't plan dinner around me." Well, who the heck else am I going to plan it around?

After unloading the groceries, I call for Ozzy to follow me out back. Sitting under the covered porch, I watch him make his usual circle around the yard, marking everything as he goes.

I check location services again just in case the phone needed to be connected to Wi-Fi or something. Nope, it's still disabled. I try texting again, "How's work going?" It's an unusual text from me. I never ask him that anymore. But I'm not sure how to question what he's doing, why I saw him drive right by me, without coming straight out and asking him. I could just ask, but I want to see if he will be forthcoming. I hold my phone in my hand. Watching. Waiting. Eventually, the screen goes black.

I don't know exactly when it stopped, but Levi and I used to talk no less than three times a day while he was at work. We would text just as much. He would send me a message every morning when he made it to work saying something like, "'I hope you slept well, miss you already" or "You looked so beautiful under the covers that I didn't want to go into work today." It was cheesy and adorable. He would call me mid-morning just to say hello, and again around lunchtime so we could share how our days were going. Later in the afternoon, he would call to give me an estimate of when he'd be home. These phone calls often only lasted for two or three minutes, but that's all they needed to be. They were our check-ins. Our touch base to say, "Hey, I'm thinking about you." Some people may think that much daily contact is over-the-top, but I loved it. Over the years, the calls steadily decreased, and then eventually texts were only used to communicate specific requests, such as, "Going to the store today. Need anything?"

Thirty minutes later, I'm still sitting, waiting. Apparently, a response is not coming any time soon. Ozzy is softly snoring at my feet, and I hate to disturb him, but I need to shift before my foot falls asleep. My tired boy doesn't even notice.

I take a peek at the Mom Group and note that there is a new event scheduled.

"Attention all bibliophiles! Mom Group proudly presents our new book club called 'On the Same Page.' We named it that because, as moms, we are all on the same page in terms of our journeys. This first meeting will be to establish the club, choose our first book, and mingle. We hope to see you there with your reading glasses on!"

This is an event that I actually might be interested in. I am an avid reader, but do I want to subject myself to yet another outing where I leave feeling deflated? Obviously so. Before I confirm that I'll attend, I text Liz.

"Hey there, a new Mom Group book club event has been scheduled. Want to go with me? It's a week from Friday. We could wear our plant shirts?"

I add a laughing emoji and hit send. Even though she works at a school library, Liz isn't much into reading. She isn't into reading at all. She told me that the last book she read was "The Count of Monte Cristo" in high school, and she thinks she used Cliffs Notes. Liz prefers art. That is her creative outlet. She doesn't paint or sculpt or anything like that herself. But she loves and appreciates it. She has spent hundreds of hours walking around museums, planning vacations around them the way some people take vacations to see the Eifel Tower or the Statue of Liberty. Personally, I don't understand art. Sure, I think some paintings are pretty or interesting, but when they become too abstract or complicated, I'm totally lost. Give me a story with a beginning, a middle, and an end any day.

I stare at my phone once again, waiting for a reply. None comes. Where is everybody? I go inside and find myself incredibly antsy, pacing around the house. For some reason, I'm too worked up to sit and read or watch TV. I decide to clean. I start by vacuuming the down-stairs, moving the furniture to clean underneath it. I use the hose attachment with the angled edge along all the baseboards. Next, the brush attachment is used on the couch and chair. I look up at the fan, then get a step ladder so each blade can be wiped down. I probably should have done this before I started vacuuming. Or maybe vacuuming just kicks up more dust. Who knows? I move to the kitchen, rinsing the few dishes in the sink and wiping down the counters. I dampen a dishcloth and set it in the microwave for thirty seconds. I nearly burn my hand taking it out but am pleased that everything in the microwave wipes away easily. I stand there, looking around, trying to determine what to clean next. Before I know it, everything from inside the refrigerator is sitting on the kitchen counters and center island. I wipe down each shelf in the fridge, removing the produce drawers to wash them in the sink. I'm sitting on the floor scrubbing the bottom shelf when my phone dings. The time on the phone shows that it's just after eight. I've been cleaning for hours.

It's Liz responding to my text, "Sure, sounds good."

I have to read my last text to remember what she is referring to before replying, "Great. See you then."

Before I forget, I go to the Mom Group to RSVP for the book club event. I get sucked into scrolling for just a few minutes when Levi walks in.

He looks around at the mess that's been created for the sake of cleaning. "What are you doing?"

I follow his gaze around the kitchen and say, "Cleaning. How was work?"

"It was fine."

"Were you there all day?" I ask, unable to help myself.

"What do you mean was I there all day?"

I slow down, enunciating each word. "Were you at work all day?"

"Yes," he says, matching my tone. "Where else would I be?"

I stare at him for a second, contemplating my next move. If I press on, the night could end badly with us in a full-blown fight. On the other hand, it's at the point where the truth is more important than keeping the peace.

"I saw you today," I begin, "driving."

"You saw me driving," he echoes.

"Yes, stop repeating everything I say. I saw you driving."

"Okay, where did you see me driving?"

"I was at the grocery store, in the parking lot, and I saw you drive by. Where were you going?"

He pauses for a moment. Something flashes across his face, but I'm not sure what it is. I stand up now, so I can better look him in the eye. Plus, my back is hurting.

"Oh, that," he says, "David was home sick today, so I needed to drop off a report to him."

Now I'm the one who pauses, staring. Waiting.

"Anything else?" Levi prompts.

"You took a report to David? In the middle of the afternoon?"

"Yes. Stop repeating everything I say," he retorts.

I give him a look.

"Okay," he says, "if there's nothing else, I'd like to get myself something to eat." He looks around the room again. "But it looks like it's all over the kitchen."

"Wait," I say, "I'm just wondering—" Levi looks so impatient, almost irritated, as if I was the one driving around instead of at work. "I'm wondering what year it is."

"Excuse me?"

"Like are we back in the 1990s?"

"Erika, I have no idea what you're talking about. Do we have any chicken salad left?"

I ignore his question and continue. "Because if we were back in the 90s, that might be believable. That is if David didn't have his own fax machine. But we live in a time when we email reports and print them at home. Like you, David is also a vice president. And like you, I'm sure he has access to email and a printer at home. So, it just seems, I don't know. Like it doesn't make much sense."

Levi turns away from me and starts sifting through the food on the counter. "Well, I don't know what to tell you. I took a report to him. End of story."

Suddenly I feel very clammy. "I'm going to take a shower."

"What about all of this food?"

"Put it away," I call over my shoulder as I walk out.

On Friday morning, I wake up feeling excited. It's the day my baby girl comes home, and I'm tremendously eager to see her. It's been nearly five months since Cora has been here, when she and three of her girlfriends stopped by one night during their drive to Austin for spring break. This time will be different. The pang in my chest reminds me that Brandon will be coming with her.

Around lunchtime, I receive a text from Cora advising that they are a few hours out. I, in turn, text Levi so that he can make plans to leave work early. "I'll be home by four," he replies.

I take another peek into the guest room. I know I didn't overlook anything, but I'm fidgety. The bed has been made up with clean sheets, and an extra blanket is folded at the foot of the comforter. There are two bottles of water placed on the nightstand along with a box of tissues. The freshly washed towels are stacked in the adjoining bathroom, topped with a new bar of soap. This room doesn't get used very often, which is a shame because it's beautiful. The gray wood furniture is simple, yet rich. The lush white comforter is accented with gray and black pillows, and a black chair with tufted upholstery sits under a tall, brushed nickel reading lamp. There is a simple white bookshelf in the corner, stacked with classic banned books, such as "To Kill a Mockingbird," "The Catcher in the Rye," and "A Clockwork Orange."

It's not that I'm trying to impress Brandon, but I do want him to feel comfortable. Comfortable people show you who they really are. If this grown man is dating my young daughter, I want to see his true colors, aside from the negative assumptions I've already formed. It will take more than a nice room to make someone comfortable, but it's one of several small steps designed to show that we are making an effort. In truth, the only effort I want to make is to kick Brandon out of Cora's life. But alas, that would only push Cora away. Push her further towards Brandon.

I hear the front door open. "Hello," my daughter sings into the empty entryway.

I run downstairs and take Cora into my arms, squeezing her a little too tight. These hugs have become further and farther between so there is a need to hold on whenever the opportunity presents itself.

When I finally release her, she says, "Mom, this is Brandon."

"Hello, Erika, nice to meet you."

At first, I'm taken aback by the use of my first name. Levi and I aren't formal people by any means, but it sounds odd for Cora's friends or a boyfriend to call me Erika without me first inviting them to. But I suppose it would be weird for a man my age to call me Mrs. Thompson.

"Hi, Brandon. It's nice to meet you. Welcome," I say motioning towards the living room. "Come in, come in. You can set your stuff down here for now. Do you guys want something to drink? Come sit down."

"Mom, we've been sitting for hours. We're fine, but thank you," Cora says.

"I still can't believe you drove all this way for just a weekend trip. It's such a long drive for such a short period."

"It was a nice drive," Brandon chimes in. "I had good company." He smiles at Cora.

"Well then, Dad will be home soon. Do you guys want me to cook dinner? We're having enchiladas."

"Sure, that sounds good," Cora says.

Brandon adds, "But no cooking tomorrow night. I'm taking us all out to dinner." He gives me a thumbs up and smiles, holding my gaze.

"That's really nice of you, Brandon. Make yourselves at home. It'll take me a little while to make dinner, so I'm going to get started."

I set a pot on the stove to start some vegetable broth boiling and begin chopping tomatoes and dicing onions. I hear the sliding door open. A peek out the kitchen window finds Cora and Brandon walking hand in hand through the yard. She is pointing at various things, the fire pit, some potted plants. Brandon says something to her, and Cora's face lights up. She leans into him, her body language showing me exactly what I don't want to see. They share a brief kiss. I go back to preparing the meal.

I love cooking, but I don't do it very often anymore. Baking is something I was never good at. I think that's because I have a hard time sticking precisely to recipes. I've tried baking several times throughout the years. The kids would have bake sales at school or need treats for classroom parties. But I learned quickly that if you aren't carefully following along, it just doesn't turn out well. It became easier to cook the food and buy the dessert.

Levi arrives home and walks into the kitchen. "Hi. Are they here?"

"Yes, out back," I say, moving toward the window.

Levi stands next to me, both of us watching. "What's he like?"

"I only just met him a little while ago. We didn't talk much. He seems nice, though. He's a good-looking man." I feel a twinge at my use of the word "man." She is just too young. I add, "I can see why Cora likes him."

"I guess I better go meet this guy," Levi says, as he turns to go out back.

Several minutes later, the three of them come back inside, and I offer them all spicy water.

"Spicy water?" Brandon asks.

"Yes," I explain, "when Cora was little, she called sparkling water 'spicy water.' It was the cutest thing. We've called it that ever since."

Brandon gives a little laugh, clearly humoring me.

Once we are all seated at the table and have begun eating, I glance around. Awkward is the word I would use to describe dinner, but who knows what everyone else is feeling. Cora seems a little on edge. But I definitely didn't have to worry about Brandon feeling comfortable. He seems right at home, dominating the conversation.

"Basically," he says, explaining his career in chemical engineering, "I have oversight of the team that conducts test-production methods. As new pharmaceuticals are created, we assist with the implementation piece. Establishing health and safety protocols, things like that. It can be very stressful." He shoves a bite of food in his mouth. "There are a lot of deadlines."

"I can imagine," I say.

"Sounds interesting," Levi says. "How long have you been with your company?"

"Only about a year. There were some issues with the last lab I was at. It just didn't work out. So, yeah, that's where I ended up."

"These enchiladas are amazing, Mom," Cora praises, changing the subject.

"Thanks, honey. I know you like them." I smile.

"I love them. Really good," she replies.

"Yes," Levi says patting my hand, "they are very good. Thank you."

I catch his eye for a second, and we smile. Our mutual contempt for Brandon putting us on the same team once again.

Later in bed, I turn to Levi and ask, "Do you think she will sneak into his room?"

Levi laughs rolling on his side to face me. "I don't think so. They aren't high-schoolers." Then his face turns serious. "Wait, do you think so?"

"I don't like it, Levi. Not one bit. He's a grown man. He has no business being with Cora. She has her whole future ahead of her."

"I don't like it either," Levi agrees, "but I don't know what we can do about it that won't drive her away. If we make her choose, it won't be us. And she still has a future. It's not like she's running away with him."

"Yet," I add, flopping onto my back. "I think we need to go hard at him over dinner tomorrow. Ask him the tough questions."

"Yes," Levi says, "we need to find out what he is doing with Cora. Why he likes her. We just have to be diplomatic about it. Maybe you should start. You are the level-headed one. You won't do or say anything demeaning or hurtful."

A thought flashes through my mind, and I am reminded of the demeaning and hurtful things I've said and done recently to some of the local moms. "Okay," I say, "but I need your support. Will you back me up?"

"Absolutely," Levi says.

I can't lose Cora. Not yet and not to Brandon. Motherhood is such a balance of holding on and letting go. We do our best to guide our children, to support them, to trust them. It's difficult to remember that sometimes they will make decisions that we don't agree with. And when they do, we are tasked with the difficult decision of knowing when to push and when to back off and let them choose their own paths, even if we know it's a mistake. Cora's new boyfriend is definitely a mistake.

Brandon chooses an upscale restaurant in downtown Fort Worth. They have a large rooftop seating area, but it's a little warm to be outside. We sit at a table near the window offering beautiful views of downtown. The flickering candle in the centerpiece is bouncing off the glass, intermingling with the lights of the surrounding city.

The waiter comes by to take our drink order. I order first, then we all look to Cora to go next, but Brandon speaks for her. "She'll have sparkling water with lemon." Cora smiles, placing the black linen napkin in her lap.

"So," I say, looking directly across the table, "tell me, Brandon, why do you want to date our daughter?"

"Mom," Cora cries, furrowing her brows at me. Then turning to Brandon, she says, "You don't have to answer that. Why we are together is nobody's business but our own."

"No, it's fine," Brandon says. "Actually, I've always preferred younger women. Women in their thirties have ticking clocks. They are always saying things like 'When are you going to propose,' or 'How do I get you to pro-pose' or 'I want to have a baby.' I'm not about all that."

I'd like to point out that even women in their thirties are younger than he is, but I let it go. "So, what are you about?" I ask.

"I'm about fun, you know. Life's too short. I can't have a woman nagging me all the time. It's like, older women already have a past. They are bitter. No offense," he says, looking directly at me. "It's like their self-worth is hinging on whether I'll marry them or not. They're sick of dating and just want to latch on to anyone. And they lie about being on birth control just to trap you."

I am flabbergasted. This is the most disgusting speech I've heard in a while. I'm not even sure how to respond. I look to Cora who is smiling, drinking her sparkling water. Glancing at Levi, I can tell he is upset. His eyes are boring into Brandon who is completely oblivious.

"Has that happened to you before? A woman lied about being on birth control to trap you?" I ask.

"Well, no, not me. But it happened to a buddy of mine. I don't have time for any of that. I just want a good girl like I have here." He squeezes Cora's shoulder at the same time Levi squeezes my knee under the table. Levi is losing his patience. Mine is already gone.

Brandon, clearly unable to read the room, continues. "You see, older women are already established and successful. It's like, I go into the relationship having to prove my intelligence, my success. I get enough of that stress at work. But with Cora, she is just young and free. She isn't concerned with my status. She is googly-eyed and easy to impress."

"Just wait a minute," Levi's voice booms, as he stands up.

"Dad," Cora says, pleading with her eyes, "sit down, please."

A few of the other guests have turned to look our way, but I don't care. Brandon is out of line. Levi sits back down, lowers his voice, and continues, "My daughter is a highly intelligent and amazing person. She is beautiful inside and out. And you better be trying like hell to impress her every second of every day. If you aren't being your best self, you don't deserve her. You actually don't deserve her anyway."

Cora's eyes glaze over as she fumes. "Oh my God, I knew this would happen. That's why I didn't want us to come home. I knew you guys would act this way."

"Cora, we aren't acting," I say, trying to control my own rising voice. "We are reacting. To him." I point at Brandon, who is busy digging into hors d'oeuvres.

The rest of dinner is quiet, and we primarily focus on our plates. On the drive home, I text Liz to recap the night. "Wow. That's crazy," she replies.

"Yes, and the thing is, he didn't even realize that what he was saying about women was completely gross. I can't believe Cora chose this guy."

"Hopefully she comes to her senses. How's Levi handling this?"

I text back, "Levi? The same as I am. We're on the same page here. Trying to be a united front."

I'm holding my phone in my hand, but no more texts come through. Levi's phone dings. He glances at it and turns off the screen. "Work," he says to me.

The next morning, there is still tension between Levi, Cora, and me. Brandon couldn't sense tension if it smacked him in the face. I'm not surprised when Cora announces that they are gathering their things together and heading out.

"Don't you want to at least stay for breakfast?" I ask.

"No, thanks, though. We can grab something on the way. We better get on the road."

I was hoping to have some alone time with Cora. To dig a little deeper into this relationship she has. "Can you come out back with me for a second?" I ask her.

"Mom, we really need to get going."

"Just give me a couple of minutes."

She sighs and heads outside with me on her tail.

"I love you," I begin, "and ordinarily I trust your judgment. But this? This is wrong, Cora."

"Why? Why is it wrong? Because he's older?"

"It's not even that anymore. He's just kind of a jerk." I realize that as soon as the words are out of my mouth, I've lost my opportunity. I wish I could take them back. Any chance I had at having an in-depth discussion about Brandon is lost.

"He is not a jerk. You and Dad just don't know him. You didn't even try to get to know him. And now we're leaving. You've lost your chance." She goes back into the house, they pick up their bags, and say goodbye.

My heart aches as I watch them drive away. There are hundreds of books on raising kids. You can read about sleep schedules, breastfeeding, potty training. There are guides on the best way to teach a child how to ride a bike, how to spot bullying, and how to not raise a bully. There is information on public school versus private school versus homeschool. There are parental books about anger, happiness, and loss. But nobody tells you how to let go. How to fall asleep at night with your children under a different roof. I suppose that's because telling a mom not to worry is like telling water not to be wet. The fear courses through our veins. It beats through our hearts. No matter how old they get, we, as parents, will never stop worrying. We never let go.

"What did you say to her?" Levi asks.

"I told her he was a jerk. I know I shouldn't have. It just came out."

"But it's true," Levi says. "That guy is a real piece of work. Cora can do much better."

"Right?" I say, shaking my head in disappointment. "She really can. Want some breakfast?"

Chapter 12

The Mom Group book club is tonight. To say I'm excited is an overstatement. However, now I have Liz, so it will be much better than traversing these things solo. At least I don't have to think too hard about my outfit, as Liz and I are planning to wear our farmers market plant shirts.

This event starts at seven and is at Allison's house. That part makes me leery, as I'll no longer be on neutral ground. That is definitely enemy territory.

Levi is home from work well before I plan to leave, which is surprising. He usually uses Friday nights as his catch-up time at work. He laughs when I come downstairs. "Nice shirt," he says.

"You like it?" I say holding it out, so he can fully admire it.

"Yes, it's totally you." He offers a smile, which is returned.

"Okay, well I'm off to the book club. Wish me luck."

I pull up in front of Allison's house. There aren't very many cars out front, so I double-check the address, then glance at the time. I'm at the right address, and it's a few minutes past seven. I twist around, scanning the street for Liz's SUV but don't see it. I text her to ask if she's here, then check the event in the Mom Group to ensure it hasn't been canceled, and it hasn't. However, there are only six confirmed attending. Six including Allison, Liz, and me. My body tenses. I don't know why these things make me so nervous. I've been through enough unpleasant Mom Group experiences that they shouldn't phase me anymore. I get out of my car and grab my purse and the dessert tray from Costco. It's filled with bite-sized brownies, cheesecake cups, and strawberries. My stomach rumbles either because I'm hungry or nervous. Logically, I knew I'd run into Allison considering this is her house. But I didn't plan on so few people attending. I thought I'd be able to mingle and avoid too much face time.

There are broken toys scattered in the yard, the grass looks like it hasn't been mowed in a while, and weeds have invaded the flower beds. Considering how put together Allison always seems to be, I'm surprised by the exterior presentation of her home. Perhaps her husband works a lot and just hasn't had time to take care of it. Right before pressing the doorbell, I hear yelling coming from inside the house. It's a man and a woman arguing, but I can't make out the words. I'm not sure what to do. Even in the evening, it's hot enough to melt the cheesecake. I go ahead and ring the bell, and the shouting immediately stops. A minute later, the door opens, and Allison is standing there, a huge smile plastered on her face. As soon as she sees me, her smile falters. She tries to quickly recover it.

"Erin, it's so nice to see you. Come in," she says, holding the door open wider.

"It's Erika. Thank you for having me."

"Yes, well. It was an open invitation to everyone in the group."

Not exactly the warm welcome I would have liked, but about what I expected. I walk into Allison's house and am taken aback. It isn't awful exactly, just surprising. The living room is neat in that toys are piled into a large bin in the corner and the bookshelf is filled with framed family photos, books, and faux plants. Vacuum lines run diagonally across the living room, but evidence of spilled juice or soda remains. In the kitchen, I set my platter on the counter that is cracked and worn on the edges. There is nothing wrong with this house, per se. Truthfully, it is much nicer than the place I grew up in. Bigger too. It's just unexpected considering how Allison continuously presents herself. She is always so haughty, walking around with this privileged air about her.

I shouldn't have sent that email that got her fired. It's obvious she needed her job, as it looks like they aren't doing too well. For the first time since it happened, guilt hits me. I am responsible for the loss of someone's career. A paycheck. I hurt not only Allison but her family. In a matter of minutes, my guilt turns to shame. I decide right then and there that I will be a better person. I can be a friend to Allison. She may need friends, someone to talk to. Losing a job is a significant life change that requires support. I can be that supportive person. Maybe nobody showing up isn't an accident. Maybe the universe is trying to tell me something.

"You're the first one here," she says, "but I'm messaging the other ladies who said they were coming. I'll try to find out where they are."

She turns around to grab her phone and gasps, noticing my shirt. "What are you wearing?"

I look down and smile. "Oh this. It's funny, right? Liz bought a similar one. She's supposed to wear it tonight too."

"It's kind of crass, don't you think? Definitely not book club appropriate. Sure, we are moms and like to cut loose once in a while, but we hold ourselves to a higher standard than that," she says, motioning to my top. "You said Liz? Do you mean my sister-in-law, Liz?"

It is suddenly very clear what the universe is trying to tell me. It's saying, "Screw you, Erika. You get a whole evening with the bitchiest person you know. Enjoy."

"Actually, no, I don't think it's crass. I think it's funny, as do most people with a sense of humor. And yes, Liz, your sister-in-law. Where is she by the way?"

I send another text to Liz, "Are you on your way? I need moral support. Your husband's sister is getting a bit crazy up in here. The shirt was not a hit LOL."

The doorbell rings. Thank God. Allison hurries off to answer it, and I hear two more ladies talking excitedly, but neither of them is Liz. I join them in the living room.

Allison says, "Tanya and Sheila, this is—" she turns to me. "I'm sorry, what was your name again? I never get it right."

I know this game. Pretending to forget someone's name is a sure-fire way of letting that person know just how unimportant she is. I am so insignificant that Allison can't be bothered to even remember my name. But that's okay. If Allison is testing my waters, she better know how to swim.

"Erika," I say, directly to the other two ladies. I make eye contact with Sheila. She knows who I am. She must remember blowing me off when I first joined the Mom Group because she quickly averts her eyes, turning back to Allison. I have just about had enough. I'm ready to leave, and this book club hasn't even officially started yet. But I know that Allison also wants me to leave, and that's why I decide to stay. She should be uncomfortable, irritated even. That, and I am still hoping Liz shows up.

"Everyone, grab some wine and snacks and meet back in the living room in five, so we can begin," Allison says, resuming command of the evening.

I put only the items that I brought on my plate and sit down in the chair. The other three ladies are packed together on the couch.

"To get started, we will go around the room, and everyone state your favorite book genre, your top three favorite books, and the worst book you've ever read. This will give us a sense of where we are at in terms of choosing a book that we'll all like. I'll start," Allison says.

I glance at my phone to see if Liz has responded to my plethora of texts. She hasn't, but I notice the time and can't believe I've only been here for about thirty minutes. It feels like it's been hours. After playing Allison's book discussion game, then another hour of listening to the three of them chit-chat, I excuse myself and say that I need to get home.

"Thank you for hosting, Allison. It's been riveting," I deadpan. I can be snarky right back.

She gives me another one of her smirks and closes the door behind me without another word.

During my drive home, I try to figure out just what the heck is wrong with her. I think this was the worst Mom Group event yet and don't understand why Allison dislikes me so much. Perhaps she acts that way towards anyone who refuses to kiss up to her. Her bosses were probably glad to have an excuse to fire her. I wonder how her husband can stand her or how anyone can for that matter. People must either worship her or loathe her. There can't be any in-between.

I pull into the driveway and notice that Levi's car is gone. I wonder if he decided to go back into the office. Once inside, I pull out some leftover eggplant parmigiana from the refrigerator and warm it in the microwave. Ozzy wanders into the kitchen to investigate the smells.

"Hey there, Oz. You want a treat?"

He looks at me but does not respond. Then he lays down. This is weird behavior, as Ozzy loves treats and is well aware of what the word means. I go over to the treat jar, but he doesn't follow me. Only after I open the jar and offer him one of the peanut butter nuggets does he begin thumping his tail. He crunches the goodie, then lays his head back down.

I take my food to the living room and turn on the TV, channel surfing. A few minutes later, Levi walks in.

"Where've you been?" I say, between bites of breaded deliciousness.

"I went for a walk. On a trail."

"A walk," I repeat, laughing as if to say good one. Levi lifts weights in our home gym, but he doesn't go trail walking.

"Yep," he says back.

"Wait, really?" I sit up, interested. "Where did you walk to?"

"I went over to the Bear Creek trails." He sits on the floor and begins untying his tennis shoes.

"All the way over in Keller?" I ask.

Bear Creek in the city of Keller is a huge park with several walking trails, ranging from less than a mile to over five miles long. It isn't that far away, but far enough to wonder why Levi would go there on a Friday night when there are several other trails located much closer to our home.

"It isn't that far," he says. "I like it over there. It's nice."

"Okay, it's just—" I stare at him as if looking harder will help me see something more.

"It's just what, Erika?" He stops what he's doing and looks up at me. "What? Am I not allowed to go to whichever damn walking trail I want?"

"You can go wherever the hell you want," I snap back. "I don't care what you do."

"Obviously you do," he says. "Obviously, since I get twenty questions every time I'm not exactly where I'm supposed to be."

"What's that supposed to mean?" I feel my voice rising.

"It means that while I'm at work all day, you're at home doing God knows what. But heaven forbid I go out walking one evening without asking your permission," he thunders.

"Doing God knows what?" I yell back. "You know exactly what I'm doing. Not a damn thing."

"Well, whose fault is that? Nobody told you not to do anything."

"Nobody told you not to do or not do anything either," I continue, infuriated. "I never said you had to ask my permission. I just asked where you were. Didn't know it was so top secret. What are you really out doing, Levi?"

"You're impossible," he yells, going up the stairs. "Ridiculous even." I hear the bedroom door slam.

As I get up to go into the kitchen for a glass of water before bed, I notice an odor wafting through the air, very subtle. It's not a scent I've been aware of previously in my house. I'm not sure how to even describe it. It smells yellow if yellow had a smell. But not yellow like sunflowers and sunshine. It smells more like the dull stain of cigarette smoke. Stale.

The next morning, I wake up to an empty bed. I sarcastically wonder if Levi is out walking trails again but find him in his office. Without a word, he gets up and closes the door as I walk by. My heart sinks a little. He's really upset. Maybe he actually was just out for a walk last night. Maybe. But something doesn't sit right. When you've known someone for a long time, a really long time, you understand their habits, their patterns, the way they think. You can almost anticipate their behavior before it happens. But this. This is different. I wouldn't say I necessarily distrust Levi, but I also can't ignore this nagging suspicion. I attempt to push it down, but it continues to occupy space in my mind.

In the kitchen, I pour myself a cup of the coffee. My taste buds protest that first sip so down the sink it goes.

A quick check of my phone finds a text from Liz, "I am sooooo sorry for missing last night. Please don't hate me. I'll make it up to you. Promise! By the way, how was it?"

"Where were you? It was awful. Too much to text. I'll tell you next time I see you."

She responds immediately, "How about you and Levi come over for dinner next weekend? I'll cook something fantastic. Make it up to you."

"I thought you didn't cook," I reply.

"Okaaaay, then I'll order in some amazing food. What do you say?"

"That sounds nice. I'll talk to Levi about it and let you know."

A great cup of coffee is always available at Sip & Spin. I consider leaving the house without saying anything to Levi but decide against it, trying to demonstrate considerate behavior.

"I'm running to the coffee shop for a while. I'll be back soon," I call through the closed door. I wait for a beat but get no response, then go ahead and leave.

What a pleasant surprise to find that Sip & Spin is not very busy. I missed the early morning coffee rush and now it's that off time before lunch. I smile when I see Jimmy behind the counter. He is looking pretty adorable, moving about with purpose, a smile plastered on his face. He is always so pleasant. I feel at ease just being in his presence.

He turns around, sees me, and his whole face lights up. "Hey you, I haven't seen you in a while. How're you doing?"

"Hi, Jimmy." I feel a flicker of butterflies, which surprises me. It's just sweet, coffee guy, Jimmy. Nothing to get worked up over. "It's been pretty busy for me lately. My daughter came home for a visit and other things going on."

"Yeah?" he says, still smiling. "Well, I'm glad you're here now. What would you like?"

"Can you make me that special latte you made before? The one with the vanilla and cinnamon?"

"Anything for you," he says, before ringing me up.

I take a seat facing the window and notice that some trees are shedding their leaves. It's already almost fall. Now, in terms of temperature, that means nothing here in the northern part of Texas. It could get cold in October, or it could be hot until December. Mother Nature is finicky, so the weather is totally unpredictable from year to year. Some tree leaves do change their color, turning yellow or a deep red, but mainly they just fall, leaving us with huge piles and lots of raking.

Jimmy sets the steamy cup of goodness in front of me and says, "Iced Buns Latte."

"Cute name. I like it."

"Glad you approve," he says, taking a seat across from me.

I enjoy Jimmy's company. We talk a lot about nothing in particular. He tells me about a recent camping trip. I tell him about my girls' day with Liz. We laugh about the guy who comes into Sip & Spin for a muffin and gets upset that they don't also serve beer.

"What are we listening to?" I ask, motioning to the speakers mounted to the ceiling.

"It's just an early 2000s Billboard hits mix. Do you have a music request?"

I tap my chin, pretending to think. "How about Poison? Their 'Open Up and Say...Ahh' album. Do you have that?"

"The music is streaming from my phone, so we essentially have everything." He gives my hand a quick pat, and says, "Be right back."

A minute later "Love on the Rocks" is flowing out of the speakers. With good coffee and even better music, I instantly feel in my element. The prior night's issues with Allison and Levi are washing away. Jimmy comes back to the table, this time sliding into the seat next to me. I'm taken aback for a second but chalk it up to Jimmy just being his friendly self. He is uncomplicated, easy to talk to. And he really listens to me. Not that I'm talking about anything too complex or deep, but I appreciate his attention. He's busy, but he always makes time for me.

"This album," I begin, "reminds me of tenth grade."

"Oh, yeah? How so?"

I tell Jimmy about my friendship with Amy. How we were two outcasts who somehow found each other early on and stuck together all the way through high school. My love for rock music seemed so out of character. Olivia used to tease me that I looked like I should be listening to Genesis or Peter Cetera.

Many people loved heavy metal and rock music at my high school, but they dressed the part. They were the kids who looked like they could be in those bands themselves. The girls wore fishnet stockings, acid-washed denim skirts, leather boots, eyes heavily lined with black liner, and even black lipstick on occasion. The guys wore ripped-up jeans, band t-shirts, one dangling cross or a lightning bolt earring. Some of them had leather or jean jackets covered in button pins displaying names or images of their favorite bands.

My style, if it could be called that, was much more subdued by the way of baggy jeans with sweaters or flannel shirts. I didn't wear much make-up. Nobody in a million years would have looked at Erika Gatlin and thought "rocker chick." But on those Saturday nights when my mom and Olivia were both out, Amy would be at my house and the stereo in the living room would be blasting AC/DC, Aerosmith, Twisted Sister, and even Black Sabbath. We would raid what little snacks we had in the cupboard, pour ourselves Dr. Peppers, and sing and dance our hearts out. No doubt we looked ridiculous, but we didn't care. We were having the time of our lives. Those Saturdays were special. I make a mental note to call Amy. Our last call was cut so short, and I'd really like to catch up.

My story is interrupted when I feel Jimmy's knee brush against mine. At first, I think it's accidental and move it away. But when I start to talk again, his leg touches mine once more, lingering there. I pause for a second, unsure what to do. We are now the only two people here in the shop.

"Women like you don't happen often, Erika. You're a special one. I can see it."

My raw self tells me that Jimmy is fantastic. And I feel this magnetism, this pull towards him. Levi has been so distant, almost pushing me away. I can't remember the last time we actually talked about anything other than the kids without arguing. It's just so comfortable hanging out here with Jimmy. Uncomplicated. It's nice to be able to share things with someone who listens, to laugh, to connect. I feel something else on my leg and glance down to find Jimmy's hand resting on my knee. I look up, and he is looking right into my eyes, leaning in ever so slightly. I hold his gaze, my eyes wandering down to his mouth and back up again. He takes his other hand, moving a piece of my hair back behind my ear. I suddenly stand up.

"Thanks for the coffee," I stammer. "And the visit. But I have to go."

"Wait, Erika—" he says, but I cut him off.

"I'll see you next time. Thanks again," I say, hurrying out the door. But there won't be a next time. I can't go back to Sip & Spin ever.

Chapter 13

I let a few days pass before broaching the subject of dinner at Liz's house. Levi needed to cool off, or he might be quick to say no. We spent several mornings passing each other in the hall with barely a nod, and at night, I'd be asleep before he was home from work. Truthfully, it didn't appear to be all that different from any other day, but the tension in the air was there. His anger continued to linger.

Then one evening, I couldn't take the silence and blurted out, "I'm sorry, okay? I didn't mean to insinuate that you were lying. It was just weird to me. That's all."

"Thank you, but there wasn't anything weird about it. You go to the cemetery, and I go to Bear Creek Park. We are just different people doing different things."

That last sentence was a jab to my heart. I never considered us as separate. Of course, logically, we are two people, yes. And we are different, yes. But we had always been one unit. One unified team. Now we are individuals, each playing for our own sides.

"We got invited to Liz's house for dinner on Saturday. It will be Liz and her husband, Alec, and us. Can I tell her we'll go?"

Levi was back engrossed in his phone but suddenly looks up. "Go to Liz's house?"

"Yes, Levi, for dinner. Can we go?"

"Sure, I guess so," he says. He has a strange look on his face, so I ask him again to be sure. We don't need another blow-up fight, so I'm trying to be conscious of his feelings.

"Yes, I'm sure. That's fine."

That Saturday, I go back to the hair salon to get my roots touched up. Levi and I haven't been out together in a while, and I want to put in the effort to look extra nice. I'm excited about the evening, about getting to see Liz and having a fun night with my husband. I decide to pamper myself and get my make-up done, as well. And Levi is supposed to be out picking up some wine for tonight.

But nervousness is creeping in, mingling with the excitement. It's as though I'm going on a first date with a stranger rather than the thousandth date with my husband. I suppose that's because it technically is our first date in a very, very long time. Tonight needs to go well.

At home, I look at myself under the bright LED lights. Whoa, my eyes are smokey. It looks much darker than it did at the salon. In an attempt to fix this, I wipe most of the charcoal eye shadow off my lids, going back and forth, trying to even them out. I wanted to look done up, not like I got in the ring with Muhammad Ali. When I think it's as good as it's going to get, I get dressed.

Levi comes into the bedroom and sits on the bed. He looks up at me, taking in my fresh hair and make-up, and says, "You look nice tonight."

"Thanks. What should I wear? I'm thinking my sheer pink blouse over a black tank top and jeans? Maybe it's too hot for jeans. I mean, we'll be inside, but still. What if we go outside? Well, if we go outside, I probably do need to be in jeans, so the mosquitoes don't swarm me."

"You're overthinking it," he says gently. "Jeans will be fine. I'm wearing jeans, as well. But I didn't get wine."

I give him an incredulous look. "What do you mean you didn't get wine? That's the only thing I asked you to get."

"I know," he says, grinning. "I decided on champagne instead. I bought four bottles. It seemed like a good night to celebrate."

"Oh, nice. A bottle for each of us." I give him a genuine smile.

And he smiles back. "Exactly."

Liz opens the front door. "Come in," she exclaims, hugging and kissing both Levi and me. "Alec is in the living room. Make yourselves at home."

Liz's house is stunning. It's a contemporary home, decorated in a modern style. There is a mix of beautiful elements, including one raw brick wall and rich oak ceilings. The floors are hand-scraped teak. All the furniture is white but in a variety of patterns and textures. The granite countertops in the kitchen are also white, as are the cupboards. The only true colors in her home are found in the art, which hangs on every wall. They appear to be oil paintings, some realism and some abstract. It feels like the most comfortable, welcoming museum ever.

"Oh boy, we are in for a night," Liz squeals, taking the champagne bottles out of Levi's hands.

"Anyone want a drink before dinner?" Alec asks. He looks to be several years older than Liz, his mostly gray hair blending into the lighter brown. He is tall, stocky, and not as handsome as Levi, but he has a good face. A kind face.

"Absolutely," Levi says, making himself comfortable on the couch.

They begin to make small talk, and I follow Liz into the kitchen.

She pours us a glass of wine from a bottle that's already open. "Tell me everything about the book club at Allison's."

I describe every detail, from Allison's disappointed face when she opened the door and saw me standing there to her even more disappointed face when she realized it might just be her and me.

"Oh my God. Nobody else showed up?"

"Two more," I say, holding up two fingers. "Those two were Allison's saving grace."

I continue about the "What the Fucculent" shirt, and the horrified look on Allison's face.

Liz breaks out in laughter. "I would've loved to see that."

"You were supposed to see that." I'm laughing, still caught up in the humor of the story, but curious about Liz's absence too. "Where were you?"

Liz's laughter dies down. "I know, I'm sorry. I just got caught up with stuff at the house and didn't check my phone. I guess I just forgot."

"It's fine," I say to reassure her, trying not to be a little miffed about it. "But you missed out."

"Sounds like it. Want to help me get this food to the table?"

Liz has ordered Thai food. There is an entire feast that includes spicy fried wontons, tofu satay, pho, Pad Thai noodles, pineapple fried rice, and yellow curry with vegetables.

Liz has set out one plate and two very small ceramic bowls in front of each place setting. Like the rest of the house, the table is dressed in white. I try to be extra careful not to splash as I spoon the curry and pho into my bowls. The first bottle of champagne Levi bought has been evenly divided into our four flutes, so close to the top that the bubbles are dancing above the rim.

Levi raises his glass and says, "Here's to those who wish us well, all the rest can go to hell."

Everyone laughs and takes a drink. The food is delicious, the company is even better. We are laughing and talking, sharing stories, and telling jokes. Levi is in his element, more talkative and animated than I've seen in a while. It's the Levi I love. The one I've been missing. Both Alec and Liz are eating it up, engrossed in his stories. Levi has turned up the charm.

After dinner, we all get a champagne refill and head to the living room. Alec is sitting in one chair, and Levi is seated on the couch between Liz and me.

"Erika," Levi says, "remember when we used to hotel surf?"

"God," I say, laughing, "don't tell that story."

"I have to know. What is hotel surfing?" Liz asks.

"Okay," Levi begins, as I bury my face in my hands, "when Erika and I first started dating, we were poor college students, right? So, we used to try to be creative and come up with ways to save money. And this one time, Erika, comes up with hotel surfing."

"Hey," I interrupt, "I didn't come up with it. It was your bright idea." I smile at Levi, remembering the fun we had.

"Well, whoever had the idea, it was fantastic. We would go to local hotels during their free buffet breakfast time—"

"You didn't!" Liz exclaims.

"We did," Levi continues, "except we had to be smart about it. We couldn't just walk in off the street and go straight to the buffet. So, we would try to be as nonchalant as possible, and head to the elevator first, pretending to be guests going up to our room. We would ride up and down for about ten minutes. Then when we thought enough time had passed, we would come downstairs, go to the buffet, and sit down and have breakfast."

Liz squealed, playfully slapping Levi on the thigh. "That is genius. We have to try it sometime."

Now Levi laughed. "No way. I'm beyond stealing free breakfast. You'll have to count me out. I'd feel so guilty now, I'd pay for a night's stay just to make up for it."

"Anyone want more to drink?" I ask, holding up my near-empty glass.

"I'll get another bottle. Be back in a flash," Liz says, jumping up.

"No more for me," Levi says, "I'm driving."

"Nonsense," Liz sings on her way to the kitchen. "Y'all can just stay the night. We have plenty of room."

I try to give Levi a look to signal that I most definitely do not want to stay the night. I'm having fun, but I don't want to sleep here.

"Then pour me another. I have to use the little boys' room." Apparently, he missed my nonverbal cues. Levi then gets up to use the bathroom, leaving Alec and me in the living room. I ask him about the art on the walls, but he explains that he is not the art lover. "I don't know too much about them, other than they're amazing. You'd have to ask Liz. I'm more into music."

"Me too," I practically yell. "What kind of music do you like?"

"Mainly Jazz. The modern stuff. Jason Moran, Esperanza Spalding. I also like some of the classics."

"Cool, cool," I say, deflated. I know nothing about jazz.

"I also like musicals," Alec adds. "'The Phantom,' 'Wicked,' 'A Chorus Line.'"

"I loved 'A Chorus Line.' And 'Evita,'" I say. "But I've only seen the movie versions. Michael Douglas. Madonna."

He stares at me for a moment, and then we burst out laughing. Alec and I talk more about this and that when I realize my glass is still empty.

"Time for that refill," I say, standing up. The alcohol rushes to my head, and I have to stop and steady myself on the arm of the couch before trying forward move-ment again.

I part walk, part dance my way toward the kitchen, the champagne accomplishing its job perfectly. The self-consciousness that always looms over me, washed away. Before I step foot into the kitchen, the sight in front of me stops me dead in my tracks. Liz is standing by the sink, her arm on Levi's arm. They are only a few inches apart, speaking in hushed tones. I take a step back, trying not to be seen. I strain to listen to their words but can only make out whispers. Whatever they are talking about seems important, urgent. My head is not clear, the alcohol adding a hazy layer to my reality. Liz is looking up at Levi, smiling. I can't see his face, as he is partly angled away from the doorway, but whatever they're talking about is keeping him in that same spot. Close to Liz. Too close. I choose to not interrupt. I want to watch. I want to see what my husband is going to do when he thinks I'm not there. Suddenly, Liz turns my way and catches sight of me. She takes a step back from Levi, creating the distance that should have been there to begin with.

"Ready for more champagne?" Liz asks me. She is acting overly casual.

Levi turns around. His eyes flash a look of surprise and something else. Guilt, maybe? It's there for just a brief moment, and then he gives me his stupid crooked grin. I'm not sure what is going on here and don't want to jump to conclusions or make any accusations. This is my husband and my good friend, and they were just talking. It's perfectly normal for two people who are friends to have a conversation. Alone. Whispering to each other.

Standing no more than six inches apart. Her touching him. I'm not going to make a big deal out of this. It's been a fun night, and this doesn't need to ruin it. It's fine, I tell myself. It's fine. I repeat this mantra several more times in my head, not sure if I'm confirming that it's fine or if I'm trying to convince myself that it is. I try not to cry. I realize that I hate champagne.

"Actually, no. Thanks. What were you two talking about?" Just because it's fine doesn't mean I don't want to know.

Liz looks at Levi, and he says, "Liz was just telling me about her job. And how much she enjoys it."

Liz adds, "Yes, and how I can't believe school is starting up next week, and I'll be going back. The summer just flew by."

I don't say anything. Not at first. I'm still just watching as if I will suddenly get some sort of superhero power that allows me to read minds or detect the truth. My superhero name would be "ERI-KAught You Lying." I snicker to myself, buzzed me finding myself quite funny considering the situation.

"Well," I say sarcastically, "once you two are finished discussing the pleasures of your careers, we should probably be going." Levi looks like he's about to protest but decides against it.

The car ride home is quiet for the first few blocks. I'm watching the expansive homes as we pass. Some have their porch lights on, and others don't. I've always wondered why everyone doesn't keep their porch lights on. It's a deterrent against would-be burglars, vandals, or any other type of mischievous person, as they'd prefer to work in the dark, not directly under a bright light. Levi interrupts my random thoughts, breaking the silence. "That was a lot of fun. Did you have fun?"

"Yes, it was fun," I reply dryly.

He glances at me. Now he looks like he wants to ask me what's wrong, but I know him well enough to know that he changes his mind to avoid opening that can of worms. Not tonight. Four or five glasses of champagne plus a heaping teaspoon of irritation is not a good combination. He turns on the radio, eyes focused back on the road.

Every relationship has its ebbs and flows. The beginning is the peak, the spark, the excitement. It's that uncontrollable giddiness you feel when you're about to see the other person. Your person. The sadness you feel when it's time to part. There is the longing. The feeling like you will die if you aren't together. But feelings are fleeting. They change. Love isn't just about feelings. It's commitment. It's about showing up every day. It's filled with disappointments and hurt, but also forgiveness. It's trust and the ability to have someone to count on no matter what. No matter what.

I glance at Levi and wonder if we still have that commitment. I remember a time when I never would have questioned it. We showed up for each other every single day, even if we were busy. Even if we barely saw each other. I knew he was there, supporting me. And I was supporting him. We had a common goal of raising the kids, providing a happy, structured home. Now the kids are raised, and Levi has his busy career. And I have me. All I have is me.

I wake up the next morning with a headache. Levi has set some Tylenol and a bottle of water next to the bed. He also left a note: "Going for a walk at Bear Creek Park. Be back later." He has drawn a happy face at the bottom of the paper. Okay, whatever, I think. But then immediately feel grateful that he was considerate enough to let me know. And that he left me some hangover help.

I pop the Tylenol into my mouth, tasting the bitter coating before I'm able to twist off the water bottle cap. I knock back half of the bottle before trying to plant my feet on the floor. I wasn't pass-out drunk last night, but too much champagne always leaves me feeling like I should be seriously reevaluating my life choices. The older I get, the worse the repercussions. I would vow to never drink again, but I don't like liars.

I look in the mirror and decide I definitely need a shower. I also know that standing for any length of time at this juncture sounds like too much effort. I opt to just wash my face, then slowly head downstairs with Ozzy on my heels. Food should be my next priority, but the thought of it makes another bout of nausea wash over me. I compromise and decide on a glass of orange juice, just managing to pour it and sit at the table when Olivia calls.

"Hey," I say.

"Hey," she replies, matching my less than enthusiastic voice.

"What's wrong with you?" I ask.

"I went out last night. It was bad," Olivia replies.

"Why? What happened?"

"I drank tequila shots and who knows what else, acting like I was in my twenties."

I sit back, laughing. "You too? Same here, but with champagne. If you were taking shots, I think you win."

"Great," Olivia says, "I have the perfect prize. Pick me up and take me to get my car."

"Where's your car?"

"Well," she explains, "the girls at the shop asked me if I wanted to go out for a drink with them after we closed. At first, I said no, but they were hounding me."

"Right, I'm sure they were twisting your arm."

"They were. Anyway, I drove over to meet them at a bar, but then we started taking shots. I left my car there and took an Uber."

"You took an Uber home?" I ask.

"Eventually, but first we took an Uber to a few more bars. I didn't get home until after two in the morning. I hardly remember going to bed. It was a lot of fun though. But I was quickly reminded that I'm closer to fifty than twenty. Ouch."

"Your head?"

"No, I mean yes, my head is pounding, but it hurt me to say that I was close to fifty. I don't feel like I'm in my late forties. Well, when I'm sober I don't."

"If it's any consolation, you don't look like you're in your late forties. You don't look a day over forty-five."

"Ha, ha, very funny," Olivia says. "So, can you pick me up to get my car? I'll buy lunch."

The thought of lunch makes my stomach turn, but I know I need to eat. The drive will be awful. It's not like it's around the corner. But she would do it for me.

"Sure," I tell her. "Give me about an hour."

I do a minimal amount of moving around to get ready, only brushing my teeth and running a comb through my hair. I stop to give Ozzy extra kisses and cuddles before I leave. He looks so cute curled up in his oversized, fluffy bed.

The sun smacks me right in the face when I step outside. Sunglasses are a must before taking another step. The drive over to Olivia's is rough. Not because there is a lot of traffic, but more so because I'm expected to keep my eyes open while driving. I pull up in the driveway and nearly hit a bunch of plants haphazardly strewn about. They are still in their nursery containers, waiting for transplant to the nearly bare flower beds. I should help Olivia with the yard, but not today.

I text that I'm here, and Olivia comes out a few minutes later. She is dressed in an orange, pale yellow, and white sundress. Tan espadrilles are on her feet, thin straps tied around her slender ankles. Her face looks flawless, every bit of make-up meticulously applied. Meanwhile, I'm sitting over here looking like I lost a fight.

"You don't look hung over," I say as soon as she gets in.

"I feel it on the inside, but I refuse to let it show on the outside." She takes a glimpse at me and adds, "I see your hangover has seeped out."

I look right at Olivia, hold my head up high, then hold my middle finger up even higher. She laughs, and with that, we are on our way, choosing to stop for lunch first.

The restaurant has a shaded patio with fans, so we opt to sit outside. There is also a slight breeze that keeps the stifling heat from ruining our meal.

"I think someone has a voodoo doll of me, and they are jabbing pins in my head," Olivia says.

"I wish whoever had my voodoo doll would stop forcing me to make bad decisions."

The waiter comes over. "Can I interest you ladies in a mango mimosa or a Paloma. It's really good. Made with tequila and grapefruit with a twist of orange."

We both groan at the mention of alcohol. "We'll just have water for now," I say.

"So, tell me about your evening. What has led you to your current state?" Olivia asks.

I tell her about Levi and I hanging out with Liz and Alec at their house. I talk about the four bottles of champagne, plus the wine that was already there. I relay stories and stupid jokes that were told, trying one out now.

"How do you organize a space party?" I pause, allowing Olivia's eyes to scrunch before continuing. "You planet."

I wait for a smile, but Olivia is staring at me like I've lost my mind.

"So, yeah. We had fun. But then—" I stop, not sure how much I want to share with Olivia. How deep I want to get into my insecurities about Levi and my marriage. My relationship with Olivia is what I would call tumultuous. We love each other, but we have definitely had our ups and downs throughout the years. We rarely see eye to eye. And yet, I would do anything to protect her, and I think she would too. She has. There was a time when she was the only one who ever did.

Growing up, our mother was constantly gone or pre-occupied with work or men or the men at her work, and

Olivia and I were left to often fend for ourselves. I tried to be grown up, to shoulder responsibilities that weren't typically expected of a kid, but it was hard. With Olivia being the older sister, many decisions fell to her.

When the heater broke one winter, our mother left the house to stay somewhere warm, likely at some man's place. She literally left and told us that we were old enough to figure it out. I was eleven and Olivia was fourteen. It was an especially cold week that winter, with daytime temperatures only reaching the twenties and the nights falling to the teens or lower. Olivia bundled us up in several layers of sweaters and coats. The outer-most coat layer that we wore was taken from our mother's closet so that it would be large enough to fit over everything else we were already wearing.

One afternoon, we left the house and walked toward the community church. The cold burned our faces, making the two-block walk seem much longer. The church had an outreach program and would feed the homeless twice a week. Olivia wanted to get us a hot meal. I felt uncomfortable about taking food from them. We weren't homeless. We had a place to live. A place to sleep. I told Olivia that we were taking food from people in need. She asked me if I saw the food that was in our refrigerator and cupboards. I told her no, and she said that was correct because there wasn't any. We are people in need, she had said. We each took a pre-packaged boxed meal which included two pieces of chicken, green beans, macaroni and cheese, and a roll. The church also had a huge bin full of new blankets, each one folded and individually wrapped in plastic. Olivia and I took one of those, as well.

The food was cold by the time we walked back home, but we were glad to have dinner. We reheated our food in the microwave and sat on the new blanket which she spread on the living room floor in front of the TV. It's like a picnic, she had told me. I don't remember what we watched or what we talked about, but I remember how I felt. My big sister took care of me. And as long as I had Olivia, everything would be okay. She was there for me. Sure, maybe she didn't want to hang out with me when she was with her friends or be associated with me at school, but when it mattered, she was there.

The waiter brings out our food, and it looks delicious. Both of us pick at our plates, trying to get down what we can. I opt to come clean about my feelings toward Levi. About my suspicions.

"I think that maybe, possibly, Levi could be having an affair."

Olivia stops eating and stares at me. "Why would you think that?"

"Lots of reasons, I guess. For one, he's never home. I mean sure, he works a lot, but still, who knows where he is. One time I saw him driving when he was supposed to be at work, and he said he was taking a report to one of his associates."

"So?" Olivia says.

"So, isn't that just a little suspicious? And then, one time, he was supposed to be home, but he said he was walking at a trail over in Keller. He never walks."

Olivia is all but rolling her eyes. "Did you catch him cheating? Did you find proof on his phone? Is he sending naked pictures of himself to women on the internet?"

"No. Gross. At least not that I know of," I say.

"So, you think he's cheating on you because he drove to a coworker's house and went walking?"

Okay, hearing it like that sounds ridiculous, I admit. But I know my husband. Something is off. "Oh," I cry out, "then there was last night."

"What happened last night? I thought you guys had fun."

"We did, but right before we left, Liz said she was going into the kitchen, and Levi said he was going to the bathroom, and I found them both in the kitchen. Together."

"And?" Olivia asks, raising her eyebrows, interested.

"And, they were whispering, like saying something they didn't want Liz's husband or me to hear. And she was touching his arm."

"Okay," Olivia says, now clearly unimpressed. "You spend too much time worrying about nothing. You really need to find something to do."

"Will everyone stop saying that to me," I say loud enough that the only other table sitting outside glances over. "I know it sounds like nothing. But something is happening. My marriage is—"

Olivia looks at me, waiting for me to finish.

"My marriage is unsatisfactory." I finally decide.

Olivia breaks out in laughter.

"It's not funny. What's so funny?" I ask.

"Erika, everyone's marriage is unsatisfactory. I think that's actually like a requirement for marriage."

"I don't believe that to be true. How can it be true? We used to be so good together. Perfect. Everything was perfect. But these last few years, I've been so lonely I can't even stand myself anymore. I think I need to be sure. Levi keeps his phone locked, but I know his email and text messages pop up on his tablet. They are connected somehow. I haven't checked it out myself, but I remember him telling me about it when he set it up. Oh, I have a better idea," I continue, feeling slightly hyper. "I am going to get one of those car trackers. I can hide it inside the vehicle. That way, even if he doesn't have the location services active on his phone, I can see where he is."

Olivia is shaking her head. "I don't think 'Wrangler' is cheating on you. And if I were you, I wouldn't be pressing that issue. You're going to drive yourself crazy. And him. You haven't caught him doing anything untoward. He is just being Levi. Being a guy. Sometimes guys are inconsiderate. But that doesn't mean they're having affairs. Stop being wary and stop expecting him to screw up. Trust your husband. You have no concrete reason not to."

I sigh, taking in Olivia's advice. She's right, I suppose. When I laid it out and heard myself say the reasons I had my doubts, it did seem ridiculous, like I was definitely stretching.

"If he isn't cheating, fine. But what about our marriage? I'm not expecting Levi to be perfect. I just want to be loved like he used to love me. Like he promised to love me when he first said those words. I know he's busy with work and tired and stressed out all the time. But I have bad days too. And when I do, I want someone—Levi, I want Levi to put his arms around me and hold me tight and tell me that it's going to be okay. To say that he's there for me. That we have each other so we can overcome anything. These days it's like we are two strangers sharing a house, roommates almost. Do you think I need to spice things up in the bedroom? Not that there has been anything to spice up lately."

"No, definitely not," Olivia says. Her answer surprises me. Olivia is many things, but a prude is not one of them.

"Why not?"

"I just think you need to talk first. Get to the root of your problems before you start breaking out the sex toys."

"I'll try, but I can barely get a normal conversation out of him, much less one about our relationship. He isn't around long enough."

Chapter 14

I'm trying to get ahold of Levi. His assistant said he is out of the office, at lunch maybe, but she isn't sure. It's almost four in the afternoon.

Cora has called me no less than five times today and is having a complete meltdown.

"Mom, he is scum. Complete scum." I can barely make out her words amongst the sobs.

"I know, honey. You don't need him. You can do so much better. Besides, you're busy with school. You don't really have time for a boyfriend," I say.

"School? Who can possibly go to class at a time like this?"

So, the creep Brandon has broken her heart and is the cause of her missing a semester at school. Just perfect.

"And you know what really sucks?" Cora whimpers. "He said he loved me. He said that he could see a future with me. He said I was special."

"Honey, you are special. He's just too stupid to see it. He's a piece of crap, Cora, and you are better off without him."

"How can you say that?" Her cries are now turning to wails. "He was the ideal guy – smart and good-looking and funny." I must have missed the part from their visit where Brandon was funny.

"And," she continues, "he has already found someone new. He didn't even tell me. He just started dating her behind my back while we were still together. When I found out and confronted him, he literally shrugged his shoulders. That's it. A shrug." Okay, that sounds more like Brandon.

"You don't need him, Cora. You'll find a guy who puts you on a pedestal. Someone who treats you the way you deserve to be treated. A guy who is so focused on you, nothing and no one could pull him away."

"Like what you have with Dad?" She sniffles.

"Sure." I choose to go with the white lie, figuring it's needed at this moment. "One day, you'll find a relationship like the one Dad and I share." God, I hope not. "Sometimes, the biggest blessing is a goodbye. It just takes time to see it." That last sentence hits me hard the second it's out of my mouth.

I continue, carefully. "But you need to still go to class and do the things you have to do. Life doesn't stop. Don't let Brandon take more from you than he already has."

"I know. I just need a few days of hibernating in my room, watching TV, doing something mindless."

"Ice cream," I suggest. "Get ice cream."

"Did you tell Dad yet?"

"No, not yet. He's in a meeting at work." Another lie. "I haven't been able to talk to him."

"Okay, well tell him for me, will you? But tell him not to call. I think I'm going to try to lay down. I'll call you guys tomorrow."

"Okay. I love you, Cora, and I am sorry. A broken heart is the worst kind of pain. But you will get through it."

Where is Levi? I have texted him several times, but no reply. The location on his phone is still turned off. I need to ask him about that. When we originally decided several years ago to share our location with each other, it was for safety purposes. If, God forbid, one of us didn't come home one day, we would at least have some idea where the police could start looking. It had nothing to do with a lack of trust, so him just turning it off seems a little shady.

Normally, I wouldn't think twice about Levi not being home from work yet, but today isn't a typical day. I try his office phone again, and it goes straight to voice mail.

By 7:30, my irritation turns to worry. I text Liz, "Hi there. Poor Cora. Her jerk of a boyfriend left her for someone else. I'm happy about it, not that she is hurting, but that he's out of the picture. She is really upset though. I tried to calm her down and make her feel better. So that's what's going on here. How's your day going?"

"Oh, I'm so sorry for Cora," Liz texts back. "Time heals all wounds. She is tough like her mom. She will be okay."

About ten minutes later I get a text from Levi, "Hey, what's up? I got your message."

He got my message? More like fifteen texts and six voice mails left on his cell phone, plus a few voice mails left at work. He got my message. Is he insane?

"Where have you been? I've been trying to reach you. What if it had been an emergency?" I text back.

"Was there an emergency?"

He is unbelievable. "That is not the point. The point is, Cora needed both of her parents and you were nowhere to be found. So where were you?"

I hold the phone in my hand waiting for a reply. I see the dots, indicating that he is typing, then they stop. Then the dots start again. Then they stop. It takes so long for his reply to come through that my screen goes black, forcing me to reenter my passcode.

Finally, his text appears, "I was in a meeting. I must have forgotten to turn my phone back on after."

"Well, that's strange, because when I talked to your assistant today, she didn't know where you were. She said maybe you had gone to lunch. But I thought no way he is at lunch this late."

"She must have missed it on my calendar or something. But I was in a meeting. Don't know what to tell you."

His casual, minimal responses are making my nostrils flare. I begin pacing around the living room, talking out loud to myself. "He is so full of crap. I don't believe him for one minute. Not for one damned minute. He forgot to turn his phone back on. Please. That man lives and breathes through that phone. Does he think I'm an idiot?"

I'm so worked up that I cannot wait until Levi gets home. When that smug face walks through the door, I'll let him have it. Cora needed him. I needed him. But he wasn't here. And I don't believe for one minute that he was in a meeting and forgot to turn his phone back on.

If someone had asked me ten years ago to describe my husband, I would have said hard-working, kind, smart, funny, thoughtful, amazing father. I never would have said liar. Sure, we've both told lies before. Everyone lies. We've crafted detailed stories about the tooth fairy flying through the house for the kids. We've pretended to be sick to avoid going to my mother's house that one and only time she invited us over for Thanksgiving. I've let the kids stay home from school on their birthdays, writing them false excuses so that we could spend the entire day together. I think I've even told Olivia she was the best sister ever after too much wine. So, yes, I've lied. Levi and I, we've both lied. But we've never lied to each other. Not that I know of anyway. Not until now. I'm not sure if Levi no longer respects me enough to be truthful about what he's been up to lately, or if he thinks I'm not smart enough to recognize the lies that roll so casually off his tongue.

As time passes, with Levi not yet at home, the fight slowly drains out of me. Hour by hour, my stress and anger have morphed into determination. I still believe he is lying, but I'm not yet sure how to handle the situation. I'm less ready for a fight, as yelling and arguing seem pointless. There will be no confrontation tonight. But something is going on, and I'm going to find out what it is.

I wish I had someone to talk to about all of this. I tried talking to Olivia, but she thinks I'm overacting and creating things that aren't really there. I don't want to open up to Amy about this. She has always been easy to talk to, and I love her dearly, but we talk so infrequently these days that it would feel bizarre to unload my marital issues during a catch-up phone call. Then there is Liz. I am fairly uncertain about Liz. On one hand, she has been a good friend. We laugh so much, and I love hanging out with her. On the other hand, she gives me an uneasy feeling that I can't quite put my finger on. I want to trust her. But, I rationalize, if I'm having doubts about whether she can be trusted, maybe she can't.

I open the Mom Group to see what has been posted lately and scroll through the typical posts, searching for something related to my current situation.

"I want to get my eyebrows microbladed and my teeth whitened. Where do you go and how much do you pay?"

"Is anyone else absolutely thrilled that school has started back up and the kids are out of the house? I'm so excited to have my mornings free again."

"Is there a local women's bowling league? I'm not the best bowler, but I love it, and would be interested in joining."

I continue reading through posts, not finding what I'm hoping to find. There is a little magnifying glass to enter specific words to search. First, I try "cheating" and get a few results. One is about a kid who was caught cheating on test at school. Another is asking if anyone had experience cheating on a drug test with borrowed urine. The next word I search is "infidelity." There is a post that says write one word that comes to mind when you think of marriage, and someone commented with the word infidelity. Another woman wrote that her marriage ended due to infidelity, but the post focuses primarily on juggling shared custody.

I stop to think, trying to come up with other similar words. I'm not sure exactly what I'm looking for, but I am trying to find other women in my situation, hoping to glean some ideas or advice. I search for the word "affair" and read the results. One is about the movie "An Affair to Remember." Another post is about a 5K charity run called "A Family Affair." Yet another post is included in my search because the mom wrote that a visit to a local museum was an all-day affair. Suddenly, there is something that piques my interest written by a woman named Beth Smith.

"I'm not sure if I want advice or if I'm looking for reassurance, although I'm not certain if I will get that in this group. I'm having an affair with a married man. When we are apart, I'm wracked with guilt. I know this would cause tremendous pain to his wife. I try to justify that with the knowledge that their marriage is on the rocks and has been for a while. When we are together, I feel happy. Really alive. It's like he has woken up something inside me that has been asleep for a long time. He is the sweetest man. He is kind and makes me laugh. I'm tired of sneaking around, but not sure if he plans to leave his wife or if I even want him to. I like being with him, but don't want to marry him or anything. I've just felt empty for so long and this man fulfills me. There is not a specific question for you all, but I am interested in your thoughts. Please don't crucify me too badly."

I set my phone down and try to steady my shaking hands, utterly appalled. I don't care how wonderful a man makes this Beth woman feel, he is married and that means hands-off.

I log off HollerHub as myself and log back in as Candace. I haven't used the Candace account in a month or two, as there's been no need. The Beth post was added approximately three weeks ago, and there are over a hundred comments. I begin reading through them, trying to gauge the typical reaction of the other moms. About ninety percent of the women are as horrified as I am. They shame Beth for interfering in a marriage. Some call her a home wrecker and other harsh names. But the remaining small percentage of moms are not as critical. They are empathetic, which is shocking. They have written supportive comments, not necessarily condoning the affair, but understanding it. They tell Beth that she is still a good person. One lady even congratulates her on finding a great guy.

"A great guy?" I scream out loud to my phone. "A great guy does not cheat on his wife no matter what." A deep, dull pain is forming in the back of my head down into my neck. My palms feel sweaty, and I wipe them on my pants before going back to the Mom Group.

I notice one of the comments is from Allison. Of course. She wrote, "Beth, you are a strong, fearless mom and human being. Things happen for a reason. I truly believe that if you two are together, it's because the Gods above believe that to be the best for everyone. You should embrace your time with this man and explore your relationship with him. You have to take care of yourself first. I'm always here if you need to chat. Hugs!"

It's as if Allison hasn't already given me a hundred reasons to hate her. Being supportive and uplifting to one woman doesn't mean trampling on the rights of another. The wife has the right to fix or not fix her marriage, and she should be able to do that without interference from anyone else. How can this married couple have a fighting chance if Beth is inserting herself into the equation?

I click on Beth's profile. Her primary picture is of a field of flowers, a stock photo she grabbed off the internet. But I want to see her face. I want to see who this woman is and try to grasp what kind of person sleeps with another woman's husband. Unfortunately, her profile is private, so it's fairly limited, with only a few photos of some landscapes. That's it. I can't read any posts or see who her HollerHub friends are. Nothing.

I go back to Beth's post in the Mom Group and begin to comment, to write all the ugly, vile things I think about her. How she is a sorry excuse for a woman. But I stop due to another idea. Beth needs to be held accountable, I just need to figure out who she is. I come up with a plan to try to flush her out. It isn't the best idea, and probably won't even work, but I have to do something. As Candace, I type up a private message to Allison, mimicking the way Allison herself would craft a message.

"Hey girl, I've only been a member of your Mom Group for a few months, but I love it! I think it's the perfect place to meet other incredible women, such as yourself. You are such an inspiration to me and moms everywhere. I know I need to attend a few events. I'd love to meet you in person. I think we could be besties! I was wondering, has the group ever played 'Hot Seat' at an event? It's super fun, and a great way to really get to know people. It's built on friendship and trust, just like your group. Anyway, thanks for your time, and I hope to hear from you soon."

I read through my message one more time, adding "Hugs" at the end. Once the gagging stops, I hit send.

During college, I was invited to a "Hot Seat" party by my then-roommate, Hailey. After a lot of convincing, I said I would attend with her. It was at a house that a few guys from a neighboring school rented together. When we arrived, there was a person at the door demanding an entry fee. To be admitted, we each had to pay five dollars and take two shots of tequila, then we were handed some sort of alcohol-laced punch. There were about fifteen people there, sitting around the living room and standing in the hallway. I sipped my punch feeling kind of buzzed and kind of bored. Over the next hour, another dozen or so people came through the door. Our host then announced that it was time to begin.

"The rules of the party," he said, "are simple. Thirty questions have been written down, folded into squares, and placed in this box. I'll pull the first question out and choose someone who must answer it. If someone else also wants to answer the question, that's fine, but the person who was originally selected is required to answer it. Then that person draws the next question, chooses who to ask, and so on. Some questions are bizarre, some risqué, some tame. You may never be asked a question, or you may be asked several questions if you're chosen more than once. There are three things you all must absolutely do. First, you must be totally and completely honest. This can't work if everyone isn't truthful. It's the only way to really get to know each other. Second, if you choose to not answer a question, you must remove a piece of clothing. That piece will be chosen by the person who asked you the question. And third, you must keep drinking and having fun."

I remember looking at Hailey like she had lost her mind. What was she thinking inviting me here? Why did she want to be here? I didn't know or want to know these people. I sure as hell didn't want to tell them about me. Not that I had any secrets, I just preferred to be a private person. And I was not taking off my clothes.

I spent the evening avoiding eye contact each time a new question was selected. Eventually, someone chose Hailey. He asked her something about the craziest place she had sex. After she answered, she reached her hand in the box and came out with a question. She unfolded the paper, read it to herself, then looked right at me. "Erika," she said. I was going to kill her. "If you were a chef and were creating a recipe for the perfect life partner, what ingredients would you include?"

Everyone turned to watch me, and I remember suddenly feeling very warm. It wasn't a difficult question, but as I said, I didn't want to be here much less share with these people.

"Well, I guess I'd add in a fun personality and a good work ethic."

"No, no," someone called out, "you have to go deeper than that. It's supposed to be your fantasy guy."

"Take off your shirt," someone else had yelled. "You didn't answer the question."

"Fine," I said, "I'm answering it. I guess I would want a lot of humor. Like a full cup's worth. He has to be attractive. Well, I need to be attracted to him. I would add in a pair of gentle eyes. The kind of eyes that smile when he's happy. A lot of integrity. Honesty. Faithfulness. He should have a dash of mystery just to keep things exciting, but I'm not looking for a bad boy or anything. Strong, working hands that like to hold mine. A few days' worth of stubble. And yeah, I guess that's it." I looked down at my hands, unable to make eye contact with anyone else.

Then some guy called out, "and a humongous wiener." And everyone laughed because we were drunk college kids. I laughed then too, but when I looked up and caught Hailey's eye, I remember her smiling at me, silently agreeing that what I had said was what we all wanted in a partner.

Chapter 15

I've just hung up with Cora, who seems to be doing better. She has resumed her classes, and even mentioned a cute boy she met in one of them. Thank God. She is so young and should be out with friends and boys her own age, having a fun, drama-free time. She doesn't need older men mucking it up. Brandon isn't mentioned, and I don't ask. But I know her heart is still hurting. I try to listen and be encouraging. Cora is a strong young lady, and she will be back to her old self in no time. I'm just angry that Brandon stole her time this past summer. Time she could have spent with people who love and care about her. I likely won't see her again until Thanksgiving or Christmas.

Things have been strained between Levi and me since that day I couldn't reach him. Who am I kidding? Things have been strained for a long time before that. But now it feels different, almost final somehow. We go about our lives as if nothing happened when in reality, everything is happening. I'm just not sure what to do about it. Levi is gone most nights. He says he's working, but I don't try to text him. I don't try to check his location. I don't try.

I've only seen Liz once since we were there for dinner. Her daughter was in the high school play and Alec was out of town, so she asked me to come along. We didn't get the chance to talk much beyond small talk. After all, you can't chit-chat while watching a play. She invited me out for ice cream afterward with her girls, but I declined, needing to get back to Ozzy. He hasn't been feeling too well lately, and I hate leaving him for long periods. Sometimes he has accidents in the house, poor boy. I know it's not his fault. In his older age, he just can't hold his bladder like he used to.

I pour myself a glass of sweet tea and take Ozzy out back with me. He loves the sunshine. I intend to let him get all he wants before winter takes over, and he is stuck in the house more often. As I am just sitting down, Olivia texts, "It's almost someone's birthday! What do you want to do? Shopping someplace fabulous and a fancy dinner?"

I almost forgot about my birthday. It's still a couple of weeks away, but with all that has been going on, I'm just not in a celebratory kind of mood. I text back, "I don't want you to go to any trouble. I wasn't planning on doing much of anything. Maybe you can just stop by, and I'll make lunch."

"Nonsense," she replies, "we have to celebrate. Think about it."

I don't want to think about it. Another year gone. Another set of wrinkles. Another fifty gray hairs. Getting older is not for the faint of heart. One good thing I have realized is that even though my eyesight is getting weaker, my ability to see through people is getting stronger. And my tolerance for bullshit is shrinking.

I check in on HollerHub and see that there is a reply message from Allison.

"Hi Candace, thanks so much for reaching out! I'm so glad to have you in our beloved Mom Group. I hope you are feeling as welcome and included as I personally try to make each member feel."

I literally snort out loud. Ozzy, apparently roused from his sleep, rolls over onto his side. I keep reading.

"I'm not familiar with the type of game you mentioned, but I would love to learn more. As you know, we here at Mom Group love to get together in person. That is an important part of our little community. If 'Hot Seat' turns out to be something the Mom Group would like to do, I may ask you to help plan it. I'm just so busy these days. I look forward to hearing from you. Hugs!"

I immediately respond to Allison from the Candace account, explaining the primary idea of the game. I emphasize how it is designed to bring people together, allowing them to bond over our true honest selves, leaving out the parts about the mandatory drinking and removal of clothing. I'm not sure what my end game with this Mom Group event is just yet. But I'm hoping to lure Beth out, to figure out who she is and find out more about this affair of hers. Expose her for the husband-stealing tramp she is.

It takes a full day for Allison to respond to my Candace account. She loves the idea and asks me to find a place and design the questions. I get to work.

I begin scouting for locations. It can't be in a place where everyone from the Mom Group is segregated in just one room. I need to be able to blend in, as I will not be officially attending, but rather, plan to sit nearby the group and listen. Three restaurants have been checked off the list before I find an ideal spot. It's a place that will allow us to reserve several tables together, near the bar. The women from the Mom Group can either sit or stand and mingle around the bar-height tables. The other, unreserved tables will be full of the restaurant's regular guests. I look around and see that even on a Wednesday evening, this place is crowded. It will be perfect.

I don't reserve the space right there and then, as nobody who works here should be able to associate me with the Mom Group event. The next day, I call and reserve the space for one week from today under the name Candace. I then set up the event in the Mom Group and also send an individual message to Beth.

"Hi Beth, I'm one of Allison's friends and am helping her with our next Mom Group event. I don't think that you've attended one of our events before, so I'd like to personally invite you. We would love to have you there. Hope to see you!"

The weekend before the event, I create a box with questions, the majority of which revolve around marriage and infidelity.

"Have you ever cheated on your spouse?"

"Has your spouse ever cheated on you? If so, did you take revenge and cheat back?"

"Have you ever slept with a married man?"

I throw in a few other random questions so that they aren't one hundred percent about adultery.

I hope this plan of mine works because I am absolutely fed up. Fed up with men like Brandon who think they can run around on those women they've pledged to be faithful to. And Levi. I'm fed up with his deception and his stories. God knows if he's sleeping with someone else, but I know he isn't sleeping with me. I'm also fed up with women who tear apart other women, acting high and mighty, as though their actions have no consequences. And women who cheat and lie. I'm over it all. It was easy when I exposed Nicole, as she had pictures of her husband and his friend tagged in photos on her page. It took a little more snooping to expose Allison and figure out where she worked, but it was simple enough. Now, Beth deserves whatever is coming to her and more. I just need to know who she is.

A few days before the event, I message Allison from the Candace account. "Hey girl, I have a little bit of a cold but don't worry. I'm taking medicine and getting plenty of rest. But just in case I can't make it to the event, can I drop the box of questions off on your porch sometime? You don't have to be home. I can just leave it. But like I said, I'm doing everything I can to make it."

Candace will not make it to the event because Candace does not exist. But I will be there.

Allison replies immediately, "Oh no, girl! Get rest, because for sure I want to see you. You can drop it off anytime. Knock on the door. I'd love to meet you in person. I'm out at lunch now, but I'll be back later. Feel better! Talk soon!"

Allison provides her address, which I already have. But I won't be knocking on her door. If Allison is not home, now is the perfect time to go.

I put on a hoodie even though it's ridiculously hot out. I highly doubt Allison has cameras on her home, and I don't remember seeing any when I was there for the book club. But I wasn't looking for cameras either.

I park a few houses away, out of the line of sight of Allison's house. I pull the hood up over my head, tuck in my hair, and put on sunglasses. It isn't much of a disguise, but I'm banking on the fact that Allison isn't home. I can run up to the porch, set the box down, and run back to the car.

Creeping up into the yard, I feel like a burglar or some sort of stalker. A really sweaty stalker. There is one car in Allison's driveway, which must be her husband's. I pray he does not come outside. My head is pointed down the entire time, causing me to nearly walk into a large tree limb that needs to be trimmed. Setting the box on the porch, I turn and jog back to the car. Once inside, I peel off the hoodie and drive back home.

I message Allison, "I left the box. Wanted to get back to bed to rest. Sorry I missed you!"

Anxiety grows inside me as I wait to see if I've been found out. I'm half expecting Allison to blast me in the Mom Group, telling everyone that I'm impersonating people and harassing her. But that post never comes. Instead, about an hour later, I get a response.

"Thanks, Candace! Game sounds fun. I peeked at a few questions. But only a few. I couldn't help myself. It's going to be a racy night! You better feel okay and be there!"

Relief briefly floods through me until I remember that I need to figure out what I'm going to do about the actual event. I keep checking the RSVPs. Beth has not yet responded, but Liz says she is going. Crap, I did not anticipate that. It's going to be difficult enough to hide from Allison, but there is no way to hide from Liz. I need to come up with a plan to keep her from there. I send Liz a text.

"Hey, want to meet me in Dallas on Thursday? I'm going to be there that day and would love to grab dinner and go shopping with you. Maybe around 6:15?"

I, of course, will not be in Dallas. I will be at the mom event.

She responds within a few minutes, "I was planning on going to a Mom Group event. You know, supporting Allison, keeping the family peace, whatever. You should come with me to the event. When will you be back from Dallas?"

"I was actually going to treat myself to a spa day. I won't be back for the mom thing. Are you sure? I thought maybe we could meet up and celebrate my birthday a little early." Maybe guilting her will entice her to agree.

"Okay, sure, that will be great. Much better than my other option LOL. Just let me know when and where to meet you, and I'll be there."

I let out the breath I didn't realize I was holding. I feel bad writing this lie, causing her to drive so far for nothing, but I need to do this. Beth must be stopped before she causes more hurt. I owe it to this guy's wife, to Cora, to all the other women whose boyfriends and husbands cheat on them. I owe it to myself.

I sleep horribly on Wednesday. When I wake up throughout the night, my mind starts working, playing out scenarios. Once, I am excited about my plan and wish it was already Thursday night. I'm ready to be there, ready to find Beth and figure out who this cheating man is so I can warn his wife. Another time I wake up and think that I've made a horrible mistake. This is a terrible idea. What if Beth does something drastic? What if I get caught?

I glance over at Levi who is deep in sleep. He kicks his feet occasionally, but other than that, he is silent. He is having no trouble sleeping, not a care in the world. I suppose feeling no remorse is a blessing. Those people can go about in the world doing and saying what they please. Those of us with a conscious, with a soul, well, we want to right those wrongs. We want to ensure people are treated the way they deserve to be.

My eyes open to light pouring in through the window. I glance at the clock and see that it is just after eight. I'm exhausted and not ready to get up, but I feel like I still have a lot of things to do before tonight. I already have a text from Liz, "Have fun at the spa! Let me know about forty-five minutes before you are ready to leave there, and I'll start heading to Dallas."

I don't respond but instead, go to the Mom Group so I can check the RSVPs for tonight. I audibly gasp when I see that Beth has said she will attend. She never did reply to my message, well Candace's message, so I'm pleased she will be there. I take a few minutes to study the photos of the other ladies who will also be there tonight. Since I don't know what Beth looks like, maybe I can figure out who she is by process of elimination.

I walk downstairs calling for Ozzy. He isn't in his bed. I start looking around the house calling his name. Panic is rising in my chest. It's unlike him to not come when I call. After checking the living room, I walk into the kitchen and find him sprawled out on the kitchen floor. "Ozzy?" I call out. I don't get a response. "Ozzy," I shout louder. I bend down to check him, to touch his soft fur. At my touch he jumps, causing me to jump in return. He gives me a sleepy look and thumps his tail. "Ozzy, you scared me. Why didn't you come boy? Are you hungry?"

When he sees me pick up his food dish, he sluggishly stands up, ready for his breakfast. I talk to him while preparing his bowl of food, telling him how much I love him and that he is my best boy. I set his food on the floor and wash out his water dish, giving him a fresh bowl. A dog's water dish must be thoroughly cleaned every day. After all, dogs lick their butts and then stick their faces in those bowls over and over. Although, Ozzy probably licks his butt and then kisses me in the face. I shrug, not minding. I love Ozzy's kisses.

I spend the rest of the day trying to focus on regular chores and errands. Those things I do over and over, like laundry, dishes, and vacuuming, are much more difficult with the weight of anxiety on my shoulders. Finally, it's time to get ready. I take a shower but don't do much in the way of hair or make-up and don't fret about which outfit to choose. Instead, I put my hair up in a ponytail and add a baseball cap, looping the pony through the back. I take a look at myself in the mirror. I am ridiculous. I don't pull off hats very well anyway, but this. This is no disguise. I look like a mom ready to go watch her kid play soccer. I take off the hat and opt for a scarf. It's a nice scarf, one that Olivia gave me for Christmas one year. It's viscose in a rich crimson color. The fabric drapes like butter, naturally flowing into the perfect shape. It looks pretty tied around my head, less like Jackie Kennedy, and more like Eva Mendes. It goes well with the black pants and black shirt with maroon pinstripes I've selected. I have this vision of me having to hurry out of there tonight and tripping over high heels, thereby eliminating any chance at anonymity, so I opt for a pair of flats.

At just after five o'clock, Liz texts me to ask if she should head to Dallas. I tell her she should and give her the address to a restaurant I won't be at. My stomach begins to toss and turn. I know I'm not being very nice, but maybe she would understand if she knew what I'm trying to accomplish. Not that I'm going to tell her. We haven't been talking much these days. Still, Liz has a husband so she could imagine how horrific it would be if he cheated. I push down any last remaining doubts about this entire evening and head out the door.

The restaurant is crowded again, and I'm thankful. I'm about forty-five minutes early on purpose. I want to be able to position myself at the bar, close enough to hear what is going on, just on the outskirts of the reserved area. The stool swivels, allowing me to angle myself just so. I order a glass of Pinot Noir. The cool, dry flavors of blackberries and cloves swirl together on my tongue. It's good, and I quickly take another swallow. The waiter asks if I'd like to order food, but I can't imagine eating right now. Suddenly, Allison and two of her cronies walk through the door. They are carrying bags of something that I can't make out. I glance over my shoulder after a few minutes and see that they are dressing the tables with flowers and some sort of glittery frames. It's show-time.

I open Candace's HollerHub account and send a message to Allison, "I'm so sorry. I'm still feeling sick. I don't want anyone to catch anything from me. I hate to miss tonight, but I know you will do a fabulous job running the game. Miss y'all, but we'll get together soon for sure!"

I intentionally waited until Allison was here before letting her know that Candace wouldn't be coming. I couldn't risk her canceling the event. She takes her phone out of her purse, glances down, and makes a face. She appears to be telling the other women that she will need their help running tonight's event. They smile and nod like eager beavers.

More and more moms trickle in as the event time nears. Some of them I recognize and know they aren't Beth. But a few I'm not familiar with. I need to concentrate on those women. The moms all get a drink and spend time talking and laughing. I feel a quick pang, wishing for just a brief moment that I was one of them. A text from Liz interrupts my thoughts, "I'm here. Where are you?"

I ignore it, turning my attention back to the moms. Once it appears that everyone is here, Allison gives her usual opening speech about friendship and community and a bunch of other sickeningly sweet garbage.

I study the women I don't know, stealing glances whenever I can. One of them is wearing tan corduroy pants. I didn't even know they still made those. She has on a white button-down shirt tucked in, and her shoes are extremely sensible, simple canvas sneakers. Her hair is light brown, pretty, and hangs past her shoulders. Her face is girl-next-door cute. She doesn't seem like the type of person who would go after another woman's husband and then brag about it on social media. I mentally check her off my list for now.

The next woman is wearing distressed skinny jeans, which show glimpses of her thighs. Her black bra is visible under her thin, sheer black blouse. She must have an affinity for jewelry as she has several silver bracelets on one wrist and rings on almost every finger. She is also wearing large silver hoops and a silver necklace with a charm dangling from it. I lean back a little to check out her shoes. Snakeskin strappy sandals with a two-inch heel. She is definitely on the list of possible suspects.

The other two women that I don't recognize are maybes. Definite prospects. They are both in jeans. One is wearing a white cropped tee showing a hint of her stomach. The other is in a longer fitted teal blue blouse with one sleeve and one bare shoulder.

My phone is on silent, but I can see that Liz is calling repeatedly. I don't answer it. It starts blowing up with texts from Liz, "Where are you, Erika?" "Why aren't you answering me?" "I drove all this way. I can't believe you."

And finally, "I'm leaving. You better have a good reason for not being here."

I wait about fifteen minutes and then text back, "I'm sorry. I felt sick and had to leave. I thought I sent you a text, but just realized I forgot to hit send. Again, so sorry!" I watch my phone for a few minutes, but no response comes through.

I turn my attention back to the moms just in time to hear Allison say, "Everyone, make yourself a plate. We will take about thirty minutes to eat and visit and then we will play a really fun game. You're going to love it."

I use this time to run to the bathroom and ask the bartender to please hold my seat. I can't risk losing my place. I'm too close to figuring out who Beth could be. I'm alone in the bathroom, trying to hurry, grateful none of the moms have decided to visit the restroom at the same time. As I wash my hands, I stare at the woman in the mirror. She looks like me, same eyes, same nose, same darkly dyed hair poking out from underneath the scarf. But she doesn't feel like me. She is missing something. Kindness? No, I still try to be kind. To those people who deserve it, anyway. Logic, perhaps? Some of that has likely gone to the wayside. Sanity? Probably so. I do feel sort of absurd. Is this an irrational thing I am doing? I contemplate this entire plan of mine, my effort to weed out cheating Beth. I conclude that no, this is not crazy. I am not crazy. It's these cheating men who are the problem. It's possibly Levi. It has got to stop. If we as women don't take a stand, then who will?

Back at the bar, my stomach no longer feels like I'm on a roller coaster. I order a sample appetizer and an iced tea. No more wine for me. The game is about to begin, and I need to focus.

Allison explains the rules. Of course, she decides she will go first. She reaches into the box and pulls out a piece of paper. As dramatically as one can unfold a two-inch square, she does. She reads the question to herself, smiles, then turns to one of the ladies. "Tanya." The other ladies squeal, some patting Tanya's arm or shoulder. "Who is your favorite celebrity crush?"

Favorite celebrity crush? I didn't write that question. Oh no. Allison said she read some of the questions ahead of time. She must have added some of her own. If she replaced them all, they won't ever get around to talking about infidelity. This was a terrible idea. I have completely wasted my time. This was so far-fetched, I was an idiot to think it would ever work.

Thirty minutes go by, and I have listened to questions about books, fetishes, and fears. I've learned that some of them like Stephen King, get turned on when their feet are tickled, and are afraid of snakes. Others like Danielle Steel, get turned on when their husbands do the dishes, and are afraid of heights. This is not what I came here to do. Then I hear her resounding voice. Liz.

She walks into the restaurant and saunters straight to the bar. There are three people between us. I turn completely away from her, holding my breath as though that will keep her from seeing me. I have to get out of here.

"I'll take a margarita on the rocks with salt. Make it a double with a shot of tequila on the side," she orders.

"Liz," I hear Allison say, "over here." As if Liz were unable to notice this large group of women on her own. Allison continues. "We are still playing. Come join us."

"I've had a crappy afternoon. I'm going to try to catch up to y'all drink-wise. I don't want to play any games, but I'll be over in a minute," Liz says.

I'm not looking in her direction, but I know she's still there. Still at the bar. I wish she would leave so I could leave. When she finally moves over to the set of tables with the other women, I grab my phone, pick up my purse from the floor, and start to get up. I abruptly sit back down when I hear Allison ask the next question.

"Is it ever acceptable for a spouse to cheat?"

Every last one of my nerve endings is on fire. My pulse is racing. Everything in my body is telling me to get out of there double time. But my brain is curious. My brain now knows that at least one of the questions I wrote was still in that box. Could my other questions be there too? I have to stay and listen. I have to know.

Someone who I know is not Beth answers the question. I hold my breath, waiting to see if someone else will offer up an answer and then see that Liz is walking back to the bar. Dang it. Why can't she wait for a server to come to the table like a normal person? I turn back around, tilting my head down as I hear her say, "One more shot and one more margarita with salt, please."

She is on a mission tonight. When she rejoins the group, I hear her loudly talking over some of the other women saying, "I'll ask the next question."

"That's not how it works," Allison says, "but you're welcome to answer any question you'd like after the selected person finishes her answer."

Liz becomes bizarrely angry at this response. She and Allison step aside from the rest of the group and are speaking in heated whispers. I can't make out what they're saying, and I don't know if the other ladies can hear them, but they're looking a little uncomfortable.

One mentions that she needs to get going. No, it can't end, I need to know more.

"No," Allison says, "please stay. We are so close to finishing the game. It won't be the same without everyone here." The mom resumes her seat.

Allison continues, "There are only a couple of questions left in my little box. If it's okay with everyone, I'll ask the rest of the questions and everyone who wants to answer is welcome to do so. Now, let me see. Ah, okay. The question is, 'Have you ever slept with a married man?'" Ding, ding, ding pops in my head.

I bravely turn my seat just a little more to get good view of who says what. I wait and wait, but the women are silent.

"Okay," Allison says, "I will take that as a no." I take another sip of my tea feeling defeated.

"Wait." I hear a familiar voice say. Even slurring, I recognize it. "I did, okay? I've slept with a married man. Are you all happy? Are you happy, Allison? Yep, I cheated on your precious brother. And you know what? He deserved it. Because he cheated on me too."

Allison doesn't say anything. Nobody says anything. Liz continues, her voice rising. "Is this what you ladies do? Come here to shame each other?"

"Nobody is shaming—" someone begins.

"Shut up," Liz shrieks. "Just shut up. You don't know me. Don't you dare talk about me. He was married, and his wife treats him like crap. And they have a bad marriage, okay? So, I did it, okay? Are you all happy? I'm an awful person. There. Now I'm going to go home, and you all can talk about me."

"Liz," Allison says, "you cannot drive home. But under the circumstances, I don't want to drive you home either. Is there someone here who will volunteer?"

"I don't need any of your charity." Liz cuts Allison off, her voice so loud I'm expecting a manager to escort her out any second. "I don't need your charity or your friendship or nothing. I don't need anything from you."

"I'll take her home," I hear one of the other ladies tell Allison.

Before anyone makes a move for the door, I grab my things and rush out. The night air cools the sweat dripping down from under my scarf. I pull it off my head, dropping it in the parking lot. I am running to my car. Running away from here. Away from Liz, whose full name is Elizabeth. Beth.

Chapter 16

I drive only so far as to be out of sight of the restaurant. I keep waiting for the tears to come, for that release, but they never do. I'm slumped over in the seat, the weight of the night holding me down. My mouth begins to salivate, that telltale sign when you're about to throw up. The vomit is quickly working its way back up towards my throat. I lunge forward in the direction of the door, reach for the handle, and am barely able to hang my head out before it comes. Blackberry wine, dark like blood. I search around for something to wipe my mouth with, wishing I had the scarf.

My mind is unable to focus as my body has taken over, shaking as if it were thirty degrees colder. My vision is blurred, protecting me from seeing anything that could cause further damage. I wanted to know the truth and I got it. It slapped me right in the face. My husband and my friend.

The signs had been there all along. I knew I wasn't crazy when I relayed my fears to Olivia. I'm angry it took me this long to put it all together. Angry that I let Olivia talk me out of what I knew my gut was telling me. Liz is also Beth. And she was sleeping with my husband. It makes sense. Liz is fun and beautiful. She is adventurous and exciting. She isn't me.

I am finally able to pull myself upright in my seat but can't do much more than that for a few minutes. I have no energy left. There is nothing left. I don't know what my next move should be. Where do I go from here? I mean this metaphorically in terms of my marriage, but also literally. I can't sit on the side of the road all night.

I drive to a gas station down the street and go inside to wash my hands and face and rinse my mouth, buying a bottle of water on the way out. Back in my car, I continue to sit. Staring, but not seeing. I pick up my phone, needing to hear a friendly voice, some reassurance that everything will be alright. But there is no one. Nobody to call. I am alone.

I'm not sure how long I've been sitting here but decide it's time to go when a group of men start gathering outside near the gas station doors, loudly talking, and stumbling around. It's nearly half-past ten. Levi is likely home, but who knows. He could be out comforting Liz, ensuring that she is okay, holding her while she cries. Making her promises that belong to me.

I start the car, waiting for a moment. The adrenaline that was coursing through my body is dissipating. I take the long way home, past the cemetery and consider stopping, slowing down just before the gates. A cemetery that feels so peaceful and comforting during the day seems ominous in the dark. Headstones scarcely visible in the moonlight. Trees casting sinister shadows. I keep driving.

Eventually, I pull into the driveway and turn off the ignition. Levi's car is here. I can see through slits in the window blinds that the house is dark except for the lone light that is on in the downstairs front entryway. It's the light I always leave on for Levi when he is working late. I breathe a sigh of relief that he will be asleep, as I'm not yet sure how to handle all of this. I need time to think.

I go inside and just make it to the couch, needing to sit, to be in a place that is familiar to me. Home can be comforting even if it's not the home you thought it was. The last thing I want to do to top off this atrocious night is lay in bed next to Levi. I walk down the hall to the linen closet and pull a few blankets out of there, tossing them back on the couch before heading into the guest bathroom. I open the cupboard under the sink, searching for mouthwash and completely rinse my mouth out several times. It will have to do. I don't want to go upstairs and risk waking Levi. There is an old bottle of Tylenol in the medicine cabinet, but I need something more.

I lightly creep into the kitchen where we have one cabinet dedicated to pills. Throughout the years, people who have opened it looking for a glass have been surprised to find medication stored in the kitchen. It began years ago when Levi and I were following a fad vitamin regimen. We decided that it was easier to take them in the morning with our coffee or juice, so we kept all of the bottles here. Then, when my allergies seemed to worsen, I put my antihistamine in here. Newly purchased bottles of ibuprofen or acetaminophen and all prescriptions were also eventually placed in this cabinet. It became the all-encompassing pharmaceutical storage spot.

I rummage through the bottles, not sure what I want to take. Something that will make me feel a little less sad.

A little less broken. A little less. I decide on Xanax, left over from some major dental work that Levi had two years ago. He is terrified of the dentist. There are two pills left in the bottle. I dump one pill from the bottle into my hand then pause before adding the second. I've never taken anything that isn't prescribed specifically to me, particularly Xanax. But I am in a near panic, which justifies my decision, but not before returning one pill to its bottle. I need to relax, but I don't want to be asleep for eighteen hours. One pill should be enough. I wash it down with a swallow of water.

I lay on the couch, trying to get comfortable. These pants feel like they are making a permanent indentation in my skin. I take them off and try again, covering myself. My mind is working overtime. I'm not sure what to do about my marriage. I suppose it's much easier to make a decision when a relationship is volatile. When there is constant fighting and screaming and name-calling. Sure, Levi and I argue. But it's the silence that is most harmful in our marriage. The quiet that screams so loudly there is nothing left to say. The connection has been broken, and we are two separate people living two separate lives.

And Liz. I know I've only known her less than a year, but we also had a connection. At least I thought we did. I felt it every time we were together. I wonder if she only pursued a friendship with me after meeting Levi to get close to him. Or if my friendship with her was genuine, but somehow along the way, she strayed towards him. What I do know is that friends are supposed to be there to support you when you cry. They aren't supposed to be the reason you cry.

The Xanax is doing its job. My senses, my feelings are becoming numb. It's as though a barrier has gone up, anesthetizing the fresh sting of tonight's events. Tomorrow, I think as I drift off to sleep. Tomorrow, I will figure it out.

"What are you doing on the couch?" I hear Levi's voice filtered through my sleepy haze. I don't open my eyes but can tell that it's morning, the sun permeating through my heavy lids.

"Erika?" he tries again. "Why are you on the couch?"

I stay silent, rolling over away from him. He walks out of the room. I can hear him in the kitchen fixing himself a travel mug full of coffee for his drive in to work. I think about how he woke up this morning and must have seen that I was not in bed like usual. Did he come running downstairs looking for me? Did he call my cell phone a dozen times out of concern? No. He got completely ready for work, showering, shaving, and dressing. He sat on the bed like he has a thousand times before, to put on his socks and oxfords. He applied his usual two spritzes of Giorgio Armani, which I smelled when he came downstairs. I was not his first concern. I never am. Not anymore.

His keys jangle as he gathers his things before heading out the door. "I love you," he says indifferently, and then he is gone.

I love you. It's a phrase that used to hold so much meaning. At first, it was the signal of something perfect and new. It created butterflies and nervous laughter. Love was the unspoken word when Levi reached for my hand or gently touched my face. As our relationship grew stronger, "I love you" was a verbalization of our feelings. A promise of a life together. A commitment to always be there for each other, in good times and bad. He was my person, and I was his.

It's strange how those same three words have morphed to mean something else. Something much less. A quick phrase said meaninglessly before hanging up the phone. Often a phrase used in place of goodbye. A phrase that we were once terrified of saying is now merely a habit. I'm not sure when that phrase changed for us, for Levi and me. It was likely just a slow conversion, like a caterpillar turning into a chrysalis before becoming a butterfly. The stages of life cause the end to be so much different from the beginning.

I sit up and a nauseating sensation, much like a hangover, washes over me. I call Ozzy, but again he doesn't come. I'm not sure what is wrong with him. I used to nearly trip over him every time I took a step. If I moved, he would be right there moving with me. I trudge upstairs calling his name and find him asleep on my bed. He must have crawled up there after Levi left. Levi hates when the dog is on the bed. But I let Ozzy up there whenever Levi isn't home. So, Ozzy is on there a lot.

I lay down next to him, snuggling against his warm fur. I know he's almost ten years old, but the thought of losing him kills me. This whole horrific situation with Levi is overwhelming and frustrating and hurtful. But if I lost Ozzy, I would be completely broken. When Henry and Cora became busy teens and then eventually left the house and with Levi always working, Ozzy has been my one constant. Always there. Always loyal. Plus, he is just the cutest stinker ever. I kiss the top of his head and leave him to sleep.

Back downstairs, I hear my phone ping. It's a text from Liz, "Hey, I was driving back in from Dallas when you texted me and I didn't see it until this morning. I had a rough night. I'll tell you about it later. I hope you're feeling better."

I feel sick all over again, and my body becomes warm, the anger quickly returning. She had a rough night? She has a lot of nerve contacting me after making a spectacle of herself while admitting to having an affair with my husband.

I pour myself some of Levi's leftover coffee. Again, it has a stale, bitter taste. I find myself longing for a visit to Sip & Spin, not necessarily to see Jimmy, but to get something hot and decent to drink. But that is the last place I need to be in my current state. One wink from Jimmy, and I'd probably be ready to run away with him. I sigh at the speck of humor still there amidst all of this.

I grab my purse and make a quick run to a Starbucks drive-through, ordering the Cinnamon Dolce. The vehicle in front of me pays for my drink, which is such a kind gesture. I want to return the favor to the car behind me, but I'm the last in line.

The drink is hot and good, but not the same as Sip & Spin. "It will have to do," I say out loud.

I consider driving out to Olivia's shop to share what happened last night. Tell her how wrong she was about Levi and Liz. I start to steer towards the highway but don't get on. Olivia is not the warmest, most comforting person. She would likely criticize me for setting up that entire artificial event in the first place. No, I don't need that right now. I have an entire empty house in which I can think, I can plan. I turn in the other direction and head home.

I don't even go inside, stopping to sit on the front porch. My birthday is less than a week away. I'm hoping to still have lunch with Olivia, a little shopping afterward. But then Levi will expect to take me to a nice dinner at a restaurant of my choosing. And I would choose it based on the dessert menu and not the main course. The dessert is the best part. But I don't know if that dinner will be happening. My birthday. How silly to be thinking of that when there is so much more going on. My marriage is ending, and here I am worried about birthday plans.

I need to focus, to come up with a strategy. And finding proof is key. Levi's phone must be overflowing with proof. He isn't much of a texter, but Liz is, so she probably texts him constantly. I wonder if he knows what she did last night. Would she have told him that? Surely not.

But Levi's phone is always locked, and I don't know the passcode. It isn't that we have never shared our passcodes because we were doing something inappropriate and didn't want the other to see. It was actually the opposite. We always trusted each other and, thus, never felt the need to access each other's phones. Not anymore. Although, even if I did have the code, he has his phone on him 24/7. Even when he takes a shower, he sets his phone on the bathroom counter. I never thought anything of it before, but now it just seems shifty.

My latte is now lukewarm, but I toss the rest of it back, eager to get inside. I head straight upstairs to our bedroom. Straight to Levi's underwear drawer because that's where people tend to hide things. Olivia once said that she keeps her adult toys and condoms in that drawer. My hidden treasures are much less exciting, consisting of a small jewelry box that contains a few special pieces and that's about it. I open Levi's drawer and rummage around, moving his carefully folded boxer briefs. Surprisingly, there is nothing here. I check his sock drawer but come up empty-handed there too.

In the closet, I open every stacked shoe container and look through everything on his shelves, searching through a mixture of belts, unopened boxes of cologne, loose change, a watch tray. I move to the hanging clothes, inspecting at each piece. Moving fast and faster, I stick my hands inside jacket pockets, feel around the inside of every sports coat pocket, reach into every pants pocket. Nothing. There is nothing.

I go back to the dresser, pulling each one of the drawers out and dumping it on the bed, contents spilling onto the floor. There are t-shirts, shorts, joggers, tank tops, muscle shirts. Ozzy, noticing the commotion, climbs off the human bed and onto his own bed on the floor.

"Where is it?" I say aloud. "I know it is here somewhere. It has to be." I have no idea what "it" is, but I'll know when I find it.

I stop, looking around at the now completely disheveled room, but don't bother picking anything up. There is more work to be done.

I run back downstairs and into Levi's office. I don't come in here very often, as there is rarely a need unless

I'm running the vacuum or dusting a bookcase. It's a grand room, larger than a standard office. One wall is covered in built-in bookcases with walnut wood that is varnished just enough to give off a slight sheen. There is a mixture of books on the shelves, some work-related, such as programming manuals and system training guides, and some historical fiction and non-fiction. One shelf holds a vintage 1945 Encyclopedia Britannica set, the complete twenty-four volumes. Interspersed between the books are knick-knacks – a small globe, a glass award from Levi's company, a faux plant. There is one framed photo on Levi's desk, just to the left of the pencil holder. It's a picture of the four of us, Levi, me, Henry, and Cora, on a family vacation in San Antonio.

I love to plan family vacations. It's been years since we've all been on one together, but we used to go fairly regularly. Sometimes we would fly, but other times, it was nice to go somewhere within driving distance. This trip to San Antonio was filled with fun, albeit interesting activities.

We went to the Alamo and shopped at El Mercado, where the kids picked out authentic souvenirs handmade in Mexico. We took a short ride in a boat on the Riverwalk and toured Natural Bridge Caverns, walking nearly two hundred feet below ground to the large caves. But the most fun and strange thing we did was visit an old western town located just outside of San Antonio. The main street was lined with saloons, a general store, and other shops reminiscent of the Old West in the late 1800s. Movies and commercials had been filmed there, but it was a lesser-known tourist attraction. At the time, the owners used the property as an amusement park of sorts.

I sit down in Levi's office chair smiling at the memories. First, we went to a bird show, which consisted of one man and one pigeon. The pigeon would fly around the room and come back to the man's hand to eat the sunflower seeds he was holding. The bird also deposited droppings on the tables and floor as it flew around. That was the extent of the bird portion of the show. For the remainder of the time, the man attempted animal impressions.

Next, we saw an outdoor performance by Cowgirl Carrie. She was a hoot with her pistol twirling, target shooting, and bullwhip act. She also took the time to stop and talk to the kids and take pictures with them. They loved her. As a service the ranch offered, I paid an extra five dollars for Cowgirl Carrie to "arrest" Levi and Henry. She rounded them up and put them in a covered wagon complete with jail cell bars. To be released, they had to perform a rendition of "My Little Teacup." Cora and I were doubled over laughing.

Finally, it was time for the safari ride, which was essentially a flatbed trailer pulled by a tractor. On our safari, we saw a turkey, horses, and one zebra. The whole experience was the most fun and the most ridiculous day we'd had together. We laughed so much about the bizarre experience both while we were there and for several weeks after. I miss who we all were, that family in the photo.

I meticulously set the picture back on the desk. I need to be very careful when conducting my search of this room, as Levi has his things set just so. I open the top drawer and find post-its, paperclips, pens, a calculator, and a letter opener, all the usual desk drawer stuff. In the drawer to the right, there are some CDs, several papers that I rifle through, nothing of importance to me. The bottom drawer won't open. I pull on it harder, hoping it's just stuck, but it is definitely locked.

I grab the letter opener and try sticking it in the lock. This totally does not work like it does on TV. I rummage through the top drawer again, hoping I missed the key, but it's not here. I start moving things around, sliding over the monitor on the desk and picking up the pencil holder and the keyboard. I check under a stack of papers and peer inside file folders. I move a small Dallas Cowboys helmet bank and hear something inside. Coins would be the logical assumption, but there is just one thing clanking. With a twist, the bottom opens and out falls the key.

My hands are shaking so it takes a few tries to get the key into the lock, but once I do, it clicks. I slide open the large drawer, both wanting and not wanting to know what's inside. There are numerous hanging file folders with several loose papers in each. I go through them one by one. The first few contain mortgage statements and other miscellaneous bills. Then I see it. A plain brown envelope. An envelope sounds uninteresting, sure, but it's the only one in here. I lift the envelope out, not having any idea what to expect. Opening the flap, I pull out a few papers that are stapled together and see that it's an itinerary for travel. Ordinarily, finding an itinerary would be commonplace considering all the travel Levi does. But this is for an Airbnb. I start reading – Tree

House Hideaway. Number of guests: 2. Add-On Options: Catered in-room dinner; Champagne; Floral.

This is definitely not work-related, and it is definitely not for me. Levi has never planned a trip for the two of us in all the years we've been married. Plus, he is keenly aware that I am substantially more indoorsy than outdoorsy. I would never want to stay in a tree house. I suddenly feel sick. How many of his so-called work trips have been him gallivanting around with women? With Liz? I want to call Levi. I want to call him and scream at him and tell him that I know everything. The jig is up. Call him the lying, cheating, bastard that he is. My heart is beating out of my chest. I click on his stupid picture on my phone. It rings once before I hang up, changing my mind. I'm so confused about what to do but calling to yell at him at work is not how this should be played. Instead, I use my phone to snap a picture of the itinerary, making sure to capture the address and dates. This tree house place is in Oklahoma, only about three or four hours from our home.

I sit there at his desk waiting for the torturous pain slicing through me to pass. I feel like a rabbit being tossed around by a pack of coyotes, pulling at me, piercing me with sharp teeth, the agony almost unbearable. But once I make a plan, once I decide how the game will end, knowing it will be on my terms, a weird sense of calm dulls that pain. Only fury remains. It fuels me forward. I'm going to let him go on his little trip, then I'm going too.

I take my time to carefully put everything back as it was. Papers go back in their folders, office supplies and other junk back in the top drawer. I finish by replacing the key in the helmet, closing the bottom seal, and returning it to its exact spot. I stand up, push the chair back in, and take my time looking around. Everything has to be in its exact original location. Just in case, I quickly run the vacuum through the office. If anything is slightly out of place, at least Levi will know why I was in here.

Next, I go back to the bedroom. Clothes are strewn about as if a tornado blew through. This room will take more time to rectify. Every pair of shorts, every t-shirt, and all the other pieces of clothing that came from the drawers are carefully refolded and put in their rightful places. I go back into the closet and fix the hanging clothes, straightening items, tucking in sleeve arms that are bent every which way due to my haphazard search. When I'm straightening the loose items on a closet shelf, a cuff link is knocked to the floor. I bend to retrieve it and notice a small plastic bag tucked behind clothing on Levi's side of the closet.

There are three pairs of women's underwear inside – a black lace bikini, a white lace bikini, and a red silk thong. Tears instantly well up in my eyes. One might deduce that these are gifts a husband would purchase for his wife. This might be especially true if said wife's birthday was coming up, such as mine is. But there are two issues with making this assumption. One, Levi and I have not had sex in over six months. Six months. And the last time we did, it was awkward because we were so disconnected. You don't buy panties like these for a woman that you aren't sleeping with. And two, I am a solid size twelve. I have been a size twelve for the past ten years. These panties are a size eight. The thin straps on the sides of these would rip before they made it halfway up my thighs. But you know who would fit perfectly into these? Liz. They fit her personality too. As much as it pains me to do so, I put the bag back where it was.

Since Levi's and Liz's love trip is not for another three weeks, I'm going to have to play it cool until then and do everything I can to avoid him. I'll go to bed before he gets home and get out of bed after he leaves for work. I'll hang out at the flower shop or the library or even the cemetery on the weekends. Anything to stay away. I do not want to speak to Liz at all, but she has texted me a few times. I suppose a response is required to keep things normal for now.

Playing dumb this week has been a struggle. So when I wake up on the morning of my birthday, celebrating is the last thing I want to do. Levi made plans to take me to dinner tonight. I thought about pretending to be sick but don't want to raise any suspicions. Plus, a part of me wants to sit across from Levi, look him in the eye, and listen to his lies.

I go into the kitchen to make a cup of hot tea, having given up on our coffee maker. We desperately need a new one. I think for a second that I'll ask Levi to get me one for my birthday, a fancy one with options for both espressos and cappuccinos. But then I remember that I hate him right now and am not asking him for anything. Removing a simple Earl Grey from the tea tin, I fill the kettle and set it on the stovetop to boil. On the center island, sits a blueberry muffin in an individual bakery box and a note from Levi:

"Happy Birthday, Erika! I hope you have a great day. Looking forward to dinner tonight. Love, Levi"

I crumple up the note and throw it and the muffin into the trash.

I'm nervous about tonight's dinner. It's so strange to be nervous about something you've done hundreds of times before. Of course, before, I didn't know Levi was a cheater, but still. I don't realize how tense my face is until my phone rings, and I smile seeing Cora's beautiful face on the screen.

"Happy birthday to you, happy birthday to you, happy birthday dear Mom, happy birthday to you," her voice sings out.

"Thank you, honey," I chuckle. "I appreciate that. How are you?"

"I'm doing fine. I miss you though. I wish I could be there on your birthday."

"I know. I miss you too. But it's okay. You're busy with the school semester just taking off. And I'll have plenty more birthdays."

"I don't know," she says, hesitantly. "You're getting pretty old."

"Ha ha, very funny. You should drop out of school and become a standup comedian."

"I really should. I'm a riot. So, what're your plans for today?"

"I'm not sure yet. Your dad is taking me out to dinner, but I don't know what I want to do before then. Any suggestions?"

"You could get a massage?"

I laugh. "The thought of that sounds stressful. What else have you got?"

"Mani Pedi? Maybe go see Aunt Olivia at her store and get a cute new outfit?"

"Your aunt and I did talk about going out to lunch today, but I don't want to eat a big lunch and a big dinner. But maybe a little shopping would be fun."

"There ya go," Cora says. Then she adds, "By the way, Brandon's been calling."

My smile falls flat. "Oh no, what does he want?"

"He just keeps apologizing and trying to get me to see him. I've thought about it."

"Cora—"

"Wait," she says, "I thought about it, but I decided that I'm happier without him. He was kind of a lot."

I release the breath I'd been holding. "Good. You deserve better."

"Yeah, I know. Okay, well, I'm sorry, but I have to run to class."

"No need to apologize. Go get smarter. I love you."

"I love you too."

I decide to spend my day walking around some shops. Maybe I'll do a little impulse buying of things I probably don't need. I could use some retail therapy. As soon as I get in my car, a text from Liz pops in, "Happy Birthday! Do you want to grab lunch? My treat." Liz only works half days at the school and is usually home by noon.

"Thanks. I can't today. I have a busy day planned," I reply.

"No worries. We can have a belated birthday lunch this weekend."

No, we can't, I think.

On my drive to the shopping square, my mind runs through scenarios of things I would like to text back to Liz. "Would it be Liz or Beth taking me to lunch?" or "How can you possibly make time for lunch? Won't you be too busy screwing my husband?" In the end, I don't bother replying.

I drive around the parking lot, deciding where to go first. My stomach grumbles loudly, and I wish for that blueberry muffin now. I stop in one of the coffee shops for a toasted everything bagel.

The next stop is at a shop that only sells kitchen items. It's kind of like a Williams Sonoma but locally owned. Checking out the coffee makers is a priority, but wow, the aisle is overwhelming. There must be fifty options here, ranging in price from forty dollars to over a thousand. I find a decently priced all-in-one coffee machine and add that to the cart. There is an amazing selection of coordinated kitchen accessories, such as towels, potholders, spoon rests, measuring cups, and the cutest set of wooden spoons with ceramic handles. My kitchen is currently a hodgepodge of items collected throughout the years out of necessity. No thought was put into it, and nothing matches. I want to replace it all, choosing a complimentary floral and gingham pattern in white, gray, and black. Olivia is the bold sister, her home decorated in bright colors, such as orange, aqua, and yellow made warm with green houseplants and wood accents. It sounds ostentatious, but she has a great eye, and it looks very lovely. I have always been drawn to muted colors. They feel so clean, and I love the simplicity.

The total at check-out is shocking – nearly seven hundred dollars. Even though we have the money, I'm not usually a flashy spender. I think a part of me remembers where I came from and knows that I never want to go back there. I almost change my mind, but then Levi pops into my head, and I make the purchase. He owes me much more than a bunch of kitchen stuff.

My phone dings, and it's a text from Henry, "Happy Birthday. I'm sorry I can't see you today, but I'll be by this weekend to take you to lunch. Love you."

"Thank you! No problem at all, I know you have school. I can't wait to see you. I love you!"

I walk a few stores down to a shoe shop to find some new boots. It's still quite warm, but time is going by so fast, cooler weather will be here before we know it. If I want boots, they must be purchased now, or they'll all be picked over. I'm looking for something short and simple to wear with leggings and jeans. I giggle at the sight of both silver and gold glitter knee-high boots. They may look great on someone younger, but definitely not on me. Still, I want to take a picture of them to text to Liz, and teasingly tell her I'm buying them. She would get a kick out of them. But I don't. I can't. Not anymore.

I stop when a beautiful pair of boots takes me back in time. The black leather is rich, with tall shafts that hit just below the knee and lace up the front. I had boots like this in my early twenties, and they were my favorite. I always wore them with skinny jeans or a denim skirt. They eventually fell apart, but I didn't throw them out right away. I just couldn't get rid of them. When they were finally discarded, I never replaced them. I felt too old to pull them off anymore.

But these. These are fantastic. I pick them up and am pleased to see there is a hidden zipper on each one. My old ones didn't have a zipper, and they were a hassle to lace up. Nobody has time for that anymore. I find a size ten and try them on. They are genuinely cool. Now I really do wish I could text Liz, to send her a picture and ask her opinion. I already know what she'd say though. She would tell me they're great, and if I love them to get them.

I decide to go for it so I can wear them to dinner, as I have to look fantastic tonight. If I must sit across from Levi during our meal, he needs to think I'm pretty. I want him to remember that he is, or at least was, attracted to me. He should see what he's about to lose.

At the other end of the shopping center is a large bookstore. Surrounded by books is one of my favorite places to be. Spending the next couple of hours walking up and down each aisle is heavenly. I choose a few memoirs that sound fascinating. One is about a guy who had a lobotomy and the other has to do with hitchhiking around the country. I also get a few books that were recommended in the Mom Group, including "The Invisible Life of Addie LaRue" and "The People We Keep." The Mom Group has been good for something.

The Mom Group. I haven't checked the group since the night of the "Hot Seat" event. I sit at one of the tables in the bookstore and open HollerHub. The group is alive and kicking, per usual.

"What are some of your favorite ways to sneak veggies into meals so that your kids will eat them? My kids won't eat anything that isn't covered in cheese or in the shape of a dinosaur."

"My son needs volunteer hours. He got in a bit of trouble and part of his punishment is to give back to others. What ideas do you have? Where can he go?"

"I finally did it. After years of gaslighting and manipulation. I finally decided to file for divorce. Now I need your advice. For those of you who have gone through this, what paperwork do I need to gather? Which lawyers do you recommend? How should we divide things? I need all the help!"

I open this last one and take screenshots of several of the comments. I don't plan on sending these screenshots to anyone's husband or employer. This information is for me, just in case.

I then check to see if Liz has posted anything in the group as Beth. I search Beth's name and see her original post about having an affair with a married man. My stomach becomes tied in knots upon reading her words again, "...When we are together, I feel happy. Really alive. It's like he has woken up something that has been asleep for a long time. He is the sweetest man. He is kind and makes me laugh..." I feel sick.

My shopping day is over. It's already late afternoon, and Levi said he would be home around five because our dinner reservations were at six. As I head home, my mind again is overcome with all of these thoughts, and my body is overcome with all of these feelings. I wish I was strong like Olivia. She got divorced in the morning and was back at work in the afternoon. It hardly phased her. Sure, her husband wasn't cheating on her, and they were only married for a couple of years, but still. Marriage is a commitment of the mind, body, and soul. To break that commitment feels like a sin.

I attempt to drown out everything the only way I know how. I shuffle my favorite playlist and Bon Jovi's "I'll Be There for You" begins. I only allow a few seconds of the intro music before skipping it. I love that song, but don't need to make myself cry. Quiet Riot is up next, and I sing about feeling the noise and getting wild. That's much better.

Back at home, I unload the car and set everything on the dining room table, intent on changing out the old kitchen stuff and setting up the coffee machine later. With lots of my own work to do, I laugh thinking of Sandy in the movie "Grease" after Frenchy gives her a makeover. I won't be going that far but do want to look good. Dare I say it, I want to look hot.

During my long shower, I let the hot water flow down my scalp and onto my back, trying to relax the muscles that have been tense for days. The scent of vanilla pumpkin body wash is enriched by the steam and smells heavenly. I shave my legs because they need it, not because I'm grooming for Levi.

Next, I get to work on making up my face, attempting winged eyeliner, although it doesn't turn out quite the way I'd hoped. After using a make-up wipe, I start again, going more traditional. An eyeshadow palette, gifted from Cora a few years ago, is dug out from a drawer. I don't know if eyeshadow goes bad. It must at some point, but this has never been used, the brush hasn't even been removed. I sniff at it. Honestly, I have no idea what eyeshadow is supposed to smell like, but since there is no rancid odor, I think it'll be fine. There are some sort of rules for application, which I try to follow – the darkest charcoal color on the lower lid, a medium gray color in the middle, and a lighter silver on my brow bone. A very light touch gives me the ideal effect, just a little extra zing. I brush the fallen colored dust off my cheeks, then add two layers of mascara to my lashes and a light tinted moisturizer all over my face, forgoing any blush. A red Chanel lip color finishes my look. I take a step back, pleased with the results. It's definitely me, but a more polished version of me. I don't know that hot is the word I'd use. Perhaps pretty is more accurate, and I'll take it.

My lingerie drawer basically consists of cotton underwear and black sheer pantyhose, but I find what I'm looking for – a long-lost pair of fishnet tights. I know I shouldn't. I'm forty-five years old for heaven's sake. Nobody over thirty should be caught dead in a pair of fishnets, or so they say. And yet, I can't help myself. They will go so great with my new boots. To hell with the rules.

I wriggle them on, then step into a black fitted denim skirt and pull a white blouse over my head, careful not to catch my lipstick. Then the boots. Standing in front of the mirror, I decide that maybe hot is the right word because I look darn good. And for the first time in a long time, I feel good too.

Surprisingly, Levi is not late from work. I'm sitting in the living room, waiting, and he does a double take on his way up the stairs.

"Wow," he exclaims, "you look great."

"Thank you," I reply. I can't help but appreciate the compliment, even coming out of the mouth of a person I currently loathe.

"I'll be back downstairs in fifteen minutes, then we can head out."

While waiting, I make myself a glass of birthday wine, just to take the edge off. The confidence that empowered me just a few minutes earlier is slowly fading away. I don't trust my ability to spend an entire evening with Levi and still keep myself in check. But I can't ruin my plan, as it's only a few more weeks until their trip. They must be caught in the act so there is no way to deny the affair. There can't be any room left for errors or deceitful excuses.

Dinner is good. It's very good actually. I ordered a spaghetti bolognaise topped with fresh grilled vegetables. Levi got a basil pesto agnolotti which also looks excellent.

"Here, try it." Levi holds a fork in front of my mouth.

"No, thanks," I say.

"No, really, you have to try it."

"I don't want to try it."

"But it's really good. I think you'd like it."

"I don't want to try the damn pasta, Levi."

"Okay, fine. Excuse me for wanting to share."

I hold my tongue.

My belly is full, and my skirt is tight, but I don't care. This restaurant has excellent Irish cream bread pudding, and I'm ordering it, forgoing any dairy concerns tonight.

When it's Levi's turn to order dessert, he says to me, "I'll get the chocolate mousse if you want to share both desserts?"

"No, I don't want to share," I say, making the waiter seemingly uncomfortable.

"Okay," Levi says, turning to the waiter, "no dessert for me."

"Seriously?" I ask.

"What? I'm skipping dessert."

"Just because I don't want to share?"

"I can come back," the waiter interjects.

Levi and I both say no. "Just the bread pudding is fine," I say. I don't want to send the server away and prolong the evening any further.

He returns with dessert fairly quickly, probably so we will hurry up and leave his table. The bread pudding is moist, and the caramel Irish cream sauce is delectable. I finish it all.

We are quiet during the car ride home. We have been primarily quiet the entire evening. Levi's phone dings from an incoming text message. He picks it up, reads it, and sets his phone back face down.

"Who was that?" I ask. I can't help myself.

"Nobody. Just work."

"On your personal phone? Doesn't work usually contact you on your work cell?"

"Yes, but if they can't reach me on my work cell, sometimes they try my personal cell."

"So do you need to respond or call them back?"

"No, it's fine. I can do it later," Levi says.

"It's just," I begin, pretending to think. "It's just that if work tried to reach you on your work phone and couldn't, they must have felt that it was urgent enough to try your personal phone."

Levi doesn't say anything.

"Otherwise," I continue, "they would have just left you a message on your work cell and waited for you to reply, right?"

Levi still doesn't say anything. He reaches over to turn on the radio, signaling that he no longer wants to talk about this. I turn it back off.

"Let me see your phone," I say.

"What? Why? No," he says.

"No?"

"No."

"Why not? What are you hiding?"

"Jesus, Erika, I'm not hiding anything. What's wrong with you?"

"What's wrong with you?" I ask him right back. "If you aren't hiding anything, why won't you let me see your phone?"

"Because there's nothing to see," he says.

"Well, then show me. Show me that there's nothing to see."

"Can't you just enjoy your birthday? I'm trying here. We had a nice dinner."

"Did we?" I feel my voice rising. "Did we have a nice dinner? I mean the food was great, sure, but the company sucked."

"Oh, real nice. Thanks a lot. I take you out for a nice evening, and this is how you act?"

"Show me the damn phone, Levi." I reach for it, but he moves it out of my grasp and puts it in his left pocket.

"It's her, isn't it?" I can't hold it in any longer. The words are tumbling out of me like water escaping a broken dam. "I know it is. It's her."

"Her who?" Levi says.

This really sets me off. Now he is going to deny it. Pretend he doesn't know what I'm talking about. Well, I know too much for him to pretend anymore.

"Just stop all the lying, Levi. Stop it already. I can't handle it anymore. I would hope you'd have at least one shred of respect left for me and tell me the truth."

We pull up in the driveway. Levi stops the car and turns to me. There is darkness in his eyes. He's been caught, and he doesn't like it.

"Listen," he says, trying to control his temper, "there is nothing to tell. I got a text from David. He was asking me about a new account he's working on. That's it."

"Did it take you the whole drive home to come up with that lame excuse? God, stop lying. Just stop already." I am not controlling my temper. "That was not a text from David, and you know it. You can keep denying it, but I know all about it."

It's dimly lit in the car, the nearby streetlamp just barely streaming in through the glass. I think I see his face turn pale. This is not the time to stop. I need to keep going, to keep pushing. It's time for him to come clean.

"I know," I say. "I know about you and her."

He studies my face as if trying to learn what I've already learned.

"Erika, it's your birthday. I don't know what you think you know, but nothing is happening. I don't know why you're freaking out about a work text."

"Because it wasn't from work," I scream. All of a sudden, the car feels airless and repressive. I have to get out. I undo my seatbelt and open the door.

Levi opens his door, yelling, "Wait, Erika. Can we talk about this? Just stop, please."

But I don't stop. He doesn't get to control the situation. Not anymore.

He jogs behind me, putting his hand on my shoulder, and I flinch it away.

"Baby, please, wait a minute. Can you just wait? I don't know what you're talking about."

But I walk faster, unlocking the front door using the key that was in my purse. He tries putting his hand on my shoulder again.

"Stop touching me," I scream. I open the door and barely step one foot inside before spinning around to face him. I want to see the look on his face when I say her name.

"Liz!" I shriek. "It's Liz. You're sleeping with her, and I know. You think I wouldn't find out about the two of you? You must think I am just too stupid." I begin to mimic him. "Poor, stupid Erika. I can screw her friend right under her nose, and she'll never even know." I'm shaking so hard I begin to cry, but I go on. "Well, guess what, Levi? Your stupid wife figured it out. I figured out that you are a two-faced, lying, cheating bastard. You and Liz are perfect for each other."

"Erika," Levi says quieter.

"What?" I scream. He motions behind me with his eyes.

I turn around and see them. I see them all. Olivia, my mother, Cora, Henry, Amy, and Liz. They are wearing silly party hats, and there is a birthday banner strung up over the fireplace. I feel all the color drain from my face. I can't make eye contact with my children.

"I have to go," Liz says. She picks up her purse and runs out of the house.

"So, you're screwing the best friend, huh?" my mother says to Levi.

"Shut up, Marlene," Levi says before turning back to me. "Erika, Liz texted me while we were in the car. She was letting me know that everyone was here and ready for us to come home. I didn't want to show you the text because it was supposed to be a surprise."

"Surprise!" my mother says, taking a drink from her low-ball glass.

"Grandma!" Cora says, horrified.

"Shut up, Marlene," Levi says, more sternly. Then to me, he says, "Erika, this party was Liz's idea. She planned it all. And I don't know why you think I'm having an affair with her, but I'm not, and we are not discussing it further here in front of everybody."

I nod, still looking at the floor. I have a sudden urge to get these boots off. My feet are on fire, sticky with sweat.

Always the diplomat, Olivia says, "Let's go ahead and have some cake." To Levi and me, she turns and says, "Why don't you two go upstairs to figure this out. I've got things down here."

"Thanks, Olivia," Levi says.

I go upstairs without a word. There is a roaring in my head that I can't seem to quiet, and the nausea is over-whelming. The outfit I loved only hours before is now suffocating me. My entire body hurts and for a minute I wonder if I'm having a panic attack. I am a whole sea of emotions and can't calm down. I can't focus. I also can't put one name to it. I'm mortified, hurt, angry at Levi and at myself for exploding in front of my children. I know they aren't little anymore, but it's never comfortable witnessing an argument between your parents. This is particularly true when infidelity is involved. My anger has also been infused with bewilderment. Sure, this little party explains tonight's text, but that most certainly does not explain the trip or the underwear.

Levi begins speaking, but I hold up my palm and cut him off. I'm not ready to hear him just yet. I go into the closet and remove my boots and clothes, my body nearly groaning in relief. I grab a pair of leggings and a faded t-shirt and put those on then sit on the bed, the bag of panties in my hand.

Levi glances down to see what I'm holding, then looks back up at me. "Why do you have those?"

"You tell me why you have them," I say.

"I don't even know what happened here tonight. I was taking you out to dinner, and Liz was putting together this surprise party while we were out. How did we get to this? Why would you think I'm cheating on you with Liz?"

I take out my phone and scroll to the photo of the romantic Tree House itinerary. I might as well lay it all out now. I hand it to Levi, and it takes him a minute to process what he's looking at.

"You found that?"

"Obviously," I say. "It's for you and Liz, right?"

"God, Erika, no. It's for you. Well, for us. It was for your birthday."

I try to read his face, which isn't giving much away. Definitely no remorse. Not much concern either. I decide that I don't believe him for one minute. There is no way he planned this for us. We are the married couple who hardly acknowledges each other. We barely interact. A trip like this for us would make no sense.

"I don't believe you," I finally say.

Levi throws his hands up. "I don't know what to tell you. It's a trip for us. I've been gone so much, I just thought that it would be nice for you and me to get away. To spend alone time together."

"Levi, you and I are the only two people who live in this house. We could have all the alone time we wanted. We wouldn't need a trip for that. But you are never here so it never happens."

"I know," he says, sitting next to me on the bed, his voice softer. "That's why I booked the trip. I thought that if we left, if I got away from work, we could have a real getaway."

I sit in silence for a few minutes before hastily standing up. I throw the bag at him. "And what about these?" My voice rising once again.

"I bought them for you," he says. "I was going to take them with us, and if things were going well, I was going to give them to you. For fun."

"That is such a load of bull. They aren't even my size. You're so full of crap."

"I don't know what size you wear. I told the lady at the lingerie store that she looked to be about the same size as you, and this is what she came back with. I didn't check the tags, I just bought them."

I sit back on the bed, trying to process it all. I hear my mom's booming laugh all the way up here.

"My mother, really?"

"Hey," Levi says, "that was all your sister. She insisted on inviting her."

"She can't stay here in our house."

"No, she's staying with Olivia."

I nod. My stomach somersaults when I again think of Henry and Cora. And Amy. Poor Amy flew all the way here for this. God, I am such an idiot. Could Levi be telling the truth? I knew I should have waited to see what happened with that trip. That would have been the definitive proof I needed. But I just couldn't hold it in any longer. Some secrets weigh so much you can't take another step until you unload them.

"We need to talk," I say, "about this, about us. About all of it."

"We do," Levi agrees, "but not tonight. Can we try to salvage what's left and go downstairs and finish celebrating your birthday?"

He holds out his hand to me, but I don't take it. I stand up on my own and walk out of the room with him behind me. I am not yet convinced that he's as innocent as he claims to be. I am also no longer sure if he's having an affair. I don't know what to believe. A whisper of uneasiness consumes me as we head downstairs to face our guests.

They all look fairly somber. Well, except for my mother. She looks three sheets to the wind.

I feel as though the elephant in the room must be addressed. "Hey, thank you all for coming." I go around and hug everybody before continuing. "I want to apologize for my behavior. It was inappropriate. I should've kept my composure and discussed things with Levi in a civilized manner in private. Of course, I didn't realize you were all here, but still, I'm sorry if I made any of you uncomfortable. And with that being said, I'm really happy that you're all here. Cora, you kept such a good secret about coming home. I can't believe you made it in. And Amy, you flew all the way here just for this? That is incredibly sweet. And Henry, you little storyteller." I smile at my son. "You pretended you couldn't come see me until this weekend."

"I flew all the way here too," my mother says.

"Yes, you did," I acknowledge.

Everyone tries to behave normally, but it is painfully apparent that there's tension in the air. We make small talk here and there. It's close to midnight when everyone decides to leave. My mother goes home with Olivia. Cora is going to stay with Henry. It's finally just Levi, Amy, and me. Levi arranged for Amy to stay with us, so we could visit for a few days.

"I can get a hotel," Amy offers. "It's really no problem."

"Absolutely not. You're perfectly welcome here. I want you to stay. Honestly," I say, and I mean it.

"If you're sure, I'd like that too," she says. "I've been looking forward to this visit."

Levi again tries to talk to me while we are getting ready for bed. But I can't have this conversation right now. I am completely spent. The only thing I want to do is close my eyes. My head just hits the pillow before I am carried off to a full night of dreamless sleep.

Levi left for work first thing in the morning. I put on my slippers and, with Ozzy in tow, head down to the kitchen. I need coffee. Lots and lots of coffee. I guess the old maker will have to do until I get the new one set up.

"Good morning," I say to Amy, opening the back door to let Ozzy outside. She is already up and the coffee is made.

"Morning. Did you sleep okay?"

"Surprisingly, I did. How about you? Do you need any extra blankets or pillows or anything? I'm sorry I didn't ask last night."

"No, I'm good. I slept great. But—" Amy hesitantly says, "your coffee tastes like crap."

I laugh. "I know. Sorry about that. I bought a new machine yesterday. Do you want to help me set it up?"

"God, yes," Amy says, as she pours her full cup down the sink.

She and I begin the task of removing plastic, foam, and other packing materials from the box. She reads the directions while I let Ozzy back into the house. He walks up to Amy, waiting to be acknowledged.

"Well, hello there." She bends down to meet his eyes while giving his head a gentle scratch. "Aren't you a good boy?"

With a quick wag of his tail, a satisfied Ozzy retreats to the floor, snoring within minutes.

Once our now delicious coffee has finished brewing, and we are both seated at the table with a steaming cup, Amy begins, "Do you want to talk about it?"

I sigh. I don't even know where to begin. "Oh Amy, you didn't come all this way to listen to me complain about my marital problems. That sounds like a crappy way to spend a vacation."

"I'm your friend," she says, touching my hand. "I'm here to listen to whatever you want to talk about."

The gesture makes my eyes a tad damp. "Can we start with you?" I ask. "I want to hear what's been going on in your world."

"Sure," she says and smiles. Amy tells me about her husband, Jared, and how he has joined a work softball team, so the family is dragged to the park every weekend. She also admits that it's fun and that she has made some friends with the other wives. I feel a stab of jealousy, but it's quickly replaced with genuine happiness for her. Her daughter, Courtney, just started her senior year of high school and is on the student council. Her other daughter, Sydney, graduated in May. I remember seeing Amy share graduation pictures on HollerHub at the time. She is going to community college and living at home. She also works part-time behind the counter at a drug store pharmacy.

"It sounds like they're doing great. I know you're so proud," I say.

"Yes, I am. And you must be too. Cora and Henry are both so grown up. They seem to be doing so well."

"They are. I'm super proud of them. I'm excited about their futures, to see what lies ahead."

"And what about you?" Amy asks. "What lies ahead for you?"

"I honestly don't know. I don't know if my marriage can be saved. And I don't know if I want it to be. I mean, I think I do. I'm supposed to, right? Aren't we supposed to fight for our marriages? I just feel like there is no fight left."

I tell her how life has been over the past couple of years since the kids have been out of the house, mentioning Levi's demanding job and my lack of a job or anything really to occupy my time. I tell Amy about the growing distance between Levi and me. I also tell her about the vacation he scheduled, but leave out the part about the underwear. Once I finish sharing the facts with Amy, I move on to how I'm feeling.

"I've been so lonely here at the house. Every connection I once had with my husband, with my kids, is gone."

"Erika, you have not lost your connection with your kids," Amy says.

"I know, but it's different. I suppose I should've said it has changed. And I also know they're doing what they're supposed to do. I want them to leave the house and be independent. I want them to have their own successful lives. I think what they're doing is amazing. I just thought that when they went off to college, I would have a husband left here to share my empty nest syndrome. Instead, he has become more absent than ever. Some people might view this as freedom, but to me, it's just loneliness. Some days I feel this loneliness so deep it's in places I didn't even know existed inside me.

"I'm so sorry. I hate to see you hurting," Amy says. "Have you tried getting out of the house more, maybe making some new friends? I know that isn't a replacement for a husband, but you need to have someone else in your life. Well, besides the evil sister."

A grin escapes, as I say, "Oh, believe me. I've tried. I joined this Mom Group on Hollerhub and went to some events. They were disasters. It felt like high school all over again. They were the cool, popular kids, and I was the weird oddball. And then I met Liz and she was great, but you saw how that turned out."

"Yes, so what's up with that? Levi and Liz?"

"I don't know what to believe. Levi says there is no affair. I haven't talked to Liz about it, but I'm sure she'd deny it anyway. There were just too many signs. All of his late nights, his work trips that became even more frequent and included weekends. Just this feeling I got whenever we were all together. It's like they had some sort of bond."

Amy is studying me now. "You know, sometimes your mind sees what it expects to see even if it isn't actually there. Could this be that? You decided that something was going on between Levi and Liz, so your mind started making the pieces fit?"

"I don't think so. Shoot, I don't know. But then there was the trip too. Just all of it. It feels super shady."

"Yeah," Amy replies, "but what if it isn't?"

"Even if it isn't, we still have major issues."

"You've always had major issues," Amy teases.

"Thanks, I learned them from you." I try to joke back, but I'm not feeling very comedian-like today.

"So, tell me about this Mom Group," Amy says.

Out of nowhere, I begin to cry. It rapidly becomes more than crying. Uncontrollable, ugly sobbing is happening, and I can't stop it. She goes to get me a tissue.

"Aw, Erika," Amy says, hugging me. "What happened?"

Once I calm down enough to speak, I tell her about how awful the ladies in the Mom Group were to me. I tell her about the mean replies when I would comment on posts, trying to be helpful. And Allison and her allies and how flat-out rude she has been to me. It sounds a bit ridiculous as I say it out loud. I'm a grown woman. I shouldn't feel bullied. I think the difference is that when kids bully, they target insecure people. When adults bully, they create them. I definitely won't be putting myself out there again. That has caused enough heartache. If this is what it takes to make friends, I don't need them.

"I was so angry. I did some horrible things," I finally whisper.

"It sounds like you were really hurt."

"Yes, probably. But I turned into this awful person. I hurt so many people in return, possibly caused irreparable damage. I'm completely embarrassed by my behavior."

Amy watches me and waits for me to go on. I'm so overwhelmed, so overloaded, I'm about to shatter. I can't believe the hurt I've caused. To Nicole for one. I mean, marriage is difficult enough. I, of all people, know that. I had no right to cause problems in Nicole's marriage. I created drama and suspicion over a harmless post. I hurt her and her family, probably ruined the friendship and working relationship her husband had with his friend. Who knows what effects have trickled down as a result of my behavior? And for what? Because she didn't agree with my comment? Because she told me to fuck off? Have I become the kind of person who is so thin-skinned that internet trash talk can send me over the edge?

And then there was Allison. Okay, Allison is pretty much a terrible person. Even Liz thinks so and Liz is related to her, albeit by marriage. In any event, that is no excuse. Even if Allison treated me poorly, that's no reason to jeopardize someone's job. That was a lifeline for her family. She tries to appear like she's more than comfortable in her standard of living, but I saw that her family is scarcely getting by. I witnessed this with my own eyes, and I still didn't care. I'm not sure if her family was already struggling before she lost her job and getting fired made it worse. But whatever the situation was, she needed that job, and I got her fired. I am the sole reason her family has suffered. She has young kids for God's sake. What is wrong with me? What kind of human being does that? She stuck her tongue out at me in the sandbox, and I got her expelled from school. I took it way too far.

I tell Amy everything, all about the Mom Group and what has happened with Nicole and Allison. I tell her about the Beth profile and my entire plot to set up the event to find out who she was, with the sole intention of exposing her, possibly ruining another marriage in the process. But in the end, the joke was on me.

"Liz and I met at one of the Mom Group events. I think we bonded over not bonding with the rest of the ladies. She actually became a good friend to me. I truly liked her. Of course, I didn't realize she was screwing my husband the whole time."

"But what if she wasn't?" Amy says. "You still don't know for sure. He denied it, and by the look on Liz's face when you walked in shouting about it, I don't know if she has been sleeping with Levi. She didn't act like a person who was caught with her hand in the cookie jar. She seemed genuinely horrified. Plus, you don't have any real proof, right?"

I think about Amy's words. She's correct. I don't have proof. But I have circumstantial evidence. I do know that most criminal convictions are based on circumstantial evidence so that must mean there is something to it. It has value. I share this with Amy.

"True, but there still has to be some sort of proof."

"Yeah, I don't know. I'm just so incredibly sad," I say, putting my head in my hands. "Every night I fall asleep wondering why I'm not enough. People say that the worst thing in the world is to be alone. But actually, it's much worse to be with someone who makes you feel alone. Marriage is supposed to erase the tears, not erase the joy."

Amy looks at me for a minute. "I'm not sure what to say. It sounds like an impossible situation. But you're not a horrible person, Erika. Of course, what you did to those women was not the best route you could've taken."

"That's putting it lightly," I scoff.

"And," Amy says, "from here on out you need to do better. Take the high road when they aren't kind or welcoming at their events."

"I won't be going to any more events," I confirm.

"Just remember that you were already hurting. You were lonely and merely seeking friendship, something more than what you were getting at home. So, when you didn't get that, you lashed out. I think there's room to forgive yourself. But I do think you and Levi should go to counseling."

"That's crossed my mind. But Levi can barely break away from work as it is. I don't know how he'll make time to see a marriage counselor."

"If it's important enough to him, he will do it. People make time for those things that matter."

I wince at the thought of Levi not making time for me because I don't matter enough.

Amy must see the expression on my face because she adds, "He will go to counseling with you. You two have been married far too long to throw it away. And it's obvious you can't continue on this path. He'll go."

I'm glad one of us is confident about that.

Chapter 17

I'm surprised that Levi agrees to attend marriage counseling. The Oklahoma trip, allegedly planned for me, has been postponed. On the day of our first appointment, I arrive at the office where Levi is supposed to meet me. While waiting, I begin to fill out paperwork and continually check the time on my phone, anxious that he has not yet arrived. Five minutes before the appointment time, he comes through the door.

"Hey," he says to me in greeting.

"Hi," I reply. We don't have many words for each other lately.

The paperwork is completed just as the therapist calls out, "Levi and Erika?"

We walk into her office, which is inviting, but very plain. There are wooden bookshelves full of self-help books with titles such as, "The Seven Principles for Making Marriage Work" and "Getting the Love you Want." I roll my eyes but quickly correct my face, as I do sincerely want this help. We need it.

Levi sits on the couch, and I glance at a chair, but ultimately sit next to him. It must be some subconscious effort of wanting to appear to be on the same side.

"My name is Angela. It's great to meet you both. I'll start with some simple questions to get to know you."

Angela looks older in person than in her website photo. Her brown hair is peppered with silver strands that catch the light, as though someone laid tinsel on her head. She wears small-framed glasses that apparently keep sliding down her nose. I don't see the glasses fall, but in the few minutes we've been in her office, she has pushed them up repeatedly, perhaps out of habit. Her smile appears authentic but reserved.

Levi and I are civil while answering the first few questions. Angela asks if we've been to counseling before. We haven't. She asks how long we've been married. Nearly twenty-three years. She asks us about a fun memory we share. This one throws us off. I talk about our honeymoon trip to Niagara Falls. She smiles politely and says she'd like to hear about something more recent. Levi tells a funny story about Henry. When our son was in the fifth grade, we received an email from his teacher. Henry had approached her during their quiet reading time and asked what a virgin was. She was shocked and immediately questioned, "What are you reading?" To which Henry replied, "The Bible." Levi and I both laugh at the memory. We've never been especially religious, but Henry went through a phase where he was intrigued by religions and cultures. He was such an inquisitive boy, even at that young age.

Again, Angela smiles politely and says, "That is a funny story, and your son sounds delightful. But I'm looking more for a recent fun memory that just the two of you share. Something you did together or that happened to the both of you that invokes feelings of warmth and happiness."

Levi and I both sit there in awkward silence.

"Okay, that's okay. Let's move on," Angela says. She asks us why we are there and what we each see as our major marital issues. I immediately say that Levi is an adulterer.

"Really?" he says. "I told you I did not have an affair with Liz. Don't you think we have bigger issues to discuss, like your paranoid overactive imagination?"

This sets me off. "I am not paranoid. You've made it crystal clear that you were cheating."

"How? How did I make it clear?" Levi says.

He then turns to Angela. "My biggest problem with my wife is that she's completely unsupportive. She doesn't support me or my career or my interests. It's hard to want to be around someone who nags you all the time. My house no longer feels like a home. It's just a stressful pit stop in between my time at the office."

This revelation quiets me for a few seconds as I ponder his words, before lashing out in response. "Of course, I complain about you never being home. Oh, I don't know, could that be because you never are home? It's like I'm not even married. It's just me and Ozzy."

Angela interrupts our bickering, "Who's Ozzy?"

"The dog," Levi and I both say in unison.

Angela quietly sighs then redirects us to focus on the problem, requesting that we each remain silent while the other answers her questions. "And when I say silent, that includes facial expressions. It's not helpful to shake your head or roll your eyes while the other person is speaking."

"Even if they are undoubtedly lying?" I ask. Levi rolls his eyes.

During our first three weekly counseling sessions, we discussed how we' feel about our current relationship, what bothers us most in our daily lives, whether it's worth fighting for. I'm taken aback to hear Levi confirm that he does think our relationship is worth fighting for. Sure, he joins me in counseling, which might make that seem obvious. But to hear the words gives me a smidgen of hope. Unfortunately, that hope is immediately crushed when we are asked about our sex lives. Levi doesn't respond.

"What about you Erika? Are you interested in rekindling your sexual relationship with Levi?"

"Well, sure. I mean, he is my husband. We're supposed to have sex."

Angela's response surprises me. "Actually, not everyone has sex with their partners. It's definitely an important component to consider. And if one person wants to and the other doesn't, then it becomes an issue. But if both partners agree that sex should no longer be a part of their relationship, and they're truly comfortable with that, then who's to say that is not acceptable? It's your relationship. You get to decide what works for it."

"I'd like to have sex with my wife," Levi says.

"As opposed to Liz?" I'm having a difficult time not being snarky.

In our next session, Angela suggests we go away together for a weekend. "Sometimes a change of scenery is good. You may be able to better connect in neutral territory. Plan something with fun activities if you want but leave time for connecting, whether that's over meals, going for walks, or just spending quality time together."

A knot instantly forms in my stomach as I anticipate Levi's words before he says them. "We could reschedule the Tree House."

"Sure, because going to a place you were going to take your mistress is such a good idea," I snap.

"Erika, for the hundredth time, that trip was for me and you."

"What if you take a completely new trip?" Angela suggests. "Something that you plan together."

A few days later, an overwhelming urge to spend time with Liz hits me out of nowhere. I wonder if it's specifically Liz that I miss, or if it's more about having a friend to hang out with. Amy and I spent quality time chatting while she was here, but that was several weeks ago. I don't want to further bombard her with my emotional wreckage. Liz and I have not spoken since my birthday, and I wouldn't know what to say to her. Levi vehemently denies sleeping with Liz. With time distancing me from the emotions of that night, I'm starting to doubt my prior accusations. If Levi did have an affair, I wish he would just tell me. Knowing an unfortunate truth is much better than wondering forever. But he says there is nothing to tell. In any event, I can't contact Liz. Either she betrayed my friendship with the affair, or I betrayed her friendship by accusing her of something she didn't do. There is no coming back from either. I call Olivia.

"Hey," she says. "How are you?"

"I'm doing okay. If you're not busy, do you want to stop by today?" I ask.

She pauses, then says, "Sure. I have a couple of things to wrap up, then I'll head your way."

The deli sounds like the perfect place to pick up some sandwiches for lunch. On my drive, I crank up the air conditioner. Even though we're in the middle of autumn, it's still quite warm. It's so strange to see Halloween decorations displayed in front of homes and in stores when it's ninety degrees outside. I grew up in Texas, but the weather seems to have changed from when I was a kid. I have memories of cold Halloweens and being upset about wearing a coat over my costume while trick-or-treating.

I choose my favorite cucumber and tomato sandwiches on thick sourdough bread then grab a container of potato salad and a fruit bowl. While paying for my items, Liz walks in with Allison right behind her. My heart sinks. I try to turn away before they see me, but it's too late. Allison speaks first.

"Aren't you in my Mom Group? It's Emma, right?"

An overwhelming desire to shove Allison with all my might consumes me. I'm by no means a violent person, but she's in my space without invitation and has pushed one too many buttons. In fact, she's so close, I can clearly see the concealer she's used to hide the dark circles under her eyes. Once again, she's pretending to forget my name, but she knows exactly who I am. Or maybe I need to remind her. So much for taking the high road.

"April," I say, with a fake smile plastered on my face. Two can play this game. "So lovely to see you again. I see you're letting your natural hair color grow out. The dark roots fit you perfectly."

Her hand immediately flies up to cover the brown growth that is now showing on her otherwise perfectly blonde head. "It's Allison," she says.

"Right, Allison," I say. "It's just so easy to forget." A flash of pain crosses her eyes but is quickly replaced with contempt. I need to stop, to not let her provoke me. I remind myself that I must leave the Mom Group once and for all – both accounts, mine and Candace's.

"Hi, Liz," I say, making brief eye contact with my former friend.

"Hi, how are you?" she asks.

Well, my marriage is falling apart. I have no friends. And basically, my life is nothing I could have ever hoped it would be. "Just fine, you?" I reply.

"Good. Same. I'm fine."

"Well," Allison says, "it's been enthralling catching up, but we need to go."

"Erika," Liz begins.

I stare at her, waiting for her to apologize. Or maybe waiting for her to yell at me. Something. But all she says is, "Take care."

I nod, grab my items, and head out the door. Once in my car, the hot tears begin forming in my eyes. I wipe them away, willing myself not to cry. I am so tired of crying.

Back at home, I try to busy myself until Olivia arrives, running a dust cloth around the living room, washing a few dishes, and wiping down the kitchen counters. I make a pitcher of lemonade, adding less sugar than I prefer knowing Olivia won't drink anything too sweet.

I hear the front door open and Olivia singsongs, "Hello."

"In the kitchen," I singsong back.

She sets her purse down on the counter and herself on a barstool in front of the island with a huff. "I'm so tired today."

"We could've done this a different day," I say.

"No, it's fine. It's not like we're going to exercise over here. I came here to relax." She smiles at me.

"Do you want to eat in here or out back?" I ask.

"God no, not outside. Let's eat here."

I place the sandwiches out and open the potato salad, sticking a serving spoon in the container. Olivia takes half a sandwich and skips the potato salad.

"Not hungry today?" I ask.

"Oh, well, I ate earlier. And trying to watch my calories, you know. I haven't found Mr. Right. Just a lot of Mr. Right Nows."

I try to control my face. "Well, I'm hungry. And I already have a man, so I'm eating what I want." Of course, the thought of eating or not eating for a man or anyone else is outrageous. Why is there this notion that we have to create versions of ourselves to please someone else? It's ridiculous.

"Do you?"

"What's that supposed to mean?" I glower, not appreciating her comment or tone.

"Oh, come on, your marriage is a wreck. You know it, I know it, Levi knows it. Everyone who was at your birthday party knows it."

"You actually don't know anything. Levi and I are in counseling. We are trying to better our marriage. We both think it's worth saving." Olivia seems genuinely surprised by this little revelation.

"Counseling? Seems to me that if two people need to try that hard to be together, it just isn't worth it. A relationship should be easy, not something you have to pay a third party to mediate."

"That statement right there tells me that you have absolutely no idea what you're talking about. And why would you? You were married for like a week." That's a complete exaggeration, and I shouldn't have said it, but in comparison to the time Levi and I have been together, it's almost on par. "Lots of people go to marriage counseling. Marriage isn't all sunshine and roses."

"But the majority of it should be sunshine," Olivia says.

"Maybe," I concede, "but there will be storms. And when there are, we need to be able to figure out how to share one umbrella and make it through."

Olivia looks at me and nods her head listlessly. I don't know that she understands what I'm going through. What Levi and I are both going through. Either that, or she really doesn't see the purpose of making such a significant effort. It was wishful thinking that Olivia could be my substitute for Liz. I wanted to be able to openly share my feelings and my fears. I wanted to hear hers. Deep down I knew that Olivia was not that person. She has been there for the tangible things, but she keeps her feelings closely guarded. I'm her sister, and I've rarely seen them.

"So, what do you do in these counseling sessions?"

"We talk about things that bother us. Things that make us happy. We try to stay focused on the fact that we are two separate people with individual thoughts, feelings, and expectations. Just because I expect something doesn't mean that is obvious to Levi. If he doesn't meet my expectations, that isn't necessarily intentional on his part. He just may not have been aware because it's not an expectation for him. We need to work on communication."

"God," Olivia cries out almost mockingly, "that seems like way too much thinking. And work. I wouldn't bother."

"So, you'd just get divorced? Break up your family?"

"If it took this much effort to survive in my marriage? Yes, without a doubt."

"It's easy to say that when you're not sitting in it."

"I guess. So, what does 'Denim' say his problem is anyway? What does he like and not like?"

"Mainly he wants me to stop nagging him. To be more supportive of his career."

"That seems easy enough."

"Apparently it isn't because I feel like I don't have a husband."

"Sounds like a perfect situation to me. You have a man who pays for everything but leaves you alone. What more could you want?"

I take a minute to compose myself before responding. I really can't fault Olivia for having a less than healthy view of relationships, as she took the brunt of our mother's manipulation for most of our lives. After Levi and I got married, my mother latched on to Olivia. When she didn't have a man, my mom would guilt Olivia into doing everything for her, paying her bills, even sending her on vacation. And they didn't even live in the same city. I've had no problem distancing myself from Marlene.

Realizing that our mother chose herself and her hordes of men over providing Olivia and me with love and basic necessities made it easy. But for some reason, Olivia has bent over backward to help her out. She still does. But when it comes to her own feelings, Olivia has built a wall to protect herself. It sounds like an unhealthy coping mechanism, but considering where I am in life, maybe she's on to something.

"I want the man that I married. I want love and happiness," I finally say.

Olivia laughs. "Don't we all?"

"Maybe. But is it wrong to think we deserve it? Anyway, the marriage counselor wants Levi and me to take a trip together."

"A trip? What for?"

"To reconnect mainly. She wants us to spend a few days entirely focused on ourselves. No work, no distractions."

"Can't you just do that at home?"

"Angela thinks that it's best to change our environment. Maybe try to ignite the flame," I say playfully.

Olivia's face does not offer a smile in return. "I don't know, Erika, it just seems like a bad idea."

"How can taking a trip with my husband be a bad idea?"

"It just—" Olivia begins, then pauses, pushing her perfectly sculpted brows together. "It just seems like a disaster waiting to happen. Like sure, you are leading somewhat separate lives, but why rock the boat when it's worked this way for years?"

"That's the thing. It isn't working," I say.

The weekend of our getaway is finally here. We are flying to New Orleans for two nights, leaving Friday and coming home on Sunday, and I'm super excited. It's almost Halloween, and New Orleans is filled with voodoo shops and ghost tours. The city is over three hundred years old, and so much of its history is still preserved today. I can't believe I haven't visited before now.

We booked a hotel right in the center of Bourbon Street and opted to not rent a car, figuring most of our time will be spent right here in the French Quarter. It's the afternoon by the time we get settled into our hotel and back out to wander the streets. There are people everywhere, some in costumes even.

We decide that our first stop must be to get a drink, and we go for the famous Hand Grenade. I'm handed a long florescent green plastic tube, the bottom of which is shaped into a grenade. The first sip simply tastes like fruit punch. It's very good. We just share one for now as we walk past bars and restaurants, many with live music flowing from within.

We've only finished about half of the drink when I say, "Are you feeling this? Because I'm a little buzzed already."

Levi smiles at me. "I kind of feel it too."

We both start laughing, sharing some little secret that only us and everyone else walking around with a Hand Grenade know.

"Oh, we have to go in here," I say, spotting Marie Laveau's House of Voodoo. It's fascinating inside, stocked full of voodoo dolls, blessed chicken feet, talismans, and some souvenir-type items, such as shirts, magnets, and shot glasses. I pick up a voodoo doll and see that the tag says "Protection." Another one reads "Good Luck/Good Fortune." I find one that is marked "Love/Passion" and decide to buy it. I also buy a t-shirt with a picture of a voodoo doll stuck with pins and the words "Thinking of You" written above it.

We stop in a jazz restaurant for dinner and music. It's only our first day here, and already I'm feeling happier. I think Levi is too. He's smiling and talking more. I even catch him bobbing his head to the music.

"Are you having fun?" I ask him.

"Yes, totally. Want another drink?" he asks with a big goofy grin on his face.

"Sure," I say, smiling back at him. A version of our old selves is sitting here at the table with us. It's like we took a huge leap back in time.

We are pretty drunk by the time we make our way back to the hotel. Sex had crossed my mind, but we still have the whole weekend. This night was so enjoyable, I don't want to risk ruining the vibe by bringing it up. We take turns showering and collapse into bed. It's the soundest I've slept in a long time.

"Beignets for breakfast?" Levi says first thing in the morning. "We have to get them."

"For sure," I say, getting up to get dressed and ready. We walk to the famous Café du Monde and get in an already formed line.

"This is going to be great," Levi babbles, and I'm happy to see him so happy.

We order beignets, of course, and a black coffee for me and coffee au lait for Levi. The breakfast is a delectable light, sugary explosion in my mouth. I share this with Levi who laughs and says, "I bet it is."

I laugh too. We are a normal couple, out having fun and being silly together. Our plans for the afternoon include a swamp tour. We Uber to our destination and meet our guide, Hank. He recommends we purchase bug spray inside because "the skeeters are big as hogs." We heed his warning and do, spraying every bit of exposed skin.

The tour is relaxing. We only spot one alligator and stop while Hank drops marshmallows into the water to lure him closer, explaining that the alligators think the marshmallows are turtle eggs. I'm perfectly fine with him leaving the alligator on the other side of the swamp.

Back at the hotel, Levi and I shower again, separately, to remove the sweat, bug spray, and swamp goo. Then we begin the second half of our day, which basically consists of drinking too much and watching live music. We move from venue to venue, and the bands are either getting better at each new place, or we are getting drunker.

"Do you still love me?" I ask, my third or possibly fourth daiquiri making me bold.

"Of course, I love you. You're my wife."

"Yeah, I know. But sometimes people truly love each other and then other times they love each other because they have to."

"Nobody has to love another person," Levi says.

The thoughts in my head seem to be much clearer than the words coming out of my mouth, so I try again. "No, I know nobody is forced to love another person. But sometimes, people love each other out of convenience. I don't want to be convenience love," I say and begin to cry. I hate this part of alcohol. One minute I'm bouncing around like Tigger and the next, I'm sad like Eeyore.

"God, why do you have to ruin a perfectly good night?"

"I'm not trying to ruin the night," I loud whisper, trying to not draw any further attention to myself. "I'm looking for confirmation. That you love me."

"I said I do. Can we not talk about it and just have a good time?"

"Now you're mad at me. I'm going back to the hotel," I announce, nearly knocking a chair over as I get up.

"Erika, sit down. We can go in a little while. Let me finish my drink."

"No, I'm going now," I call out as I hurriedly walk out of the restaurant.

I swiftly march towards the hotel, glancing over my shoulder to ensure Levi is not following me. Or maybe hoping that he is. I'm pushing past vampires, French maids, and superheroes, all of whom are drinking, talking, celebrating. Bright, colorful lights are bouncing off every building, creating a strobe effect. I turn down one street and continue, but nothing seems familiar. I try to go back the way I came, but I don't remember which way that is. My heart begins thumping in my chest, and I turn in circles looking for something familiar to grab on to, but it all looks the same. I find a bench and sit down and cry.

I don't know how long I sit there, but the street begins to thin out as people return to their hotels. With the outside noise declining, I hear my phone ring.

"Hello?"

"Erika, where the hell are you? I've been looking everywhere for you."

"Levi?"

"Yes, of course. Who else would it be? Where are you?"

"I'm not sure. Sitting down."

"Are you really that drunk? I am so incredibly pissed off. I can't believe this is how my night is turning out. Tell me where you are. What do you see around you?"

I try to describe my whereabouts. Forty-five minutes later, Levi is there standing in front of me. He mutters some choice words under his breath as I stand up to follow him back to our hotel. Apparently, I wandered pretty far from the French Quarter, following the Mississippi River.

"Can you slow down?" I ask, trying to keep up.

"No, I cannot slow down. I've been walking around in circles in the French Quarter forever. I'm tired and hungry and irritated that you ruined my night," Levi barks.

"I'm so sorry I ruined your life," I scream at him.

"I said my night, Erika, not my life. Although at this point, that wouldn't be too off base."

We don't speak the rest of the night. In the morning, I'm not sure if we aren't speaking because he is mad at me or because we are both too hungover to move any more than we have to.

"Can we order room service?" I ask. "I need coffee." Levi ignores me and continues to pack.

"I'm ready to leave," he finally replies. "Let's go."

I drag myself outside to wait for our car while Levi checks out. My head pounds with every step. I was hoping the fresh air would do me some good, but I'm hit with the morning stench of urine as street cleaners wash away evidence of a Saturday night in New Orleans.

The drive to the airport is quiet, as is the entire process of getting on the plane, and we both sleep on the flight. My entire body aches, but I don't know if that's still from the alcohol or if it's the stress over the way our vacation ended. In any event, I just want to get home.

Chapter 18

I t's been nearly a month since our disastrous trip. We went to one counseling session since then, but it too was a catastrophe. Then we just stopped scheduling them and never mentioned it again. It's funny how some things just trickle away, and others are just cut off instantly. The counseling sessions and my friendship with Liz, for example, were instant cut-offs. My marriage is a trickle. Levi and I have become acquaintances who offer polite niceties without any real interest or feeling. It's barely enough to make life in this house tolerable.

I haven't been on social media at all. In reality, I know that people tend to only post the perfect parts of themselves, sharing only those life moments that are to be admired. And yet, it is still disheartening to see so much joy when I'm suffocating in my own little world. It's as if I don't measure up. My marriage, and therefore, my life is a failure.

But I do still need to remove myself from the Mom Group. Aside from Amy, I haven't admitted my horrific actions to anyone. And I won't. It all happened months ago, so there is no point of reopening old wounds.

I open the Mom Group newsfeed, intending to leave the group, but can't help scrolling through some of the recent posts first.

"If my ex-husband gives up his weekend with our kids, does he have the right to demand extra time on another weekend? He says that he's allowed to make up the lost time, but I think that if it's his choice to not pick them up, he is out of luck. What do y'all think?"

"What is the best shampoo for dandruff? My twelve-year-old suffers from flakes and we have tried regular dandruff shampoo, and it hasn't helped."

"So, I'm still seeing the married man. I know, I know. I need to stop, but he gives me that pick-up I need to get through the day. We usually meet at a hotel after work and spend a few hours together. The thing is, I don't want him to leave his wife. And I certainly can't marry him. It's more therapeutic for me, I guess. I know I'm a dreadful person, but I don't know how to quit this man."

Beth wrote that last post. My heart stops, and I grab onto the counter and take a seat, trying to calm the involuntary reactions happening in my body. It is so very loud in my head, and I can't catch my breath. "This is not happening," I say aloud to myself. "This is not happening. Just breathe, Erika. Breathe."

I read the post again, appalled that Levi and Liz are still having an affair. I knew there was still something going on with him. He is absent more than ever, both literally and figuratively. This must be addressed, but I can't go about it the way I did previously, flying off the handle. I must get my hands on the proof that I let slip away before.

I log out of HollerHub as myself and log back in as Candace, then return to Beth's post and read through the comments. Once again, several are disapproving of the affair, yet a handful of these women are supportive of Beth. They feel for her and understand what she is going through. Screw those women. What about what I am going through? What all women married to cheating spouses go through? I begin to write Candace's comment.

"Don't be so hard on yourself. You're only human after all. I went through something similar with a married man last year. We used to meet at a hotel called The Homestead Lodge. Where do you two meet?"

Since Beth said she meets her married man in a hotel, I'm hoping she will share exactly where that is. It's a long shot, but if they're going to be caught in the act, I need to find them first. I stare at the phone for at least an hour, constantly refreshing the feed in hopes that Beth will reply to Candace's question. No such luck. When my eyes begin to ache, I put it away and find something else to do with my time.

Searching for a list of hotels in the area seems like the next logical step and requires the larger screen of a laptop. There are well over a hundred, making this seem like an impossible task. After printing a map of Fort Worth and the surrounding areas, I begin marking the location of each hotel. With Liz living fairly close to us, it makes sense that they're meeting someplace local. Honestly, I have no idea where this is going, but I need to be doing something. I highlight the ones that are nice enough for Levi, as he is very particular about where he stays. This leaves me with thirty-four. That's still a lot, but it's workable.

I go back to the Mom Group to search for other recent posts by Beth, hoping to grab on to something, and find another.

"I'm looking for tried and true ways to quit smoking. It's been a battle for me for so long, and I know it's unhealthy. I've tried the gum and hypnosis. Nothing works. Do you have any suggestions?"

Interesting. I didn't know that Liz was a smoker. But then again, there is a lot I don't know about Liz. Well, it isn't like I was with her every day, and it makes sense that if she were trying to quit, she would hide that habit. Plus, she never came across as overly health-conscious. She was more about having fun and living her best life. I don't know anyone else who smokes aside from my mother. Olivia and I tried our mom's cigarettes as kids one time, which resulted in uncontrollable coughing. Olivia smoked more of the cigarette than I did, and she felt sick the rest of the day. Now the memory makes me smile.

But that smile fades when I flash back to the night at Allison's house for the book club. Liz never showed up, and Levi was not at home because he was supposedly out walking. When he finally returned, he carried with him a faint smell of cigarette smoke. All the pieces are falling into place.

A quick check on my comment shows no response, as expected. I put my phone down and decide to do something positive to occupy my mind. The holidays are quickly approaching, and we've made no Thanksgiving plans yet. I send a group text to Cora and Henry.

"Hi! Thanksgiving is almost here. Are you coming home? Should I plan dinner?"

I get an immediate response from Cora, "Hi Mom, I won't be coming for Thanksgiving. I'm going to Friends-giving that day with some of my friends who are staying on campus. But I'll be home for Christmas. Promise!"

I send my reply, "Okay, honey, we will sure miss you. Can't wait to see you next month! Henry, I can cook for the three of us and see if maybe Aunt Olivia, Cassidy, and Minnie want to join us too."

Henry texts back that evening, "I'm really fine if we don't do anything for Thanksgiving. I could use the time to catch up on schoolwork. Finals will be just a couple of weeks later so that will be a good time for me to stay here and focus on that. Is that cool with you?"

Well, shoot. I was hoping to avoid a Thanksgiving consisting of just Levi and me. The day would go much smoother with the kids here. I may still reach out to Olivia. Or maybe not. Sometimes she adds fuel to the fire.

"Sure, totally fine with me. Your dad and I understand."

During the week, I continue to play detective, watching the Mom Group like a hawk, searching for anything posted by Beth. I check Levi's chest of drawers and the closet for anything he may have carelessly left lying around and also look around his office, noticing the key is no longer in the football helmet bank. One evening when it hits ten o'clock and Levi is not yet home, I get the crazy notion to call all the hotels on my list and ask them to ring their guest rooms providing both Levi's name and Liz's. Nobody with those names has checked into any of the hotels. My efforts have produced absolutely nothing.

Thanksgiving comes and goes. Levi spends most of the day in his office, and I hang out with Ozzy. When I called Olivia about spending the holiday together, she mentioned my mother possibly coming out, so I changed the subject and decided to skip it. Marlene is the last person I need right now.

The day after Thanksgiving, I begin decorating for Christmas. I usually love this time of year. It almost seems like nothing can bring you down during Christmastime. Almost. It's still technically November, but the house needs some cheering up. I need some cheering up. And besides, all the stores are already flaunting their Santas and snowmen, with roofs draped in colorful lights. I want to bring some of that sparkle to my home. I make myself a coffee and add a little almond milk Bailey's, then get to work.

I drag the Christmas tree out of the garage and begin putting it together. We stopped buying live Christmas trees after the kids were older, once they lost interest in going to the tree farm. It may not smell authentic, but it's much more convenient, which is especially important since I usually handle this myself.

My favorite part is unwrapping each ornament. The tree isn't color coordinated and doesn't have a theme. It's filled with handmade ornaments and photos of both Cora and Henry when they were young, including crafts and little handprints. I take out a photo ornament of Ozzy as a puppy and laugh. One of the animal shelters held a fundraising event offering pet photos with Santa. He is sitting on Santa's lap, face turned towards good ol' St. Nick. We called and called Ozzy's name, but he was too interested in the fluffy white beard to look toward the camera.

The next ornament induces sadness. It's a large metal key with a photo of Levi and me standing in front of our house holding a "Sold" sign. We were happy when we moved here and had so much fun choosing furniture and painting walls. But time passes, memories fade, and feelings change.

Once the ornaments are placed on the tree, I plug in the lights. There is nothing that evokes feelings of wonder and delight like the twinkling lights of a Christmas tree. I'm standing there admiring it when Levi walks into the room.

"It isn't even December yet," he says.

"I'm aware of the date, thank you."

"It just seems a little early."

I let out an audible sigh. I could begin telling him that it's my house too. If I want the tree up, I will put it up. I could also point out that he isn't here most of the time anyway so what does it matter if the tree is. Further-more, I could say that I didn't bother him with anything having to do with the tree so it shouldn't infringe on him one way or another. But instead, I just say, "I know, but I like it."

He nods and says, "It looks good." Then he walks toward the kitchen.

We've been in this perpetual dance. He walks to the left, and I slide to the right. He passes on the right, and I shimmy to the left. But never do we join together, we are no longer partners. And while that is painfully evident, Levi is still my husband. This means we are still both here in this house together. And if we are here, he will not be sleeping with someone else. That is something I will be sure of.

On Monday, Levi wakes me up before work. "My car has a flat tire. I've called someone to come out and fix it, but I need to take your car to the office."

"What car?" I ask, half asleep.

"Your car, Erika. I need to borrow your car. It's not like you're doing anything today, are you?"

Even bright and early while asking for a favor, Levi doesn't miss the opportunity to take a jab at me. "Fine," I say, "take the car."

"Thanks," he says, and he is out the door. No "good-bye." No "have a good day." No "I love you." He is just gone.

I'm in my PJs making coffee in the kitchen when someone rings the doorbell. It's the guy from the automotive center here to fix the tire. "It's the white car in the driveway," I tell him.

"Which tire is it?" he asks.

"I have no idea. I haven't been out there. My guess is it's the flat one."

He gives me an odd look and disappears without another word. I sip my coffee and talk to Ozzy.

"You didn't bark at the doorbell, Oz. Are you feeling okay?" I bend down to feel his nose. It's dry and warm. I panic for a second thinking that means he's sick. Come to think of it, I believe Ozzy's nose has been like that a lot. I search on my phone and find that the correlation between a hot, dry nose and illness is false. That has to do with temperature, not sickness. I sit back in relief. But still, he seems a little off. He's getting up there in years. About seventy in human years. And yet, I think I read that may not be an accurate calculation either. Grapes and raisins. Grapes, and therefore raisins, are poisonous to dogs. That's one dog fact I know for sure.

The doorbell rings again. I glance at Ozzy, but he doesn't so much as lift his head.

"It's all done. Your husband gave his credit card information when he called this in, so I'll be heading out," the man says.

"Okay, thank you." I start to close the door, but before it latches, I swing it back open. Levi's car! That is one place I haven't checked. I grab his keys and nearly jog to the driveway.

His car is very neat inside. There is no trash in the doors. The floor has been recently vacuumed. I open the glove box and pull everything out, rifling through paperwork for oil changes, an insurance card, a registration letter. There's an owner's manual in there, as well as plastic utensils and napkins. Nothing useful.

Next, I open the center console and pull out several car chargers. Apparently when one stops working, Levi replaces it but fails to throw out the broken ones. There's an opened package of gum and some reading glasses in a case. I almost laugh when I find a folded map. Who uses a paper map anymore? I find some receipts and get a glimmer of hope that I've stumbled on to something. Unfortunately, it's just receipts from Starbucks, the drug store, and some drive-thru meals. It suddenly strikes me as funny that I'm disappointed to not find evidence of my husband's affair. I suppose that's because I'm so sure he is having one. The lack of proof has become frustrating at best.

I stay in the driver's seat, unsure what to do from here. I glance in the backseat, but it's empty. I remember that there are pockets on the backs of both front seats, so I half climb through the center to reach back and stick my hand in them. One is empty and the other contains a few CDs. This strikes me as odd as Levi's car doesn't even have a CD player. I pull them out and see that they are actually my old CDs. Interesting. Perhaps when we got this car a few years ago, he just moved whatever was in his former car to this one, and the CDs were included. I return them and turn back forward-facing to think. There is nothing here.

An eyelash suddenly invades my eyeball, and so I lower the sun visor to find it and fish it out. When I do, something falls in my lap. I finish with my eye and pick the item up. It's a book of matches. The outer cover is shiny and red with the phrase "May the bridges I burn light the way" imprinted on it. When I lift the flap, I see the name I have been looking for, Fuzzy Pete's.

Chapter 19

I used to think that the internet had ruined the world. Creating chaos, worsening mental health, even diminishing our memory, as who needs to try to remember anything when the answer is always at your fingertips. But for this one minute, I am so very thankful for the world wide web and all of its glorious information. I pull up the search engine and type in Fuzzy Pete's.

The first result that pops up says: "Fuzzy Pete's offers an unforgettable dining and full bar experience. Located on the rooftop of the Lucas Luxury Hotel & Suites, Fuzzy Pete's offers a fun, upscale retreat for those who enjoy reinvented comfort foods and magically mixed drinks in an intimate atmosphere. We guarantee to provide you with a memorable experience whether dining with friends, family, or business associates." I need to delve further to learn where it's located, what it looks like, the type of food they serve. This is going to take some effort, so I grab my coffee and head to the front porch to begin the investigation.

In addition to researching the hotel, I scour our credit card transactions. Levi pays the bills each month, so I rarely review the statements. Unfortunately, there is no option to search by vendor name, so this requires a line-by-line hunt for Fuzzy Pete's, Lucas, or anything else that seems questionable. There are six charges from the Lucas hotel, all approximately four hundred dollars each, which likely signifies overnight stays. I also count up seventeen separate transactions for Fuzzy Pete's during this year. Seventeen. The last charge was just three days ago.

The Lucas Luxury Hotel & Suites is located only twenty miles from my home. There is no plausible explanation for Levi having stayed there other than him spending the night with Liz. Needing to catch them together, I devise a plan. Every night that Levi is not home by eight, I will drive to the hotel and see if he's there. I quickly reconsider this course of action, realizing that would occur most nights. No, there needs to be something better.

I go back to the Mom Group and search Beth's name again, but only find the posts that were there before. She hasn't replied to my comment either. I add another, still using the Candace account.

"Beth, since we are both going through this issue with married men, can I message you to discuss it privately? It may be helpful for us to lean on each other and be supportive in a world that doesn't understand what we're going through."

I want to wretch. Of course, nobody would be supportive of having an affair with a married man. But Liz needs to trust Candace. About an hour later, my phone dings from a new private message sent by Beth.

"Hi Candace, thanks for reaching out. I'm in such a difficult spot. I don't even think I love the guy, but I do love being with him. I try to not think of his wife.

I know her personally even though we don't see each other all the time. That makes it weird, though. How are you handling your situation?"

Her message makes me want to throw my phone. I'm sure I have made it much easier on Liz now that we aren't friends anymore. Although I'm starting to doubt if Liz has any human emotions or empathy at all. She talked to me, laughed with me, and shared meals with me all while lying to my face and stabbing me in the back. The saddest thing about betrayal is that it doesn't come from your enemies. It's your friends who stick a knife in you and then pretend to care that you're bleeding. I immediately respond, continuing my lie.

"Beth, I totally understand what you're going through, and I'm so sorry. It's hard to be us. We are the ones who are there for these men, we care about them, and then we have to struggle with the guilt of it all. It's so unfair. How do you manage to spend time with your guy? I meet mine at The Homestead Lodge, usually on Tuesdays and Thursdays. That's when his wife teaches evening classes."

Now my own message makes me want to throw my phone. But if she's going to give me the information I want, she has to relate to me. And I need to think the way she would. The Beth profile is still online, so I wait until she reads my note. The three dots that appear let me know she's typing a response. They start, then stop, then start again. Finally, there is no more typing, however, I don't get a return message.

I drink the last of my coffee, unsure what to do with all these puzzle pieces. The weather is much cooler, the breeze causing the landscape flanking the porch to sway ever so slightly. Most of the plants in the front flower bed are dormant in preparation for the colder weather. Except there is one lone rose holding on, still in full bloom. A single drop of dew hangs from its center, as if crying that it's almost over.

A distraction is needed to clear my head, so I drive to the shopping center to pick up some Christmas gifts. Cora and Henry always ask for money, but a mom can't help buying them a few gifts to unwrap. Plus, Santa always fills their stockings. I pick up some lipsticks, a set of funny magnetic bookmarks, warm winter socks, and gift cards for Cora's stocking. Henry is a little tougher to buy for, even when it comes to stocking stuffers. I get him gift cards, as well, and manage to find a cool book light, a nice razor set, and pickle-flavored chewing gum. Henry loves pickles.

Christmas time when the kids were young is something greatly missed. Seeing everything through their eyes made it magical. From the time they were about eight and ten until they graduated from high school, I gave them what I called "The Gift of Time." They each received twelve envelopes, one to open every month. The envelopes contained a piece of paper with an activity written on it. The outings weren't extravagant, things like "dinner and the movies," "visit the zoo," or "lunch at the mall." But what made these special was that it was one-on-one time with each of them. As the kids got older and their schedules grew busier, it became even more important to set aside time for our dates. They lost that child-like anticipation as they grew older, but I knew they still enjoyed that special time with mom. And I treasured it.

My phone dings as I'm walking back to the car, causing me to pick up my pace, anxious to read the message. But it isn't Beth. It's Levi.

"Where are you? I think you should come home."

"I'm shopping. Why, what's going on? And why are you at home?" I type back.

"It's Ozzy. I think he's sick."

My heart drops and tears immediately begin to form. "On my way."

I drive well over the speed limit, weaving in and out of traffic. "No, no, no," I cry out loud. I can't lose Ozzy. Not my special boy. He is my one constant. My one true loyal companion. Tears are streaming down my face and the ache in my chest is so deep I can barely breathe. A dog's only true fault is that his life is too short. I think of a quote that was hanging on the wall of the animal shelter where we adopted Ozzy. It read, "My sunshine doesn't come from the skies, it comes from the love that's in my dog's eyes." The tears are coming so quickly now that I can hardly see.

I speed into the driveway, throw the car into park, and run into the house. I didn't even notice that Levi's car was gone, but as I'm running from room to room screaming Levi's and Ozzy's names, I find a note on the kitchen island. "I took him to the vet. Meet you there."

"Dammit," I yell to Levi's note. "You could've texted me that."

I sprint back to the car and am on my way to our veterinarian's office. The lady behind the counter, Janice, greets me. "Hi, Mrs. Thompson. Your husband and Ozzy are with Dr. Porter now. Room two. You can go on back."

I call thanks over my shoulder and briskly walk to room two. Ozzy is laying on the exam table, his back is to me. When I call his name, he doesn't even wag his tail. Levi looks up at me and says, "Hey."

"Why didn't you text me that you were coming here? I could've saved time by not going home first," I exclaim. "And where's the doctor?"

"I figured you were driving and wouldn't be looking at your messages. It's not like the vet is that far from the house. The doctor took Ozzy back for some tests. She just brought him back in here and left again to get the results."

"What kind of tests? What's wrong with him?"

"He just seemed so lethargic. When I came home, he didn't come to greet me. And when I went to find him, I called his name, and he didn't even open his eyes. It wasn't until I bent down to touch him that he woke up."

Just then, Dr. Porter opens the door. "Oh, hello, Mrs. Thompson, nice to see you. Since you spend more time with Ozzy than your husband, is he eating okay, drinking enough water? His gums look pink and healthy."

"Yes, he eats and drinks fine."

"Good. And what about his temperament? Is he playful?"

"Only sometimes," I respond. "He sleeps a lot."

"Yes, well dogs do sleep a lot. And when they get older, they slow down just like humans do, so they sleep even more."

My heart sinks at her mention of Ozzy slowing down.

"But," she says, continuing, "Ozzy is in perfect health for a senior dog. Except for one thing."

Levi and I both stare at her. The anticipation is killing me.

"He is almost completely deaf. Have you noticed he no longer responds to noises? Maybe even doesn't come when you call his name?"

"Wait, so that's all that's wrong with him? But he isn't sick or anything?"

She smiles. "No, he isn't sick. Just hard of hearing. You'll want to approach him thoughtfully, especially if he doesn't see you coming. You don't want to scare him. I have a pamphlet on living with a deaf dog that I'll send home with you."

Relief washes over me, and I start to cry again for a different reason. I'm thankful and happy that Ozzy is alright. The loss of hearing is manageable. The loss of Ozzy would be excruciating.

With the immediate worry about Ozzy behind me, I again wonder why Levi was home in the middle of the day. I'm driving with Ozzy in my backseat, and Levi is in his car behind me. I see him talking on the phone, which is not unusual for the middle of a workday. But from what I can tell, he seems very animated, and possibly upset. I continue to watch him in my rearview mirror and almost run a red light. I slam on my brakes causing Levi to do the same. He throws his hands up in the air in frustration.

Back at home, as Levi is walking past me heading for the stairs, he turns and says, "I'm glad Ozzy is okay. I just hadn't seen him act like that, and I was concerned."

"He's not a puppy anymore. You just aren't around enough to notice." I should have skipped that last part, but I couldn't help it.

Levi sighs and says, "I need to finish packing."

"For what?" I ask.

"Work trip. I'm leaving tonight."

Levi rarely has same-day work trips. And he most definitely has never left work in the middle of the day to pack. I follow him upstairs.

"Where do you have to go?" I ask, wanting to hear his lies.

"Washington DC. There is a three-day conference."

"There's a work conference, and you just found out about it today?"

He cocks his head at me the way a dog would. "No, I didn't just find out about the conference. But I did just find out I was going. Someone else was planning to go, but he had some sort of family emergency, so I'm taking his place. Do you need to see my ticket?"

"Yes, actually I do," I say, calling his bluff. His face shows that my response surprises him.

"Well, I'll have to email it to you later. Right now, I need to pack and get to the airport."

"It'll only take you a few seconds to show me the ticket. It's on your phone, right?" I ask, pressing the issue.

"Yes, but I'm late as it is. Dealing with Ozzy pushed me really behind. I can't risk missing my flight."

"Just hand me your phone. I can look for it while you pack."

He stops folding the shirt in his hands and meets my eyes. "Erika, will you let me finish up?"

I almost continue further down this road but ultimately pull back. He can go on his pretend work trip, and I'll go to the Lucas hotel.

To anyone else, the remainder of the afternoon would appear to be simple and serene, but my stomach is in knots and every muscle in my body is tense. My brain is going a million miles a minute. Today is the day the truth will finally be set free. All of Levi's denials and the gaslighting will come to a head. For the majority of this year, he has tried to make me feel as though I was the crazy one, creating these scenarios in my head, while he played the innocent victim. But the truth always comes out in the end. Lies are just a temporary delay of what remains to be seen. And a husband should never underestimate his wife's ability to find out the truth.

My surge of confidence, my fight and determination, comes to an immediate halt as another thought comes to mind. The after. I'd been so focused on catching Levi and Liz that I completely overlooked how this is going to affect me after they are exposed. I'd been assuming that since Levi was the one in the wrong, the ball would be in my court, and I'd get to decide how all of this is to be resolved. But in reality, it may not work out that way. Maybe it is better to keep quiet about something because it would be more hurtful if that thing is brought to light, especially if nobody cares.

The worst-case scenario would be that Levi and Liz decide that they are in love and want to continue their relationship. That would be devastating, to say the least. However, Liz is also married with kids at home to consider, and I don't know her well enough to know what she would do. Another way this plays out is that Levi and Liz stop their affair, but I still get divorced. This seems to be a logical course considering the circumstances, but it's also frightening, as I haven't lived alone in over twenty years. I have also not worked for that same period of time. I know I would be entitled to half of the house and assets, perhaps even more than half due to the adultery, but that isn't enough to sustain me for the rest of my life. I would probably need to go back to work to build my own savings.

I slump onto the couch. The weight of everything overwhelming my senses. I spend a few minutes thinking that maybe I don't want to know. Perhaps living blissfully unaware in a safe bubble is better. That bubble quickly bursts when I acknowledge that I am already aware, and once something like this is in your head, you can't just brush it aside. It lives there, its ugliness seeping into everything you do and think, the way blood oozes from an open wound. No. I can't pretend not to know something I already do. I can't stay in the dark. My only choice is to obtain the proof, so we can move forward in the light.

I'm antsy as I wait for the evening, overthinking every-thing – my clothes because I don't want to be too con-spicuous, my dinner because if I eat, I might get sick. I pour a glass of wine and head out back. The weather is cooling down, signifying the end of fall. There is a slight breeze, and I shiver as goosebumps dot my arms. I reminisce about my old life with Levi. The life we had when our love was young. These memories used to invoke such happiness. Now, they summon the pain of a life lost.

I push the memories aside. I need to focus on the present, not dwell on what used to be. I down the last few swallows of wine and head inside, ready to tackle whatever lies ahead.

I wait until almost seven o'clock before driving to the Lucas Luxury Hotel & Suites, mindlessly following the monotone voice that guides me to the destination. I pull up front and there are two cars ahead of me in line for the valet. I wish they would hurry up. Every minute spent sitting here has me second guessing myself and wanting to retreat to my safe space at home. Finally, it's my turn.

A middle-aged man dressed in a white button-down shirt and black slacks opens my car door and welcomes me with a smile. I hand him the keys, and ask, "Where's Fuzzy Pete's located?"

"It's on the roof," he replies. "The elevators are located to the right of the front desk. When you get in, press 'R.' The pool is to the left, and Fuzzy's will be on the right-hand side."

Even given the situation, I can't help but notice how gorgeous the lobby is. Four massive glittering chandeliers reflect off the white marble floors. Plush black velvet furniture sits near a white fireplace, the blue flames almost dancing to the soft music flowing through the room. There are black and white oil paintings, each with modest splashes of color. I press the elevator button and step inside. A miniature replica of the lobby chandeliers is hanging above, creating a disco ball effect on the hammered metal walls. An older couple slips in the elevator with me before the door closes. They press floor six. I press the button for the roof.

I step out into a sea of twinkling white lights and wonder if they are always here or if it's been decorated this way for Christmas. I glance to my left and see the entrance to the pool. It appears to be closed, likely for the winter season. To my right is a sign that reads "Fuzzy Pete's Restaurant and Bar." I chastise myself for not thinking about coming here earlier to get the lay of the land, as I did for the Mom Group event.

Once through the wooden doors, a hostess greets me. "Table for one?" she asks.

"I'm actually meeting someone here," I fib. "Can I take a look around?"

"Sure," she says, waving her hand back towards the dining area. "Help yourself."

I give her an appreciative smile and slowly make my way into the restaurant. I need to spot Levi and Liz before they catch sight of me. I did remember to bring my glasses, and put them on so that the faces further away will be in focus. I move methodically through the aisles only getting close to those tables that I have positively identified as not being my husband or my former friend.

When I am sure they are not in the restaurant, I move toward the bar. A quick peek inside tells me that it's moderately full. Unfortunately, it's an open floor plan so it will be difficult to just walk in without being seen. I stand behind a wall, stealing glances. I only feel foolish when a server asks me if I need some assistance.

"No," I stammer. "Thank you. I'm just looking for someone."

"You can actually go into the bar if you'd like," he says.

"Oh, I know. But it's a surprise. I'm trying to surprise my—friend."

He gives me an odd smile but leaves me to my detective work. I can't see Levi or Liz straightaway. I'm going to have to go in.

I keep to the right side of the room, hugging the wall. There are a couple of open seats on one end of the bar. I sit in the last one, trying to angle myself in a way that seems natural, but allows for full viewing of the room. I'm almost startled when the bartender asks to take my drink order.

"Pinot Noir, please."

"I'll need to see your ID," he says.

I look up at him. "You're kidding."

"I am," he says, giving me a broad smile that shows the slight gap between his front teeth. It makes his whole face seem both friendly and charming.

I try to smile back. He continues, "Will you be ordering food? Need a menu?"

"No, thanks. Just the wine for now."

He comes back with the glass and sets it on the bar. "Expecting anyone else? We can save the seat next to you." He has the slightest southern accent. I read his name tag. It says Dustin.

"No, thank you," I say. I expect him to go away, but he keeps standing there. This isn't helping my invisibility. I meet his stare and raise my eyebrows.

"You look familiar," he says. "Have we met?"

Great. I do not need to be reconnecting with old friends or strangers or anybody right this second. "I don't think so."

"No, I think we have. Let me see—" He taps his forehead with his finger as if that will somehow jump-start his memory.

I try to help him out so we can move on from this little encounter. "Well, I go to a bookstore over on Seventh Street in Fort Worth a lot, and I used to hang out at the Sip & Spin coffee shop."

"No, no, that's not it." He shakes his head, eyes boring into mine as if he will see the answer there.

Frustration is welling up in me now, so I begin spouting off places I frequent. There aren't that many. "Shopping center in North Fort Worth? Ever After in Dallas? Cemetery in town?"

"The cemetery? Why would I know you from there?" he asks.

"I don't know." My voice is a little louder than I intended. "I'm just telling you places I hang out where I may have run into you."

"You hang out at the cemetery?" His eyes are light-hearted, teasing. But I am in no mood for playful banter.

"You must have me confused with someone else," I finally offer.

"I don't think so." Finally, he snaps his fingers. "I know! I met you at a Christmas party a few years ago."

Now I'm curious. I did go to a Christmas party that Levi's work put on three years ago, but I don't remember meeting this guy. And why would he remember me?

"Oh, yeah? Which party was that?"

"My sister works for an IT company. Her husband got the flu, and she didn't want to go alone, so she invited me. You're married to Levi."

Now he has my full attention. The fact that he would know and call my husband by name is troubling. "How do you know Levi?" I ask, semi-afraid of the response.

"I see him in here sometimes. First time I've seen you here, though. Will he be joining you?"

"No," I say, too quickly. "I mean, I'm not expecting him. I just knew he comes here and thought I'd check it out. He's always saying how nice it is here and how much he loves the food. And the hotel. He raves about the hotel." Shut up, Erika, I think to myself. I am babbling way too much.

"Okay, right on," Dustin says. "I just ask because I saw him here earlier."

Upon hearing these words, I have a difficult time swallowing my mouthful of wine.

Once I can speak, I say, "You did? When?"

Dustin holds a finger up to me and says, "Just a sec, I'll be right back." He goes to take the order of three men who have occupied the seats at the other end of the bar. Once they have been served their draft beers, he returns.

"Maybe about an hour ago. He was here with some lady."

I know he sees the immediate change in my face at these words because he adds, "Sorry, I didn't mean it like that. She looked professional. Like really put together. It didn't look like a date or nothing. Maybe they work together?"

I nod, looking down at my drink. Dustin continues, "Hey, I've seen them in here before. Together I mean. But really, I'm sure there's a reason."

"I'm sure there is too," I murmur. Then louder I ask, "How many times have you seen them here?"

"Oh, I couldn't say. Not too many. A handful maybe."

"Do you happen to know where they went after they left tonight?"

"No, sorry. I didn't talk to them. The server over there, Cindy, waited on their table." He nods in the direction of a pretty blonde woman. "Wait," he adds, "I'll be right back."

I watch as he makes his way toward Cindy. They talk for a few minutes, and she looks up and meets my eyes. She sticks her hand into her apron and produces a small stack of papers. After rifling through them, she hands one to Dustin. He studies it for a minute, a serious look on his face. The anticipation is eating at me, until finally, he heads back toward the bar.

Back behind the counter, he says, "Levi's staying here. He signed the check over to his room."

My heart is beating so loudly I feel like I need to raise my voice to be heard. "And which room is that?"

Dustin takes a step back and slides both hands into his pockets. "I really shouldn't tell you. It's against policy to provide information on our guests. I could lose my job."

"I understand, I really do. And I don't want you to lose your job. I would never, ever share the information you are about to tell me. And I know that you don't even know me, so it's ludicrous for me to even ask. But you do know that he's my husband. You remembered that. Please." When I don't get any response, I push a little further. "I don't believe that my husband is here with a business associate, so I'm begging you for help."

He looks at me thoughtfully, as if weighing his options. "Tell you what," he says, "I absolutely cannot provide you with any information that violates the privacy of our guests." I slump my shoulders, defeated.

"However," he continues, "I will say that if I were to set this particular check down in this drawer with my other checks and walk away, it is no fault of my own if you completely cross the line by opening the drawer to read it."

"Absolutely not your fault," I say. "I would be acting of my own accord."

Dustin gives me a cheerless smile, so much smaller than the one I received when I entered the bar just thirty minutes earlier. He then retreats to the other end of the bar and busies himself with the other patrons.

I stand up and reach over to the drawer, sliding it open. Right on top is a check with Levi's signature and room number on it. Room 812.

A few minutes later, I signal to Dustin that I'm done. He walks back toward me, and I ask for my check, adding a generous tip, not as a pay-off so much as a thank you. He smiles at me and whispers, "Good luck."

I make my way back to the elevator and press the down button. Despite the cool temperature, my body is overheating, a bead of sweat trickling down my back. My face is on fire, and I suddenly wish I'd asked for a bottle of water to go. I turn to go back into the bar and there he is. I don't know how we passed each other, but Levi is back at his prior table talking to Cindy the waitress. He is alone. I almost confront him right then and there, but refrain from doing so. I need to catch him in a position he can't talk his way out of. If I approach him now, he could offer up a hundred false reasons why he's in this restaurant. I turn back to the elevator and head to floor eight.

When the elevator door opens, I peer down both hallways. Confirming they are empty, I creep towards Levi's room. If he is alone in Fuzzy Pete's, that means Liz is alone in the room. I stand in front of room 812 for a few minutes, working up my courage. My anger somehow morphing into other emotions. Fear, angst, sorrow.

I knock on the heavy door, placing my finger over the peephole, so she can't see who is standing on the other side. The door opens and a woman's face appears, but it isn't Liz.

Chapter 20

No. It can't be. I'd wish for anyone, but her.

"Erika," my sister says, "what are you doing here?"

My knees buckle at the sight of Olivia's face. She half tries to catch me before I crumble to the floor. Once I regain my composure, I begin to yell, "Don't you touch me."

"Erika," she begins.

"No," I say. "No, you don't get to speak. Not yet. I can't believe it's you. Of all people to betray me. It's you." I push past her and walk into the room. I spot Levi's suitcase in the corner. Those other emotions instantly vanish. It is all rage now.

"How could you do this to me? I confided in you. I told you about my problems with Levi. And you used that information to get close to him? To sleep with him? With my husband."

"Erika—" she tries again, but I cut her off once more.

"You are a disgusting, worthless, sorry excuse for a sister." Tears are flowing down my face, but I don't bother to wipe them away. They are coming too fast. I have to raise my voice to hear myself over the pounding in my head. "I can't believe you would do this to me. That you could do this to me."

I take a seat on the bed, then quickly stand up, realizing that this is their bed. Where they have spent time together today doing God knows what. Bile rises in my throat, but I force it back down. Crumbling to the floor, my legs shake, my body unable to bear the weight of everything in front of me.

"Erika," Olivia whispers, "I'm sorry."

Her apology ignites my fire once more, and I stand, closing the gap between us. "You're sorry?" I scream. "You're sorry? Exactly what are you sorry for, Olivia? Are you sorry for screwing my husband? Are you sorry you lied to my face day after day? Are you sorry that you are a despicable person? Or, maybe, maybe you're just sorry you got caught."

Olivia is crying. My otherwise hardened, emotionless sister is crying. But I feel not one shred of sympathy for her. "You don't get to cry," I holler at her. "Nobody cheated on you. Nobody pretended to love you then stabbed you in the heart."

"I do love you," Olivia cries out, "I do."

"You don't do what you did to somebody you love."

"What's going on in here?" Levi says, walking into the room. He stops short when he sees me. "Erika, what are you doing here?"

"Why are you both concerned with what I'm doing here? What the hell are you doing here? With her?" I yell at Levi. "I knew it. You denied it over and over. Tried to make me think I was imagining things. That I was the crazy one. But I knew it, you miserable bastard."

"I was just having a hard time. Our marriage hasn't been the greatest, so I thought I'd take a little break. Olivia was just here talking to me. Helping me through this. Nothing happened between us."

"Are you actually being serious? Do you think I'm stupid enough to believe that load of crap? Your marriage to me is so awful that you have to run into the arms of my sister?"

"It's true," Levi cries out, his anger rising as he becomes defensive. "Nothing is going on between Olivia and me. It's just like when you accused me of sleeping with Liz. You're just paranoid. Inventing stories in your head to fit into your own narrative. But it just isn't true."

He tries to go on, but Olivia cuts him off. "Levi, don't. She knows."

He appears incredulous, looking back and forth between the two of us. I see Levi try to say something to Olivia with his eyes, and I have had enough.

"You two deserve each other." I turn to Levi and say, "You are a coward. Instead of addressing what's going on in our marriage, you chase Olivia? Is she the fantasy of what could be?"

"I'm sorry," Levi says, "I just don't—I don't know what I was thinking. I wasn't thinking."

"You were thinking alright. You knew exactly what you were doing, and you knew how much it would hurt me, but that didn't stop you. You did it anyway."

I turn and walk out of that room. The walls are closing in on me, and I need fresh air. Olivia catches up to me at the elevator.

"Erika, wait," she calls out.

"How could you do this to me?" I ask, tears still streaming down my face. "That's one thing I will never know because there is no logical or valid explanation for a woman sleeping with her own sister's husband."

She tries to follow me into the elevator, but I don't allow it. I can't handle any more. I have to get out of here.

I run out of the lobby and hand the valet my ticket and whatever bill I pull out of my wallet. He pauses and looks concerned, as though he's about to say something to me.

"Just go get my car. Please," I beg.

I'm so sick. Too distressed to drive. I turn into a nearby gas station parking lot and shift my car into park. I hear this gut-wrenching, piercing sound. It hurts my ears. It hurts my head, and it won't stop. Then I realize it's coming from me.

I don't know how long I sat in my car at that gas station, and I don't really remember driving home. I let Ozzy out back while I get a glass of water and that one last Xanax. I need to calm down, to stop feeling. It's too much. I can't describe the feeling of losing it all, but I know it's consuming me. Over twenty years of life devoted to this man is over. Wasted. I let Ozzy back in, and he follows me to my bedroom, climbing in bed with me. As I lie there, I fight my feelings, forcing myself to focus on anything else. Finally, the Xanax takes over. My mind relaxes first, and my body quickly follows suit. I drift into a deep sleep.

When I wake up the next morning, I check the time. It's almost eleven. It takes about ten seconds for the events of last night to come flooding back. The hurt in my heart rapidly returns, but that agonizing, emotional knee-jerk has subsided for now.

I look on the nightstand for my phone, but it isn't there. I drag myself out of bed and search my purse, finding it inside. There are six missed calls from Olivia, starting at about seven this morning. Levi has called twice, the last one an hour ago. They have left voice mails. There are also several text messages from both of them. But I don't listen to the voice mails or read the messages. Whatever excuses or apologies they have for me today will have to wait until I'm ready. One thing I do is turn my location services off. Levi doesn't get to watch me today, not that I plan on doing anything unseemly. It just stopped being his business.

I really need a great cup of coffee but don't have the energy to make it myself, plus I want an excuse to get out of the house. I drive to Sip & Spin.

Jimmy is behind the counter, and his face lights up when he sees me. Saying hello to Jimmy is the only interaction I plan on having with him. Still, it feels nice to get a genuine smile from someone who has no idea what a mess my life has become. I thank him for my Iced Buns Latte, which is just as good as I remember, and head out the door.

I drive around with the windows down, allowing the cold December air to chill me. Christmas is two weeks away and my life is entirely upside down. "All I Want for

Christmas is You" is flowing out of the speakers. I can't handle that right now, so I start my favorite playlist. Joan Jett & The Blackhearts begin and that helps just a teensy bit.

I finish my coffee but am not ready to go home yet. I need to be away from the house today. I stop at Monkey and Dog Books. There is something about being surrounded by books that improves my mood. Maybe this is why we read. In moments of darkness, we find comfort in words and stories. I take my time looking all around, and eventually decide to purchase one book from each of my favorite genres—women's fiction, historical fiction, memoirs, and thrillers. I also find a Christmas book with a beautiful cover and a cute description. If I'm going to have an awful Christmas, maybe I can read about someone else's fantastic one.

I'm not entirely sure where to go next, but find myself heading toward the cemetery. There are a few cars parked along the small, paved roads, so I continue to an empty spot, then walk to a small gray bench. The cold metal immediately travels through my leggings, stinging the backs of my thighs. I wish I'd worn jeans.

I know that I will need to have a discussion with Levi. And I also know that although I still love him, it is over. My chest aches as I admit to myself that it's been over for a long time. He obviously knew it. And I knew it too, I just didn't want to see it. What I don't want from him are any more denials or excuses. Levi's actions have already spoken the truth. Some people act like victims of the crimes they have committed. Levi is no victim here. But as angry and hurt as I am about the affair, I don't hate him for breaking my heart. Maybe that's what happens when you love someone.

When the sun begins to retreat, the temperature drops even further, and it's time to go home. Levi's car is in the driveway. I take a few minutes to mentally prepare before going inside. He is waiting by the door as soon as I walk in.

"I was worried about you. Where have you been? Are you okay?" he asks. Something in his eyes is different. The indignation and defensiveness have vanished. For the first time in a long time, I see something else. Sorrow. I know because I see it in my eyes too.

"I'm definitely not okay," I say, "but I will be."

He nods then says, "I'm sorry. I really am. I don't know what I was thinking. I never meant to hurt you. I was selfish and cruel. I know it will take a long time for you to even consider forgiving me. But I hope that one day you will. I don't want to lose you."

I sit on the couch, unable to stop the tears from spilling. "Levi, you lost me a long time ago. We lost each other. Your affair was disgusting, and then knowing it was with my sister made it even more heartless. I don't know that I'll ever get over that. But even without the affair, we were heading to this same place. You just sped it up."

He lowers his head and doesn't say anything for a beat, so I continue. "I'd like you to leave."

Now he meets my eyes and says, "You can't give up on our marriage. We should fight for it. We need to try."

"I'm done trying to fight. And I'm not the one who gave up on our marriage. You made that decision when you cheated on me. Some people may be able to come back from that, but that wasn't our only issue. We were too far gone." Then I ask, "Do you love her?"

"Olivia?"

I nod in response.

"No, of course not. I don't love her. I love you. She didn't mean anything to me."

"That just drives my point home," I say.

"What do you mean?"

"Our relationship was so insignificant that you jeopardized it with someone who meant nothing to you."

"Jesus, Erika. That's not what I meant," Levi says, his voice rising now.

"I can't do this again today. It's too much."

"I'm so sorry. I truly am," he replies softly.

"You weren't sorry when I didn't know," I hiss. Then quieter I say, "Just stop. I can't talk to you right now. My heart is too tired. Aren't you tired, Levi?"

He nods and says, "But it's almost Christmas. What about the kids?"

"It is. And this will be the first of many Christmases apart. The kids will adapt. Do you need to get some of your things out of the bedroom?" I feel him watching me leave as I walk towards the kitchen.

Levi reappears a little while later. His suitcase is near the door.

"I suppose I'll go ahead and go now," he hesitates, but I say nothing.

"What about Liz?" I call out, as he reaches for the door handle.

"What?"

"Liz. Were you sleeping with her too? Because you need to tell me the truth. You owe me that."

"No, never with Liz. It was only Olivia. I swear."

I'm not sure if this makes it better or worse. I mean, of course, it's better that my friend wasn't sleeping with my husband. But I made the accusation. I thought that she had broken my trust when in reality, I had broken hers. I will need to reach out to her at some point, but not now.

"What are you going to tell the kids?" Levi says before leaving.

"I'm not going to tell them what you did. That's between you and me. I don't want them to be angry with you or with my sister. All they need to know is that we are separating. I'll talk to them tomorrow."

I fight any more tears until the door closes behind him. All of those years ago, we started with an easy hello. And now we are ending with a difficult goodbye.

I wait a full two weeks before responding to Olivia's calls and messages, until right before Christmas day. I just couldn't bring myself to talk to her until now. I send her a text inviting her to the house.

"Headed your way now," she texts back.

In less than an hour, she is knocking at the door. When I open it, she reaches to hug me, but I take a step back and say, "Come in."

"Erika, I'm so sorry. I didn't mean to hurt you like this."

"How could you sleep with my husband over and over and not mean to hurt me? That is the very definition of hurting me. Levi and I are over," I say, not sure if I'm telling her or admitting it to myself.

"Oh, no. I can't believe—"

I interrupt her. "Olivia, it's my turn to talk. You are my sister. You were my friend." She winces. "You were there for me. When Mom wasn't, which was most of the time, you were always there. You took care of me, of us. Sure, we didn't grow up to be the best of friends, but that was okay. I'll never forget what you did for me. And that's what makes this so hard. Nothing hurts more than being disappointed by the one person who I would have sworn would never hurt me.

"You sat there and listened to me talk about Levi. I talked about my concerns for our marriage. About how lonely I was. I haven't felt right for a very long time. And the wound is still very fresh. I'm still devastated about what happened. But I also feel a small sense of relief. I was fighting so hard to be seen. I just wanted to be important to someone. Now there is nothing left to fight for."

"Oh, Erika. You are important," Olivia interjects.

"I'm not done," I say. "I know I'm important. I'm important to myself, to Cora and Henry. I'm important to Ozzy. And honestly, that's enough for right now. I can stop feeling crazy. I can finally find some joy in my days because I'm not constantly wondering what Levi is doing or when he'll be home. Do you know how exhausting that is? To spend half of your time worried that your husband is having an affair and the other half begging for his attention? But I'm finished with all of it."

"Erika," my sister begins again, "I am so very sorry. I know those words sound meaningless, but I'm also devastated by this."

I can't help but give a sarcastic laugh.

"I know my apology is so small compared to the enormous hurt I have caused," she continues. "I never meant to put you through this pain. I promise to never hurt you again. Please, please forgive me."

I don't say anything, and Olivia begins to sob, making this the second time I've ever seen my sister cry.

Through her tears, she continues, "I lost everything, and you lost nothing. I lost my baby sister, a good person, my best friend. What did you lose? A crappy, worthless, sorry excuse for a sister. God, I am so sorry." She is bawling. My heart wants to comfort her, but my brain reminds me why she is crying.

"I need space. From this situation and from you," I say.

"What about Christmas tomorrow?" she asks.

"Cora and Henry will be here. Cora's flight lands this evening. Henry is picking her up from the airport, and they're both coming here. You can come over tomorrow too. You, Cassidy, and Minnie. I don't want there to be any rifts between your family and mine. They need each other. They need you."

"I would love that. Thank you. Thank you so much."

I contemplate my next question because I don't know if I want the answer, but I ask it anyway. "Why has our relationship been so strained for all these years?"

This seems to surprise Olivia. She thinks for a minute before saying, "You married Levi right out of college. After everything we'd been through with Mom. You know, the only thing Mom ever gave me that was of value was you. And I guess I felt like you were picking him over me. You left, and it destroyed me. My entire life I've had this fear that I was going to be abandoned. It's easier to push this fear aside if I don't get too close to people."

I nod, recognizing the behavior. Olivia keeps people at bay for fear of abandonment, and I hold them too tight for the same reason. It's no excuse for what she did to me, but I understand her a little better.

Later that evening, the house has a touch of Christmas spirit now that my children are home. Since they've become older, most of the mystery of Christmas is gone, but the magic is still there. I take out matching pajamas for the three of us. The bottoms are a bright red, and a pattern of light strands winds around cartoon sheep wearing sweaters and scarves. The top is the same matching red with the words "Fleece Navidad" written on them.

Henry groans when he sees them and Cora laughs, but they both put them on, if nothing more than to humor me. I pop some corn in a huge pot on the stovetop and make us three giant bowls. We hang out together watching "National Lampoon's Christmas Vacation" followed by the original "Home Alone." We laugh at the same scenes we've laughed at for years.

When the movies are over and our bowls are empty, we continue to hang out in the living room, talking until just past midnight. Both Henry and Cora are concerned about me, their dad, and the separation. I try to explain that we were so young when we met. Young love works out for some people, but not for others.

"Growing apart during our marriage doesn't change the fact that for many years, we both grew together. We entered full-fledged adulthood side by side—" I pause, considering my words. "First, we got comfortable, and then, unfortunately, we got complacent. It wasn't intentional, it just was. But it's okay, and I will be okay, and your dad will be okay. Our separation doesn't negate all the positive parts of our lives, like you two."

I smile at them both. My wonderful children, not quite grown, yet so far from the little kids they once were. I know they are upset. They're holding on to brave faces, but I know what's behind those smiles. I don't care how old someone is, nobody wants to witness their parents' relationship falling apart. We will talk more about it on another day.

We are the first to wish each other a Merry Christmas before trotting to our respective rooms. After a few minutes, I come back downstairs and fill the stockings hanging on the mantel above the fireplace. One for Henry, one for Cora, and one for Ozzy. I didn't put up Levi's stocking this year, but I did hang mine. I put a pair of amethyst earrings, some bookmarks, and some of my favorite chocolate into it.

Before I go back upstairs to bed, I pause to admire the Christmas tree. My anger and pain still overwhelm me most days, and I expect it will do so for a while. I know it's going to be hard to adjust to my new life, but not impossible.

Chapter 21

The holidays were tough for me. Both Cora and Henry stayed here for nearly two weeks, so I found myself hiding in my room to cry. Levi continues to reach out, but I can't go there just yet. I need more time by myself. This sounds ridiculous considering I had all the alone time I could've ever wanted, and I hated it. But it's different now. I'm different now.

Typically, I would give a hard eye roll to the "New Year, New Me" statements that float around social media towards the end of each year. But now I can sort of relate. It's still difficult for me to grasp my new normal, which consists of just Ozzy and me in this big house. Of course, this will change once our divorce is final. I don't plan to live here, because it's too much for me. I just need a small place with three bedrooms so that Cora and Henry always have a place to stay. Maybe an office that I can use as a little library too.

It's pretty cold out, as January usually is. I head over to an intimate shopping circle in downtown Fort Worth. There are a couple of great shops over there, and I'd like a new winter coat. I find one in a perfect robin's egg blue color that's quite beautiful and vastly different from my usual black or gray. I purchase it along with a new matching scarf.

I wander down the sidewalk to a bookstore. It's charming inside, reminiscent of a storybook. The floor is a black and white checkered tile, with splashes of brightly colored accents, such as red doors and yellow trim. There is a wooden staircase that leads to a reading lounge complete with tables and chairs. I take my time browsing and ultimately decide on three new books.

When I take my selections to the counter, I notice a "help wanted" sign.

"Great choices. I really loved this one," says the cashier.

"I can't wait to read it," I reply, handing her my credit card. I make a split-second decision and ask about the available job.

"It's part-time. About twenty hours a week. The gal who had it before just moved, so I need someone right away. Are you interested?"

"Yes, I am." This could be perfect.

I learn the ropes pretty quickly. Some of the books are new and some are used. They even sell bookish knick-knacks and kitschy accessories, which I love. The owners, Susan and Martin, are easy to work with, and I enjoy talking with the customers and recommending my favorites. It warms my heart when a customer chooses a book I suggest. As a bonus, I get to wear t-shirts that say things like "Get Lit" and "Bookmarks are for Quitters."

One afternoon while I'm working with Susan, we're talking about Oprah's Book Club and Reese's Book Club and how it's almost as fun to talk about books as it is to read them.

"You should start one here," Susan says.

"Me? A book club?"

"Why not? I think you'd be great at it. Plus, it would be good for business."

I tell her I'll think it over, and after a couple of weeks, I decide to go for it. I print out fliers advertising the new book club. Susan also posts it on the shop's HollerHub account and creates the event for our initial meeting. I choose a contemporary fiction book for our first selection. Susan and I create a small display table with this month's pick. Within the first week, we have six confirmed attendees.

I'm excited on the day of our first meeting, which is scheduled for seven in the evening right after the store closes. I have purchased tea, wine, and cupcakes. At 6:30, I start to head upstairs to set out the goodies at the same time that Susan begins gathering up her things. She tells me to have fun.

"You aren't staying?" I ask.

"No, this is your show. I need to get home. Martin decided he's making us some fancy dinner tonight so I can't miss it. I'll see you on Saturday."

Suddenly I feel nervous. I don't know any of the women attending, but I thought I'd have an ally in Susan. I am rethinking this, wondering if I made a mistake. At a quarter before seven, a woman comes in and tells me she's here for the book club. She barely looks at me before averting her eyes. I forget my own nerves and concentrate on making her feel welcomed. I give her a warm smile, which she returns, and tell her to make herself at home upstairs.

I wait around downstairs until 7:05, before heading up to begin. Only three women besides me have shown up. We introduce ourselves and make small talk while snacking and pouring drinks. Then I take out a list of questions to help facilitate the discussion.

Before I know it, the formal questions have been tossed to the wayside, and we are just winging it. There is lots of talk and laughter, some about the book, but most of it is not. One woman works full-time and joined as a way to carve out some time for herself, to do something she loves. The other two women are stay-at-home moms looking for some adult interaction. Our meeting runs over by about thirty minutes, and I lock up the shop feeling good about tonight.

The book club continues on the third Thursday of every month. About four to five women attend at any given time, and it's always fun. Sometimes we don't even discuss the book. We just visit with each other, laughing and bonding. I started working at the bookstore as a way to keep busy, but I honestly love it. And I love these friendships I've formed. It only takes me a few meetings to realize that this book club is the mom group I have been searching for all along.

One evening after work, while relaxing on the couch with Ozzy at my feet, I take out my phone and open

HollerHub, going to the Mom Group. I scroll through a few posts.

"I am so excited, y'all! My son was accepted to a new charter school. It's dual language, English and Spanish. He started right after the winter break. It has been so great for him!"

"I just wanted to say that even though I love Christmas, I was so ready for school to be back in session. The kids were kind of driving me crazy. Anyone else with me?"

"What were your New Year's resolutions? Have you kept them so far?"

I still feel guilt for the pain I have caused the women in the Mom Group. They are just moms trying to get by. I used my own insecurities and loneliness as an excuse to hurt them. To hurt their families. And for that, I am sorry. Just because they didn't roll out the red carpet for me doesn't give me the right to disrupt their lives the way I did. Who knows what they're dealing with behind their screens? Being a mom is hard. Like all moms, they have good days and bad days, happy days and crushing days. Some days they struggle to get out of bed and other days they are super moms.

I remove both myself and the Candace account from the Mom Group, silently wishing them all the best of luck.

Epilogue

They say a woman never forgets, and that's true. Once someone has hurt us, it's really hard to let go. But the truth is, unless you make a conscious effort to let go, to forgive yourself, to move on from the past, you cannot truly move forward.

It's been nearly a year since I found Levi and Olivia in that hotel room together. I spent many nights crying into my pillow. Many nights were filled with anger at them and myself. I would be okay for a few days, and then it would hit me, and I'd fall apart all over again. But sometimes going through something that nearly destroys you can also help you figure out who you really are.

I am a woman and a mother. And a dog mom. Ozzy spends every single night in bed with me, and he loves it. I love it too.

Levi and I talked about reconciling a few months after he moved out, but it was a fleeting thought. We both immediately realized what we had known for a long time. But just because our relationship ended, we didn't stop loving each other. We just stopped hurting each other. It was time to stop watering a dead plant so we filed for divorce. It's still pending, but we are close to finalizing. It has actually been fairly amicable. We've gotten along better this past year than in the last five years of our marriage. Not all stories have another chapter, and I'm learning that's okay.

Henry graduated college in May. He got a job offer right away and moved to Austin. He lives in an apartment and has a sweet girlfriend. I am so proud of him and a little sad for me. Obviously, I'm still learning to let go. My mom heart tries to remember that he won't be too far away for weekend visits.

Levi and I both celebrated Cora's birthday with her in Colorado. We rode the Cog Railway up to Pike's Peak and took a guided tour of the Garden of the Gods. Of course, Levi and I traveled completely separately and only saw each other with Cora. It was an enjoyable trip, and everyone was cordial throughout.

I never did reach back out to Liz. I feel like I burned that bridge beyond repair. Too much time had passed to go back. I enjoyed our friendship, I really did, but it was damaged too early on. We had not yet built up enough history between the two of us to weather that storm. There was no coming back from that night at my surprise party. When I heard Liz admit to her affair at the Mom Group event, I assumed it was with Levi. But it wasn't. For all I know, it could've happened before I even knew her. I never did figure out who the Beth profile was or if it was real, but it doesn't matter. It was never my concern to begin with. I can only hope that this Beth person realized the error of her ways and changed course.

It's difficult to gauge where my relationship with Olivia stands. We weren't that close before everything happened. Her affair with my husband definitely damaged us, but in some strange way, it repaired parts of our relationship, as well. It's hard to explain. She was hurting, and I was hurting, both for different reasons. We don't need to feel shame for our struggles. We have both made mistakes, as humans do. But I still keep her at arm's length. The fear of the past, of her grave betrayal, still haunts me. I am not yet at a point where I can let her back in. But I'm working on it. I'd like to have a sister again. Someday.

I did confirm what I have always known about my relationship with Amy. There is a natural ebb and flow to friendships, and the special ones tend to survive. Living in different states presented an easy excuse to push our friendship aside. This was particularly true while we both had younger kids to tend to. But now that we have more time, we have vowed to visit each other at least once a year. I saw Amy over the summer. We decided to forgo her house or my house and instead we both flew to Destin, Florida. We spent four glorious days lying on the beach and by the hotel pool with a drink in hand, talking, laughing, reminiscing. It was the perfect physical and mental vacation. A break from my situation at home and my new routine. I didn't even have to worry about Ozzy while I was gone. Cora was home for the summer, keeping us both company.

Speaking of having a drink in hand, I have stopped buying so much wine. I used to think it calmed me down, made me feel less anxious. But it was a crutch I shouldn't have been using. It didn't help anyway. Now I save the wine for special occasions, like book club.

I also don't go to the cemetery anymore. I realized that it wasn't bringing me the joy and peace that I thought it was. It was further isolating me. And Levi was right, it was kind of weird. I no longer feel the need to hang out there to escape, as there is nothing left to escape from. Plus, if I do ever feel stressed or upset, music is still my refuge. I'm even branching out from my usual eighties rock genre, but not too far. I'll always be an eighties rocker at heart.

I still have dark days. It's hard not to after spending such a long time in my marriage. But I have also come to enjoy my own company. It's finally enough for me, and that's empowering. I was locked in a marriage where I felt so lonely, and now that I'm actually by myself, I don't feel so alone anymore. Holding on to Levi was causing more damage than letting go. It took losing him to truly find myself. That is my silver lining.

Discussion Questions

1. What was Erika's motivation for sending emails to Nicole's husband and Allison's bosses? Was she justified?

2. Even though Erika's mother, Marlene, was not the ideal parent, why do you think Olivia maintained a close relationship with her?

3. Why do you think Allison was so unfriendly towards Erika?

4. Should Erika have reached back out to Liz? Could they have continued their friendship if she had?

5. Besides the obvious, what do you think contributed to the issues in Erika's marriage?

6. Is it easier to find friendship in larger groups, like the Mom Group, or in smaller settings, like Erika's book club?

Acknowledgments

I want to start by saying thank you to my own mom, Lucille Medina. She has always been my champion, confidant, and friend. Plus, she read drafts of this book several times and was such a great resource.

My amazing husband, Lenny Jones, who I love more than words. You always support me in everything I do, and I especially appreciate your incredible support through this process (and it was a process!).

The people who made me a mom, Ryan Jones and Alyssa Jones, who always have my heart. I am so proud of you both and love you so much.

My dad, Richard Medina, who has always been there, encouraging me to step out of my comfort zone.

My editor, Caroline Leavitt, New York Times best-selling author, for your guidance and insight.

My fantastic friend, Robyn Hamilton Ragno. I appreciate you reading an early copy and always being ready for great fun, conversation, and lots of laughs. Your friendship means so much!

And thank you to several others who may or may not have even known I was writing this book. We may not

talk often, but your friendship has positively impact-
ed my life... Tracy Kirk Tadolini - my first best friend,
sharing many crazy adventures (like the hotel surfing
we did in high school). Doralynn Gonzales Pecina, my
loyal and supportive friend for over twenty years, and
who first introduced me to El Fenix. Kimberly Attaway,
who I met when I joined her book club - I'm thankful
for our friendship. Patricia Wurst who has been both
my work and personal friend for the past several years
- thanks for all of our talks. They help more than you
know! Rachel Jones, my wonderful stepdaughter. Lisa
Palisin - no matter how much time passes, our friendship
falls back in step so easily. Charlene Richardson - thanks
for always checking in! And many others. I love you all.